Jack Kraywinkle

Blue Harvest

Jack Kraywinkle

Blue Harvest

This is a work of fiction. It is an imaginary story, although based in a real setting. Some details reflect artistic license.

All names, characters, places, and incidents depicted herein are the product of the author's imagination. Any resemblance to persons living or dead or to actual events is coincidental.

Print ISBN: 979-8-9862681-2-5
EBook ISBN: 979-8-9862681-4-9

Published by

RIVER PLACE PRESS

40274 Diamond Lake St
Aitkin, MN 56431
218.851.4843

www.riverplacepress.com
chip@riverplace-mn.com

RiverPlace Press is distinctive in guiding authors through the maze of specialized publishing options, with very personalized service.

©2022 Jack C. Kraywinkle
8275 Buffalo Creek Road
Brainerd, MN 56401

FIVE WINGS
ARTS COUNCIL

This project is made possible, in part, by the Five Wings Arts Council Individual Artist Grant Award with funding from the McKnight Foundation.

Dedicated to my Mother and Father.

With grateful appreciation to my sister Nancy, without whose help I could not have managed to write this story, the story of a heritage we shared. RIP.

With loving thanks to my wife, who encouraged me and allowed me the time to work on this story.

Foreword

West-central Minnesota, not far from the Dakota flatlands, is an area of sensuously undulating land generously sprinkled with lakes and ponds, the residue and melt water of the last receding glacier. These rolling hills are covered with prairie grasses and seasonal wild flowers, intermingled with dense stands of scrubby burr oak, box elder and other hardwoods.

My widowed grandmother lived in this land with her two brothers, of the proverbial Norwegian bachelor farmer type. I visited their farm often as a boy, and spent weeks there during the summer. Left alone with my imagination, I found adventure wandering around the ponds and hilly pastures. Sometimes I'd climb the rampart bales of a haystack fortress to look over a patchwork realm of fields, farms, ponds and woods that extended to the horizon.

In the distance were church steeples pointing the way to heaven through the tree tops, little rural churches with names like: *Vang, Tingvold, Kongsvinger, Aurdal* and *Stavanger*. Each church watched over a flock of simple white gravestones, like a hen protecting its brood. On many of the stones, a starkly simple epitaph in Norwegian reads: "*Takk for Alt*" (thanks for everything).

This area of Minnesota was settled predominantly by Norwegian immigrants in the mid to late 1800s. Typically, they were farmers and laborers familiar with making their living on the land. They were hardy people, accustomed to extremes in weather in their homeland, thus suited for the Minnesota climate.

With few exceptions, they were generally quiet and conservative folks, even somewhat self-effacing. In dealings or relationships with others, they tended to be non-confrontational, avoiding conflict as though it were an embarrassment. Life afforded them a droll sense of humor, arid and understated, which usually required some time for an outsider to understand or appreciate.

Generally not inclined to follow impulses, they preferred to consider things before making a decision. Decision making itself could be an involved process, but once reached, it would be followed up with deliberate, thorough action.

Sometimes consideration was marked by thoughtful pauses in conversation, punctuated by the simple word "yah" spoken soft as a whisper while inhaling, like breathing in the word. Spoken this way, "yah" itself doesn't necessarily suggest any sort of affirmation, though it could. Among these people, it was more a subconscious mannerism of speech. The broad implications ranged from insignificant to profound, and one could never be certain of which. The inhaled "yah" might express anything from a shift in thought to the summing up of an entire philosophy, or it might simply mean one's thoughts were temporarily on hold. It was a marvelous colloquialism, which through timely insertion, was capable of filling uncomfortable gaps in conversation. Gaps which, left unchecked, might otherwise expand into ponderous voids in a conversation.

Quiet life on the little farms was routine and people were prone to be skeptical of anyone new, or that which might seem spontaneous. But then skepticism may be just a cautious form of deliberate consideration.

These Nordic immigrants probably learned a tradition of caution from the treacherous mountain environment of their old homeland or the harsh North Sea. According to legend, the old Norse god Odin who sacrificed an eye to gain wisdom. From his wisdom, expressed in the *Havamal*, came sayings like: "*Trust no ice 'til its crossed, no sword before it's tested, no maid before marriage, no ale 'til it's drunk...*". Perhaps this sort of skepticism was passed on in the genes.

Throughout my life I have heard occasional references to "stoic" Scandinavians, usually in a somewhat disparaging way. These references suggest that one who is stoic is undemonstrative, devoid of sentiment or feeling. Such traits may exist in Nordic people, as they may in other nationalities but stoicism by definition is an acquired trait, not an inborn one. An indifferent man lacks interest in a situation, an impassive man lacks feeling, but a stoic man exercises control. He has feelings or sentiments, but has learned to restrain them. For example, take the old reference to the Norwegian farmer who "loved his wife so much it was all he could do to keep from telling her". The irony and humor are wrapped in the subtle wording of the statement.

I am not a stoic. I was not raised in that discipline. I am a "baby boomer." My parents' generation, growing up in the Great Depression and struggling through World War II, seems to be the last generation in this country to experience severe and almost universal hardship and sacrifice. Perhaps they were the last generation of stoics.

Blue Harvest is about the children of those who emigrated here, who inherited their parents' struggles, their spirit and humanity. It is a story about rural Minnesota during the late 1930's, at the end of the Great Depression and just prior to America's entry into World War II. It is a story about living with life's ever-present injustices. It is a story filled with spirituality, moving like the breeze and ever-present in the lives of the characters, their situations and events. It is the love story of a late-blooming, mature love and our human need for someone else, along with the reassurance that it is never too late.

The story, events and characters are entirely fictional but based on stories, personal observations, and memories of people I fondly recall from my childhood.

They were a rich part of my formative years and their endearing character remains a strong influence on my life.

Takk for alt (thanks for everything).

"The flax was in full bloom; it had pretty little blue flowers as delicate as the wings of a moth, or even more so. The sun shone, and the showers watered it, and this was just as good for the flax as it is for little children to be washed and then kissed by their mother. They look much prettier for it, and so did the flax."

—opening paragraph from "The Flax,"
by Hans Christian Anderson, 1849

1

Smoke, thicker than the moonless night spreads like black ink on a blotter. Like a pall, it hangs in the dead air that lacks breath to blow it away. Muffled by the murky dark, crackling flames dance yellow-orange under the smoke, greedily consuming a dry grassy meal. Distant points of light are far too feeble to cast shadows of a deed done in the darkness.

Now a barefoot man comes running out of the dark, coughing and gagging on the smoke that engulfs him. Clad only in his long underwear he whirls a braided kitchen rug, attacking the snapping, snarling fire dragon that devours his precious field—a field of flax. The crop sizzles as each stem is consumed, the oily seeds crackling and flashing into flame, then gone. It's already a lost cause but the farmer-warrior doesn't know it. He fights to save his precious flax.

He's not alone. Another voice coughs and calls to him through the thick billowing smoke and flame. It's a woman's voice, the farmer's wife. Together they flail at the hungry flames advancing through the field, each unable to see the other in the darkness and swirling smoke that shrouds them. But the fire dragon has had a good head start and craves the unctuous grain. There is no stopping the beast as it undulates throughout the standing stalks. Flames leap from place to place in the dark, giving but a dim glow of light through the heavy haze.

The farmer gags on the smoke and retches as tears gush from his burning eyes. He is oblivious to the sparks that land on his skin, the flames that singe his hair. His bare feet don't feel the pain of thistles or embers; there is only the need to stop the dragon. In frustrated panic the farmer and his wife battle without any plan of attack, and against the odds there cannot be one. Still, they are compelled to fight desperately because their crop of flax is so important, and because there is nothing else they can do.

The woman tires from the effort of the battle, as well as from the struggle for breath in the choking smoke. She is further weakened by new the life she carries within her. But her main concern now is the fire, for she knows the welfare of the child to come is closely tied to the flax, and she and her husband are committed in this struggle.

Overcome by a fit of coughing and retching on the noxious smoke, she gags out her husband's name in panic but it is inaudible, lost in the muffled atmosphere. In her weakened state and for lack of breath, the woman passes out and falls among the flax, surrounded by the feeding dragon.

The farmer is not far off but can see nothing of his wife in the smoky night. He's not even aware she'd left their house in her nightgown to join in the frantic battle. He is completely focused on beating down flames that spring up everywhere around him, relentlessly devouring his field.

As he flails the rug against the dragon, all he thinks of is his crop. This one is important, an investment in their future and for the child to come. It was a risk and an investment, now going up in smoke. He can't let it happen. He has to fight it, has to stop the dragon.

It doesn't occur to him to guess at what could have started the fire. It had been a spell of dry weather, but that was normal for this time of year as harvest drew near. In the middle of the night no one was working their land, no mechanical spark or careless human hand to account for this. A cigarette from a passing motorist maybe? He couldn't know, and it would be awhile before such thoughts would enter his mind. Right now, all there is to contend with is the hot breath of the dragon consuming his field.

Now there's strange sound. There, he hears it again, though it seems far off, or maybe just weak—his name. He pauses in his mad attack and listens a moment, his breath heaving. There it is again, wild and frantic. Was it his wife calling? Was she out here? It sounded like her and yet different, not at all like her. A scream, horrible and terrified, nearby. She never sounded like that before. He spins around rubbing his eyes, trying to peer through the smoky darkness. "Nora!" he bellows. Nothing. He turns again and runs a few steps toward where the scream seemed to come from, but is stopped short by a wall of heat and flame that suddenly bursts at him. Staggering back he flails the rug, beating at the flames that now reach out to embrace him.

Theodore Bergstrom sat bolt upright in his bed, eyes wide open with the vision of that flaming figure seared into his memory, forever burned into his dreams. Shaking and drenched in his own sweat, his heart nearly burst from his chest on every beat. With a throat dry as ashes, he stared out his bedroom window at the white winter landscape and gradually came back to reality. Why did she have to visit him this way?

Bergstrom swung his legs over the side of his bed and his feet touched the cold linoleum floor. Still shaking, he got up and walked to the window, threw it open and drew in deep breaths of icy fresh air to clear his head. "Sweet Jesus," he said to himself, thinking 'why do these nightmares continue?' That happened 18 years ago, in 1921. There had been so many dreams of her, of them, good dreams. Dreams of what they had shared together and the good times before the Depression came in the '30s. Then those dreams would explode in the nightmare of that awful fireball all those years ago.

Horribly burned, Nora with their unborn child, died in his arms that night as the fire swept over his field. A few neighbors came but they were too late to save his flax. All they could do was keep the fire confined to that field. The first red light of dawn found Bergstrom still kneeling in the smoldering ashes, cradling the burned corpse of his wife in the still morning air. Before friends took her body from him, he removed a scorched gold locket from around her neck, a gift he'd given her before they were married. It would remain a keepsake by which he would remember his Nora for years to come.

Neighboring farmers and their wives hurried to the aide of Bergstrom after the fire and the loss of his wife. It was simply the way farm folks respond to tragedies among their own people. While he recovered from burns to his hands and feet, neighbors pitched in to see that Bergstrom's other crops were harvested and his cattle cared for. Farm women brought him food and baked goods and offered comfort. It was what rural people did in times of tragedy but the young man was inconsolable.

He had been deeply in love and only married a few years. Nora was everything to him, his today and his tomorrow. Raised and educated in the east, she brought sophistication to Bergstrom's life and a level of respect for the gentleman farmer he hoped to become.

Bergstrom had been a good farmer with a bright future, but the fire and loss of his wife changed all that forever. The flax was to be a financial foothold on their tomorrow. Anyone who survives the crucible of tragedy is not the same as before. Some are made stronger and some are just changed. Bergstrom became a different man.

A brief investigation into the fire was inconclusive, even for the limited legal resources of rural Minnesota in the 1920s. The sheriff had nothing to go on and was overloaded with other cases. Nora's death was regarded as accidental, if tragic, and a consequence of her fighting the fire in her condition. There were some unanswered questions as to the fire's actual cause, but over time most people were able to let the questions remain just questions and get on with life, but not Bergstrom.

Over the next six months he grew more suspicious of the fire and its origins. How had it started? Why that field, his flax, his special crop? What could have caused the fire and how could it have gotten out of control so fast? The fire had put Bergstrom in a situation that affected the financial security of his farm. It couldn't have been an accident; someone had targeted him he was sure. But who would do such a thing and why? There was no evidence to prove that the fire was set. There was that cigar butt on the shoulder of the road but that proved nothing. Yet as he walked the charred perimeter of that field, Bergstrom became obsessed by the notion the fire was no accident. The questions provided a diversion from the deeper ache of his real loss, Nora. Perhaps dwelling on the fixation became a perverse means of survival.

Memories of that awful night haunted Bergstrom, pervading his mental state and every aspect of his life. Over the months, Bergstrom withdrew more and more to himself and his farm. He began to distrust people, suspecting everyone of everything, even those who had been his friends. His behavior alienated and insulted former friends and people eventually quit visiting him. In his growing paranoia, friends and neighbors saw less and less of him. He quit going to church, except on rare occasions, and then he sat in the back pew, coming late and leaving early. Bergstrom became a recluse, rarely going to town and he was virtually never seen on the rural roads around the countryside. A few of his neighbors were quietly convinced he'd "gone 'round the bend." He was "*for galt*" (crazy) as they said in Norwegian, and was not completely safe to be around.

Living in self-imposed social exile, he fell into a state of deep depression marked by fits of rage or bouts of sobbing despair. Bergstrom never sowed that field again but went there often, walking about on the overgrown soil or around the perimeter as if searching for something. All he ever found was an that old cigar butt up on the shoulder of the road, which as evidence meant nothing. Nothing except in the suspicious mind of Bergstrom. In mid-field there was the ubiquitous pile of stones, which adorned every field in that part of the state. Upon being unearthed by the plow, stones were cast aside in a pile out of the way. Sometimes Bergstrom sat for hours on that island, lost in his dark and lonely thoughts.

Harvest season was the worst time for the man, as it approached the season of the fire. Finally, after a few years, Bergstrom could stand the mental torment no longer. He had to get away from his farm. The only place to go was the nearby town of Foster Falls, where everyone went for every need their farm couldn't supply. There was nothing in particular he was looking for, nothing he needed to do there, Bergstrom just needed to get away from his farm and the memories for awhile. He wandered the streets looking for refuge or relief from the nagging questions he knew would never leave him.

He stopped outside an off-sale liquor store staring at the sign that promised a good time. Bergstrom had never been a drinker and grew self-conscious as he stood there staring so he impulsively ducked inside. He'd never seen so much liquor in one place before as he gazed at the rows of bottles awhile, wondering which would be the proper relief for his torment. Cautiously he selected a pint of whisky and went to the counter.

"Takin' a break from threshin' or are you done already?" the liquor store man asked. It required little perception to recognize a farmer when he saw one. Bergstrom looked at him defensively and set the bottle on the counter.

"Can't a man buy a bottle when he wants?" Bergstrom challenged.

"Yah, you bet you can. Just that mosta you fellas wait 'til the corn's in to start celebratin', ya know."

"I ain't celebratin' anything," he said quietly.

"Oh. I thought it'd been a pretty good year for crops around here," said the liquor store man, still trying to be friendly.

"Huh? Oh yah, I s'pose," Bergstrom replied, softening his tone.

The man punched a few buttons on the cash register and the cash drawer popped open with a ring. "That'll be one forty-nine then," he said.

Bergstrom fished his wallet out of his bib overalls and paid the man for the whisky. As he did, the man studied Bergstrom's face.

"Say, ain't you that farmer who's field got burnt up a couple years ago?" asked the liquor store man.

Bergstrom hesitated, eyeing the man. "Yah, that was me," he replied.

"Sure," the man said, "I remember seein' your picture in the paper back then. Flax, wasn't it?"

"Yah."

"Oh hey, that was too bad about your wife," he went on, sounding genuinely sympathetic. The comment turned Bergstrom's thoughts suddenly inward as the liquor store man rambled on. At the mention of his wife, he began to feel self-conscious again about being in the liquor store. Then the man's words began to impose themselves on Bergstrom's subconscious again.

"D'ya know what started it?"

Bergstrom looked up at the liquor store man. "No, what?" he asked still somewhat distracted.

"I'm askin' you," he frowned. "It's just that I heard it was kinda suspicious, that fire, like it might not have been an accident how it got started, that's all. Just rumors ya know. Folks that come in here like to drink an' that usually makes 'em like to talk, ya know, but it don't mean nothin'."

"Nothin' to you maybe," Bergstrom said. "Who's been talkin' then?"

"Well, uh, why do you ask?" the man said shifting his weight from side to side. Bergstrom noted a hint of discomfort in his voice.

"Why do I ask?" Bergstrom asked incredulously. "Hell man, it was my field, my wife. If someone knows something about it, they got to tell me. They got to!"

Bergstrom became conscious that he'd raised his voice and put the liquor store man on the defensive.

"I don't know anything about it, an' that's the truth," he replied. "It's just that there was these rumors, ya know, an' people tryin' to put two an' two together. They've got no business talkin'," he said. "People just imaginin' who would do such a thing an' why, ya know what I mean?"

"Yah, sure," Bergstrom said. "So who was sayin' this?"

"Well uh, no—nobody in particular," said the liquor store man withdrawing. "That is, I guess I don't exactly know. Can't remember. That's it, I just can't remember."

The man began fidgeting with some receipts in the drawer and turned away from Bergstrom. Even if he knew something or someone who knew about the fire, the man was obviously uncomfortable talking about it and Bergstrom wasn't likely to get anything out of him. Probably just full of bullshit anyway, Bergstrom thought, and trying to make himself seem important. Bergstrom took the paper bag that held his bottle and with a cold look at the liquor store man turned and headed for the door. As he left, the man called out something odd after him.

"You uh... you might just try talkin' to your banker then," the liquor store man said almost apologetically.

Bergstrom didn't even acknowledge that he'd heard him. Once he left the liquor store, he turned the corner and went down the street in the direction of the Ottertrack Parkway that followed the river through Foster Falls. It was pretty this time of year.

As he walked, his mind was a jumble of thoughts, and he was unable to focus on any single one. Ideas were always popping in and out of his mind but it was difficult to concentrate on any one in particular. Theories tormented him even when he wanted to think about a different line of reasoning or even escape the subject entirely. The bank? He'd worked with the bank a long time.

On reaching the walkway along the river, Bergstrom opened the bottle and took a drink. It burned his throat and he coughed, unaccustomed the harsh intrusion of alcohol. After forcing another big gulp, he felt the heat rise in his belly. Like the current in the river, he ambled downstream on the sidewalk by the bank, through the rustling leaves and crisp autumn air. This was supposed to be a day for healing, Bergstrom thought, trying to force away the persistent questions. He took another dose of medicine from the bottle.

Stopping at a park bench, he sat and stared across the current at the opposite shore. The bank had been good to him over the years he thought. He was beginning to feel the effects of the whisky in his head, a buzzing numbness and sluggish balance. Maybe he should have stayed at the farm today, he thought as colored leaves drifted on the sluggish current. He took another pull on the bottle. "To hell with that," Bergstrom said to himself out loud.

That liquor store guy didn't know what he was talking about. Anyway, it wasn't going to interrupt this day. He sat on the bench awhile and sipped, and it seemed to him his mind was beginning to ease. The whisky was having its intended affect. Bergstrom was thinking clearer now and starting to feel good, too good to sit there on the bench any longer. He took another drink from the bottle, got up and continued walking downstream along the river, now with an unsteady gait. It didn't make any sense. Talk to your banker?

Why would he say that? What could the banker know? Somebody there must know something. Who could it be? The bank was only interested in getting their money—money he'd borrowed to plant the flax. It made no sense that the bank would be involved with what happened, so what could his banker know?

Bergstrom's thoughts flowed in one direction now and, even if he couldn't make sense of them, they all seemed focused on one area. The banks of the river widened as he reached the dam and power plant for the town. Here above the dam the river was deep and looked deceptively calm.

"Talk to my banker," Bergstrom muttered to himself. "I been workin' with the bank for years. What could... why would the bank...?" He couldn't put anything together. It didn't make sense. The bank was on his side, supporting him. Everyone there was supportive. Everyone, Bergstrom thought, unless...

Continuing on, he moved below the dam where the river became a torrent of raging white water roaring through the spillway. Bergstrom weaved unsteadily. He stood looking at the concrete face of the dam as his mind grappled with reason. "Unless..." he said to himself, "unless..." He took a last pull from the bottle and threw it hard at the face of the dam where it burst into sparkling shards. He was going to have a talk with his banker.

Hindsight would have told him to wait for another time, when he hadn't been drinking. But the whisky blinded his hindsight and bolstered his courage. He had waited long enough and now he wanted answers.

The bank lobby was quiet as dignified people at teller windows conducted financial business in hushed tones as though confessing to priests. Bergstrom was not dignified, nor was he quiet. He approached the receptionist's desk directly and addressed the woman in tones meant for the open fields.

"I'll have a word with my banker now," he declared.

The woman sensed something wasn't quite right with this farmer, and asked him who specifically that would be.

"It'll be the one that loans me money for farmin'. You know who it is."

"That would be Mr. Stordal," she replied in a well-rehearsed tone. "Have a seat there and I'll see if he's available. May I tell him who's calling?"

"Bergstrom!" he belched.

"I'll be back in a moment."

From the brief conversation and the fumes on his breath, as well as his manner, the receptionist could tell the man was inebriated. She stuck her head into a back office and addressed the well-attired and groomed man behind a big desk.

"Sorry to bother you Mr. Stordal, but there's a man here to see you. A Mr. Bergstrom? Says you're his loan officer?"

"Bergstrom? Oh yeah. Him. What does he want?" said the banker.

"I don't know, just said he wants to talk to his banker. Shall I show him back or tell him to come another time?"

"Hmmm. I wonder..." Stordal seemed distracted for a moment. "Yeah, tell him I'm busy. Tell him I'm with somebody right now. He can come back later."

"Just as well," said the receptionist. "He's been drinking. Reeks like a still and I don't think he's in—shall I say—a business frame of mind."

Stordal gave a sneer that flashed a big gold eyetooth. "Yeah, good. Tell him to come back another time."

Back at her desk she addressed Bergstrom in her most professionally formal voice. "Mr. Stordal is busy with another client right now. He asks that you come back at a better time. Can I make an appointment for you?"

Bergstrom furrowed his brow not quite able to comprehend. He was on a one-way road that didn't allow for detours. He turned from the receptionist as though he might be leaving, and she smiled condescendingly.

"To hell with that!" Bergstrom said nearly shouting. Her eyes got very large as the expression on his face declared he would not be brushed off. "I didn't come to town for nothin'. He'll be seein' me now!"

Bergstrom brushed past her restraining arm like it was a corn stalk and strode for the door he'd seen her duck into moments ago.

"Wait! You can't go in there! Mr. Bergstrom, wait!" she insisted, to no avail.

He burst through the door to the office, despite a chorus of protest from the receptionist behind him, and stood weaving in the doorway, glaring at Stordal.

"That'll be all right, Ellen," Stordal said to the receptionist after setting his cigar in an ash tray. "I can meet with Mr. Bergstrom now. It's okay."

"I'm sorry Mr. Stordal. I tried to stop him but..."

"It's okay, really. I'll take care of everything. Don't worry about it," Stordal reassured her as he got up with a sigh from behind his desk. "This won't take too long, will it?" he said turning to Bergstrom, whose glassy glare followed his approach.

Stordal took the receptionist's arm as she left and said in quiet voice, "Call security. Watch for my signal." Then he closed his door.

"Good morning Bergstrom. What can I do for you today?" he said, eyeing the farmer cautiously and extending a limp hand, which was ignored.

Bergstrom's tone indicated he was struggling for composure, but his expression showed he would not tolerate being humored. "You know..." he said. "You know something an' I've come to find out what." He approached Stordal who moved to a more defensive position behind his desk and sat down.

"Have a seat Bergstrom," he said trying to relax the tension in the man's alcohol-induced state of mind and psychologically level their positions. Bergstrom ignored the offer.

"I'm not following you," Stordal said. "What do you want to know?"

"The fire."

"Oh yes. That was so unfortunate. A terrible thing. I'm sure the bank sent you a note of condolence. Didn't you get it?"

"What happened?" Bergstrom asked. "You know something don' you. What caused the fire that night? Did you do something? What burnt up my flax an' my wife?"

"Ah. It's about her then, isn't it." Stordal's eyes narrowed as he leered with his gold tooth. "Look here, Bergstrom, you're drunk. You shouldn't be here. The bank can finance crops, but we don't give loans for wives. Sorry. Too bad she—"

"What do you have to do with it?" Bergstrom said loudly.

"Are you accusing me of something?" Stordal replied, raising his own voice. "How the hell should I know what started that fire? The sheriff didn't find out anything, did he? It's not my job to investigate your misfortunes. Besides, Nora wasn't meant to be a farmer's wife. If you want to blame anyone for what happened to her, blame yourself you stupid..."

"You son-of-a-," Bergstrom growled as he came at him. Stordal's hand went for the button under his desk.

The receptionist could hear loud muffled voices coming from Stordal's office and waited nervously with one eye on the signal light. A security guard was beside her desk, and a policeman was on the way. When the light went on, both the guard and receptionist headed immediately for Stordal's office.

Bergstrom had the banker up against a wall and had lifted him by his coat lapels so his feet cleared the floor. Both men were shouting now, but Stordal's voice was panicky. The security guard and receptionist were having no success in pulling the powerful farmer away from the banker until the police officer arrived. A sharp poke in Bergstrom's ribs from the policeman's nightstick brought the confrontation to a conclusion, and he was hauled off to spend the night in jail.

For personal reasons, E.A. Stordal decided to let the incident pass and did not press charges. The matter never went to court. Bergstrom was let off with a warning and told to keep away from the banker.

That was many years ago, and it was now late winter in early 1939. Standing at his wide-open bedroom window, Bergstrom became aware that he was now shivering from the cold as he stared blankly out over the moonlit snow. His long underwear was damp with sweat after waking from the familiar nightmare that would not quit haunting him.

Even during the day, after all these years, memories of the fire and Nora remained just beneath his consciousness. It took little for them to erupt and interfere with his thoughts and actions. Truly Bergstrom was a man obsessed. After closing the window he pulled on his overalls and boots and headed for the kitchen to make coffee. The nightmare had happened so many other times before that he knew there would be no more sleep tonight.

2

(Spring, 1939)

The fresh scent of cow manure on mild breezes announced the return of spring in rural west-central Minnesota just as surely as the return of longer days and robins. But restless farmers here are more attuned to the subtle scent of the awakening earth around the rolling countryside. The soil in wet fields began to breathe again after months of frozen slumber. Soon these men would be back cultivating their fields, preparing the earth, planting... repeating the annual rituals that still mark the seasons of life on the land.

Oscar Halvorson was one of those who worked this land, and the land in return had left its mark on him. Just over six feet tall in his younger years, his shoulders now stooped from a life of labor. At sixty, he was still fit and agile from the physical demands of his occupation. He plodded soft stubble fields with a spring-kneed gait that looked a bit odd on city pavement, but covered off-road distances with steady efficiency. The elements of every season had worked their effects on his features, and Oscar's once fair Nordic complexion was perpetually dark and ruddy from too much sun. Long, deep furrows contoured his brow and crow's feet tracked the corners of his ice-blue eyes.

He dressed somewhat like a scarecrow from a farm garden, wearing worn and patched bib overalls and a faded chambray shirt. It was a cool morning and he had on a dirty old mackinaw with so much straw chaff and hayseed imbedded in the wool it had become part of the fabric. Handles of a pump pliers stuck out from one coat pocket, while his fingers rolled the few kernels of corn that always seemed to collect in the other pocket. A lifetime of farming had made Oscar's hands hard. His thick, callused fingers—all nine of them—possessed both crushing strength to deal with stubborn, treacherous machinery and a gentle touch for newborn calves.

His background was not unlike that of many others in the area. Oscar was the oldest of six children born to Halvor and Rakel Halvorson, who had emigrated to America from Norway in the late 1800s and homesteaded in northern Minnesota. Oscar was the only child born in Norway, and was only two when they crossed the ocean. The next child, a girl, died in infancy during an influenza epidemic. Then came three more boys: Nils, Jens, and William.

Oscar was a good five years older than his next brother, and by the time they were old enough to play together, Oscar was old enough to be helping his father on the farm. It was a struggle common to everyone who homesteaded this new land, and the Halvorson family, like others in the area, had very little, but managed to get by.

When Oscar's brothers were old enough, they went to a one-room school house several miles away to learn the basics. Oscar, being the oldest needed to stay home and work with his father. Oh, he learned how to read and write a little, and even acquired some basic arithmetic skills from his brothers and mother. Not being in school, Oscar was unable to maintain the pace of learning with his brothers and he became frustrated. In his mind he rejected education, knowing that as the oldest son the farm would one day be his. He put his heart, mind and soul into learning farming from his father, and found solace in a bond with the land. In time, their separate paths formed a gap between Oscar and his brothers. Of course it was never meant to be that way, but as the parents sacrificed to provide for their children, Oscar sacrificed, too.

Halvor, the father, died after being kicked by a horse the year Jens entered high school in a nearby town. That changed the family relationship, leaving Oscar the oldest male, in charge of the farm. Oscar's mother took him aside and told him the farm had to provide for his brothers now. It was up to Oscar to see that the farm fulfilled the wishes of the father and mother to get the other children educated and prepared to become productive and prosperous citizens of this great country. The farm was Oscar's without question, but in return he needed to support and provide whatever his siblings needed to succeed in the world. It was what his father would have wanted, it was what his mother wanted, and it made sense. Oscar understood and willingly took on the responsibility, putting all of his energy into the farm and the land. Still, he knew within himself something was missing, but it went unnamed.

From that time on, the gulf between Oscar and his brothers continued to widen. Oscar put down his brothers' education and social life and belittled their friends. It started as good-natured sibling rivalry, a sort of competition among boys, but soon progressed beyond that. The younger brothers shared a common experience in attending school and gradually became insensitive toward Oscar, even poking fun at his ignorance. Rakel remained his advocate in these situations, standing up for him against their taunting. If it got to be more than Oscar could bear, he would storm out of the house to seek refuge in the barn. Sometimes he spent the night out there, falling asleep in pile of straw. His resentment grew but, though he and his brothers continued to become more distant, Oscar never questioned their needs. Everything from school supplies, and clothing to spending money, Oscar and the farm provided without question.

Nils, Jens, and William went through high school and then off to far away cities to pursue their dreams. William continued his education, enrolling at the University of Minnesota and immersing himself in his studies. Each of the brothers wrote home regularly, and Oscar's mother always read their letters to him so he knew what they were doing. She'd write a reply, and persistently asked Oscar if he wanted to sign his name to the letter as well, but he never did.

There were struggles with market prices for crops in those days too, but between Oscar and his mother, they made the best decisions they could and managed to provide well enough until the boys were settled and could fend for themselves. But it was different for William.

Before he graduated from the university, The Great War broke out in Europe and William, the youngest and most idealistic, answered the call. William was lost at Verdun, a place Oscar had never heard of, let alone knew where it was. To him it represented what getting an education could do for you. To their mother, it was devastating.

The hard life of farming, the loss of her husband, age and failing health had all been catching up with Rakel over the years, and the death of her youngest son was a blow from which she never recovered. Before the war in Europe ended, Rakel became a casualty on the home front, leaving Oscar alone on the farm and head of a shattered family.

They buried Rakel between her husband, Halvor, and William, in the little cemetery beside Eidsvold Lutheran Church, a white-frame structure that Halvor had helped build after emigrating to this land. Standing over her grave after Rakel's funeral that day was the last time the Halvorson brothers were together as a family. Oscar remained alone on the farm, taking the livestock for his family, the land for his soul mate.

Now these days, if anyone was a close friend and confidant to Oscar, it was Hektor, a four-legged farm hand. Hektor had known Oscar all his life. They took meals together and he knew Oscar's every mood. He understood Norwegian and had listened to Oscar's frustrated tirades on the bank or government policies throughout the Depression, and shared his concern when weather threatened the crops. When Oscar was melancholy, Hektor was there to comfort him, and when he rejoiced, Hektor shared his joy. He stood by Oscar without judgment.

But Hektor was getting old and only moved in slow motion these days. In his younger years he'd led the way every time they headed out to the fields. Now, when he showed up in a field where Oscar was working, it was half an hour or so late. But Oscar didn't mind. He was glad to have company and always stopped what he was doing to say a few kind words to the old fellow. He understood arthritis was why his friend didn't move fast anymore. Hektor's eyesight was going too, but he always saw what was best in Oscar.

Hektor's background was uncertain, but he could claim an itinerant black lab in his lineage somewhere. He wore his hair shaggier than a lab, and his face was long and narrow, with gray hair dominating his muzzle and ears that never knew whether to point or droop. A few cockle burrs had permanently imbedded themselves in Hektor's tail, which still wagged at the prospect of going anywhere with Oscar.

Neither of them were much concerned about looks, at least not when it was just the two of them. All that mattered to Hektor was Oscar's voice nearby, or his hand stroking or scratching somewhere. They were completely devoted to each other, and perpetually together.

Now Oscar, at sixty years old, was like Hektor and well past his prime. But fresh spring air and seasonal anticipation renewed a vigor that made him feel young again. He pushed back his greasy old felt hat and leaned an elbow on a fence post, squinting as he surveyed the soggy fields.

Oscar struggled with choices this morning. Contemplating the field and its potential crop was normal, but over the winter he'd struggled with something else. Something that involved stepping outside the comfortable, conservative character that typified farmers in this area.

Like other local farmers who had survived the Depression so far,

Oscar was in debt. In the dry years when fields didn't produce, nearly every farmer needed help to defer payments on loans and mortgages, or to borrow money to simply live. Banks all over the country had failed following the crash of '29, but one in Foster Falls had survived. It was the one owned and operated by E.A. Stordal, a shrewd businessman who had money to lend, on his terms, take it or leave it. The collateral he wanted —and usually got—was a man's property, the only thing left of real value during the Depression.

As with most farmers, Oscar's land was everything to him. Homesteaded by his parents, it was his legacy from them and a connection with them. It was his home and only means of support. The sweat and blood of his parents as well as his own was intermingled with the soil, nourishing the earth, which brought forth nourishment for him in return. He'd struggled through the Depression, just managing to hang on to the place. Well, it wasn't entirely his own doing, at least not while he still owed E.A. Stordal for the loan he'd needed during the drought. The loan would come due the end of this year, after the harvest, and he didn't have the money. His farm of course, was his only collateral. It had haunted Oscar all that winter.

The lowest point in his life was when he'd signed for the loan from E.A. Stordal, putting everything on the line and allowing a stranger access to his most personal possession. The amount was far less than the actual value of the land, but the bank and Mr. Stordal had harsh terms, and Oscar was out of options. He couldn't understand all the words, so E.A. explained the terms and details to him as they sat across the banker's desk from each other. All Oscar remembered of the conversation was the amount of money he owed, the date he had to pay it back, and the glint of gold in E.A. Stordal's smile.

As they shook hands, he felt the man had a good firm grip, but Oscar sensed something other than trust and friendship taking his hand that day. Throughout his life, Oscar's hands had shoveled manure, pulled calves, been covered in grease and grime. But somehow his hand felt unclean when he left Stordal's office that day and he stopped at a restroom to wash.

Though the Depression had been hard on all farmers, it recently seemed things were beginning to get better. Crop prices were climbing back to a level that promised to make farming profitable again. Oscar reasoned that he could get out of debt if he just had more land to plant. Like the average farmer in the area, he worked eighty acres. If he could get more land and if prices continued to hold he could, perhaps, pay off Stordal and keep his farm. It would be a start toward getting back on solid financial footing again. Not all at once of course, but it would be a beginning. But Oscar had no more land to plant.

There was plenty of land for sale, what with foreclosures and all, he just couldn't afford the risk. He couldn't even afford to rent. What if something happened to the crop and he couldn't pay the landowner? He already owed too much to Stordal and Oscar knew what had happened to others who had lost their farms: shattered lives, broken hearts, broken families. He just couldn't risk losing his farm—his father's farm—after all he'd been through. Oscar turned and ambled down the fencerow towards the thick grove of burr oak that sheltered his house and the buildings that comprised his world. Losing the farm was just not a possibility to consider.

No, it was maybe just best to be patient, he thought, wait it out a little longer and see if some opportunity would come along. Maybe the government would come up with a program... the thought trailed off. He was all too familiar with various programs and political promises. "Yah," he inhaled, he'd just have to fend off creditors for another year—if he could. With that, Oscar plodded along the fence line that headed back toward his machine shed.

He'd been tinkering with the seeder that he got from Gus Haugen just before the Haugen farm went under, and now everything seemed to be ready. The soil just needed to dry a little more. Like others in the area, Oscar was a small dairy farmer. He'd managed to keep ten Holsteins, half of what he'd had in his best years. He grew alfalfa for his cattle on his 80 acres and enough corn for fodder and sometimes a little grain to feed them and the few chickens he kept. That was about it. In good years when the yield was high, he'd sell off what his granary wouldn't hold, but it was never enough to be profitable. Oscar's farm wasn't prosperous and hadn't been since the Depression. As a one-man operation, it was all he could handle by himself. He'd done well to hold onto it for so long.

Stepping over the tongue of the planter, he patted one of the big tires of the old Massey-Harris tractor he called "*Gubbe*" (Goo-beh, a Norwegian term for an old man)—a reference to the last workhorse he'd owned. After setting the choke and throttle, he turned on the switch and went to the front end of the tractor. Oscar inserted the end of the heavy crank handle onto the starter shaft and gave a few turns. The engine coughed and sputtered a bit before disengaging the crank, then backfired and died.

Oscar had a few other names for *Gubbe* when the tractor was reluctant to start. Horses had always been easier to work with, and he understood them well. Horses were so much more reasonable. He never completely comprehended what made the engine work, and never felt comfortable around it's unflinching power.

When a farmer's tractor was reluctant to start, backfires could be dangerous. A backfire caused the heavy crank handle to be wrenched from the hand in reverse direction, which could result in a broken wrist or arm. Such disabling accidents, and others, were not uncommon.

Oscar dealt with his mistrust of the tractor the way he did with stubborn horses. He assumed an authoritative attitude to show who was in charge—or in the case of the tractor, more to cover his apprehension. Then, being an even-tempered man, he'd talk to the tractor in rational tones, soothing and persuasive. If the fussy engine continued to balk, his patient tone—and personality—altered. His voice became higher pitched, assertive, even demanding, as he fiddled with controls and cranked. If nothing else worked, he finally resorted to cursing at the great iron beast.

This profanity was always in Norwegian, because Oscar felt English lacked the dark eloquence that was sufficient to focus on the situation. Hektor usually waited patiently nearby but, trained in Norwegian, he understood everything Oscar said. When the cursing began, the old dog would get up and walk away, causing Oscar to feel a bit sheepish.

By the time the situation got to this point, the engine was usually flooded, and nothing would make it run. Frustrated, Oscar would shake his fist, turn and walk away to do something else. It was probably the best thing he could do, and it usually worked. When he returned in half an hour or so, the engine would usually start, which he attributed to the fickle personality of the machine. Such was his relationship with *Gubbe* the old Massey-Harris.

Today however, spring air in the carburetor seemed to also give a vigor to the old tractor, and it sputtered to life with the next round of cranking. Oscar hitched up the wagon as the engine warmed up and lifted Hektor up onto it before chugging off to the field to load some hay for his cattle.

The hay field lay just to the south side of the oaks that sheltered his house, and he'd stacked the hay at the top of a hill at the west end of the field, just off the gravel county road. Oscar always stacked the hay there because the ground was high and exposed to drying winds. He drove old *Gubbe* out of the shed and followed the driveway around his yard and out onto the hayfield. After chugging up the hill, he pulled the wagon along side the haystack, shut off the tractor and dismounted. Below the tractor seat was a wooden crate that served as a toolbox. From it, Oscar pulled a gunnysack wrapped around a mason jar. He unscrewed the lid and took a few gulps of strong, lukewarm coffee, then replaced the jar in the toolbox.

After arranging the hay sling, he grabbed his pitchfork and set to work loading hay onto the wagon. Soon he stopped to peel off the mackinaw, and pulled himself up onto the wagon to pile the hay.

As Oscar worked, his thoughts returned to getting another field, growing another crop. If he could just figure a way to get the land he needed. There were fields around, but he didn't like to drive far with old *Gubbe*, especially while towing equipment.

There was old man Grundsvold's north 40. It was good soil, but that tight old bastard wouldn't be apt to let someone plant on it without collecting most of the profit for himself. Besides, he'd probably be out there telling Oscar how to do everything and criticizing how he did it. No, Grundsvold's land wouldn't do.

Hanson had a sweet 20-acre field that had laid fallow for the last five years, and Oscar thought it would probably yield well. But it looked like this year Hanson was preparing to till that piece himself.

Oscar paused, leaning on the pitchfork. From the hay wagon on top of the hill he could see a long way around the township. He could make out activities on other farms, other men in their fields doing similar chores, all getting back into the rhythm of the season. As he scanned the countryside, his eyes came to rest on a cluster of trees just off the county road, not quite a mile away—the Widow Holmvik's place.

3

(Spring, 1939)

Be gentle when you touch bread—
    let it not lie uncared for,
    taken for granted or unwanted.
There is such beauty in bread,
    beauty of sun and soil,
    beauty of patient toil,
Winds and rains caressed it,
    Christ often blessed it.
Be gentle when you touch bread.
—Anon

Esther Holmvik blew out the kerosene lamp over her kitchen table as sunrise poured through the east window. Diffused by curtains, the light of a new morning set the entire room aglow in a warmth that made these early hours in the kitchen her favorite time of day.

She poked a couple hardwood sticks into the glowing firebox of her stove and closed the oven door. With the morning chill now gone from the room, she felt comfortable enough to remove her old sweater. Lifting a big crockery bowl down from the warming rack above the stove, she carried it to the kitchen table. She grabbed a handful of flour from a canister, tossed it on the work surface and brushed it around. Then, with a sort of reverence Esther removed a dishtowel covering the bowl, carefully withdrew a large dome of dough and set it on the table in front of her.

After rubbing a little more flour on her hands, she began the rhythmic process of kneading the ball of dough—grabbing, pulling, pushing down with the heel of her hand. It was an easy, rolling movement that traveled from her waist to her upper body and down from her shoulders, ending up in the dough. She'd developed the motion as a child, learning to make bread at her mother's side. Every woman had a subtly different technique or rhythm for kneading that somehow imparted a personal touch to the loaf. Esther loved every phase of making bread. There never was a recipe, just a basic process that brought her a feeling of contentment, and she unconsciously hummed "Blest Be The Tie That Binds" while she worked the dough.

Esther Holmvik had been a tall, slender woman in her younger days, but at 58, she didn't seem tall anymore. When young, she had been pretty, but years of farm life and hard work had caused the pretty young face to recede behind a mask of age. The pretty girl's face was still there, one just had to look a little deeper to see her. Esther's hazel eyes were still bright and clear, but wire-rim glasses resting halfway down her delicate nose were now a permanent fixture. Her easy, genuine smile was her most beautiful feature. It started with a crinkling around the eyes just before the corners of her mouth spread across her radiant face. Anyone on the receiving end of her smile felt better, maybe even charmed. Esther kept her hair long, but the deep chestnut brown had turned early to pewter gray. She brushed it out every night before bed but wore it braided and tightly rolled into a bun at the back of her head during the day.

A practical woman without frills, Esther's limited wardrobe consisted of a few old floral-printed housedresses, which she alternated throughout the week. Over the housedress she usually wore two aprons, sometimes three on weekends. That way, she could quickly remove the outer service apron and always be looking proper with the nice clean one if company stopped by. Esther felt, as did everyone in the area, that it was important to always present a good image, especially to strangers.

Good manners and proper appearances were instilled at an early age by farming parents who had emigrated from Norway in 1870. Esther was born in this country, her parents' only child. That's why she received so much attention from her father who showed her much of what farming was about, and her mother who made sure that she finished high school, which was unusual in those days. Esther's mother played the organ at their church, and, like kneading bread, Esther learned to play the organ at her mother's side.

After high school she helped teach children reading and writing at the country schoolhouse for a few years before moving into the nearby town of Foster Falls to work at a local mercantile store. She returned to her parents' farm often to visit, and one hot summer day during threshing season Esther met a young man who worked on the threshing crew.

The man's name was Carl Holmvik and he had just got a tract of land near a country church where he was starting out farming on his own. Carl was a handsome fellow and they took an interest in each other right from the start. The courtship went on for several years while Carl worked to get his farm established, and eventually Esther and Carl were married. She joined Carl on his farm, and through their combined efforts, the land provided and they did well. But all that was in better times, before the crash of '29 and the Depression that followed.

Nowadays, Esther was not unlike any of the other farm wives of the area in the 1930s, except she wasn't a wife anymore, she was a widow. Her husband, Carl, had been tragically killed many years before by a team of runaway horses. She and Carl had a son, Arthur, but he was too young to help with farm work after Carl's death. She never remarried, but worked the farm with a hired man for a few years, until Arthur was old enough to help. Together, she and her son managed the small farm, but she made sure Arthur stayed in school too. Esther put all her energy into keeping up the farm so her son could take it over some day, but eventually Arthur confessed he wasn't interested in farming. Soon after finishing high school, he moved to Minneapolis to find work and a faster life style.

After Arthur left home, Esther sold some land to pay debts, and held on to what was left by renting out a couple fields, since farming was too difficult for her alone. After the Depression hit, no one had money to rent anymore, so her land went fallow, except for the big garden she tended. Esther canned the produce from her ample garden and kept a large flock of chickens for food and the little money she got for eggs. She often bartered for things she needed and by taking in sewing and mending when she could, she got by.

A woman of deep Christian faith, Esther attended Eidsvold Lutheran Church. She had taken over playing the church's old pump organ when her mother gave it up, and ever since Esther played not just for Sunday services but weddings and funerals as well, all presided over by Reverend Ellerby. It was convenient for her, as her farm home was located right next to the church, just a short walk away. Because of her being so close, Esther had been given a key to open and close the church for all functions, and so she could get in for minor cleaning or for special preparations for which she received a small stipend.

Eidsvold Lutheran Church was typical of the many little white wood-frame churches around the county. Each church brooded over a flock of white tombstones, like mother hens watching over their eggs. The plain grave markers bore names and dates, and often an epitaph in Norwegian, which simply said, "*Takk for Alt*" (Thanks for Everything). Eidsvold's steepled structure nestled amid a small grove of burr oak and box elder, with a pair of outhouses—men's and women's—at the edge of the trees, and a well pump in a corner of the cemetery.

Eidsvold, like most of the other rural churches in the area, was built in the mid-1800s by Scandinavian immigrants just a generation before many of the current members. The front door of the church opened out on half a dozen steps and a sidewalk that led to the gravel parking apron, which was more or less an expansion of the gravel county road that ran by. Inside the front door was a small alcove with coat hooks around the perimeter and a bell rope descending from the steeple.

Another set of doors opened into a sanctuary, which could optimistically accommodate about sixty souls at a time, but had never been tested to that capacity. Every square foot of the hardwood floor creaked so loudly that no one dared get up in the middle of a service, for the attention they would draw. It was far better to endure the long service in the discomfort of the dark hardwood pews than risk the embarrassment that such a disruption would cause. It was a form of penance some felt. In the early days, women sat in the pews on one side of the aisle and men on the other, but this was America in the 1930s, and such old traditions were on the way out. Reverend Ellerby was considered quite progressive, as his services were in English, though most of the old timers still believed Norwegian to be the language of the Lord.

Each side of the sanctuary had three long, narrow windows that opened on the bottom to provide some ventilation and were decorated with a pointed, stained glass section at the top. In the front of the sanctuary, two steps ascended to where a plain oak altar table was centered and adorned with a white altar cloth of incredibly elaborate Hardanger embroidery made by the church women, a simple brass cross, and an ancient Bible with embossed leather cover printed in old style Norwegian text. The simple, handmade pulpit stood to the congregation's right, and the tired old pump organ sat against the wall on the left.

To the side of the compact alcove at the entry was a narrow creaky stairway that led down to Eidsvold's musty basement, which was used for social gatherings, and that meant eating. The dining area was crowded with several rows of wooden folding tables and chairs, always left in position for use. At the far end of the basement, a wall separated the kitchen from the dining area. A doorway to one side allowed serving traffic of bustling farmwomen in and out of the kitchen, and a long serving window opened to the dining area. The kitchen was equipped with cupboards of heavy, white china dishes, pots and pans, deep sinks for washing, and a couple kerosene stoves. Here and there a dull yellow strip of curly flypaper dangled precariously, and bare light bulbs in ceiling surface fixtures gave a dim incandescent glare throughout the basement.

It was here at Eidsvold Church that rural families came together, not just to worship, but to support each other in times of joy and sorrow. The church was a common bond that held area people together, offering a reason for social gathering to a group that may not otherwise have found an opportunity for relief from the arduous farm life. In addition to their faith, these aspects of the church drew and held people, including Esther Holmvik, by providing a sense of community in their lives.

Another responsibility Esther assumed for the little church was providing the bread for communion services, meals and bake sales held there. She had an arrangement with Mr. Phillips, who ran a mill over on the Ottertrack River. He would grind all the flour she needed for free, as a payment for the services Esther provided to the church. It was Mr. Phillip's way of contributing to the church, and a good arrangement for Esther as well.

Now this morning, after she finished kneading the dough, Esther used a large knife to slice it into five loaves, placed them in prepared pans and put them in the pre-heated oven. After checking the draft on the firebox, she poured herself a cup of coffee and sat down at the table to rest in the sunlight. Gazing out at the awakening countryside, Esther's thoughts wandered back over the past seven months and how her life had changed. Turning to the cupboard behind her, she took a wrinkled letter from a drawer and unfolded it in her lap. She didn't need to read it; she knew every word it said by heart.

The letter was from her son Arthur. It was the last one she received from him, and it had arrived with a surprise. His previous letters all told about working in a flourmill in Minneapolis, on the river near downtown. Then there was a letter telling about meeting a young girl named Helen while waiting for a streetcar. The letters came less frequently after that, but she gathered that Arthur was getting quite serious about the young lady.

Then, in 1929, after a period of about two years with no word, Esther got another letter from Arthur. He apologized for not writing for so long, but told his mother that he'd gotten married to Helen. Not only that, but they now had a son whom they named Henry. He had gone to work for Helen's father and everything was looking rosy for them. Arthur hoped she could come visit them sometime in Minneapolis.

To Esther, the news was bittersweet. She felt hurt being left out of such important affairs in her son's life, but was delighted to hear that she was a grandmother. She anxiously hoped she would meet her little grandson Henry some day. Esther put her feelings aside and wrote to her son to tell him how pleased she was that all was going well for him, and that he now had a son of his own. She sent gifts at Christmas—a baby blanket that she made, booties and mittens she'd knit. Arthur made an attempt to correspond, writing to thank her, but didn't include much news. Then came the stock market crash and the Great Depression.

Now, sitting at her kitchen table, Esther recalled what she was doing the past October when she'd received her last letter from Arthur. He wrote that his father-in-law's business had failed and he was out of a job. Esther was concerned for him and his little family, but she had no money to help or even travel to visit them. It was more than seven months ago that she'd had the idea to invite her son and his little family to come live with her on the farm. At least they'd have a place to live and a means of providing something to eat. She had written back to Arthur that same day, inviting him, his wife and son to come back to the farm and live with her. She was unprepared for his response.

It came a few days later by telegram; the only one Esther ever received in her life. Arthur said he was putting his son on the train that evening. She must meet him at the depot in Foster Falls the next morning. An explanation would arrive with him.

Now as she sipped her coffee, Esther recalled how thrilled she had felt knowing she was going to see her grandson for the first time. She had immediately walked to a neighbor's farm to make arrangements for transportation into town the next morning to meet him at the train depot. As she walked, she wondered what he would look like, how big would he be. Young Henry was about eight years old by then. What would he think of her? What would he be like? When would Arthur and Henry's mother Helen come? Esther had been so excited she could barely explain to her neighbor that she needed to get to town the next morning.

Smiling to herself Esther now recalled meeting Henry at the depot that morning last fall. It was no problem picking him out since he was the only boy that age on the train. He was wearing knickers and a tweed cap and coat and dragging an old carpetbag. Esther had walked up behind him and tapped him on his shoulder. When he turned around she could see he had his father's dark hair and blue eyes. He looked frightened and his eyes were still red from crying. He spoke first, saying, "Are you my gramma?" She knelt down and they melted into each other's arms. Esther remembered holding him for what seemed a long time as her own tears ran. Finally she said, "Yes, Henry, I'm your gramma."

For some of the stoic bystanders, it was an unusual display of affection in a public place, and they drew furtive stares from a few people on the platform. Esther didn't care. She was holding her son's flesh and blood and now felt closer to Arthur than she had since he'd left the farm. She was no longer alone. It wasn't until she and Henry were in her kitchen that Henry gave her the letter from his father that he'd carried in the breast pocket of his coat. Now, seven months later, Esther again held that letter in her hand as she sat at her kitchen table.

Tears welled up again in her eyes as she recalled what the letter said. Arthur had written of how the Depression had ruined his father-in-law's business, and he lost his job, his savings, everything. He and Helen, with their little son, had moved into a dingy little cold-water flat, where they struggled to pay the monthly rent. Arthur spent most of his time standing in line for menial jobs that paid next to nothing. Evenings he often went to union meetings, which didn't help his relationship with Helen's father.

Arthur had written that the collapse of his father-in-law's business had taken a severe toll on the man, ruining his health and spirit. After a while, he just sat in a chair and never left the house. During the winter of '36, Arthur's father-in-law got sick and died. His mother-in-law crumbled emotionally. When she became bed-ridden, Helen returned to her home to care for her mother and support the rest of her family.

She left Henry and Arthur and moved back home, saying she couldn't have Henry living with her sick mother, nor could she care for both of them.

It was obvious by Arthur's writing that he was hurt and disappointed by his wife's decision, and Esther's heart went out to him. He had never felt accepted by Helen's family and now she had abandoned him. He was left a single parent in the midst of the Depression, without a job and no means of supporting himself and his young son.

That had been about the time Arthur received her letter inviting him and his little family to come live with her on the farm. He wrote his mother that her letter couldn't have arrived at a better time, and it had given him an idea.

The end of Arthur's letter explained that he had thought it over, and realized he had been insensitive in excluding his mother from the recent years of his life. He had thought she wouldn't fit in with the sophisticated family he had married into. Realizing his mistake, he wrote that he now felt sorry and didn't deserve her kindness, but he hoped she would extend it to his son instead. Arthur felt the farm would be the best place for his Henry, and he was sending him by train to live with her until he found decent work and a suitable place to raise the boy.

Arthur then said that he had joined the Civilian Conservation Corps (CCC), and was going to work in the woods of northern Minnesota. He hoped she would understand and care for Henry, and he'd send money when he could.

That had been seven months ago and so far Esther had not heard from Arthur. She worried about her son and wondered where he was and how she could let him know they were doing well. She wanted so much to tell him that she loved him, that both she and Henry missed him, and wished he'd come home to the farm.

Just then, barefoot young Henry came hopping down the stairs wearing a flannel shirt that was too big for him and an old pair of bib overalls that had been Arthur's when he was young. It was Saturday morning, no school, and the boy was ready to appease a raging case of pent-up spring fever.

"'Morning Gramma!" he managed to get out as he dashed for the back door, eager to take on the day.

"Hold up there young man!" Esther's pseudo-stern voice of authority reached out like an invisible lasso. "You're not going out 'til you've washed up and had breakfast. And don't forget, you've got chores today."

"Aw Gramma, I didn't forget, I can do chores later and I ain't hungry now, can't I jus' eat breakfast at lunch?" Henry pleaded.

"At the pace you go you wouldn't make it to lunch. You know you've got to feed the fire to keep it burning," Esther said. "Just sit up here and have a bite and you won't waste time discussing it with me."

Henry turned and dragged himself obediently toward the kitchen table.

"Aren't you forgetting something?" Esther asked, turning to face Henry and crouching as she spread her arms.

Without a word, Henry's face broke into a big grin and he lunged with abandon into her embrace. After their morning hug Henry pumped water in the washbasin and smeared it around his eyes. He dried his face on his sleeves and went to the table.

Esther made milk mush: a paste made simply by adding flour to warm milk until it thickens. Butter and a bit of sugar was added to make it more palatable. It was typical fare for those who had little. Beside his plate was a cup of steaming coffee with cream and sugar in it. She poured herself another cup of coffee and sat down across from Henry as he took a seat and began to eat. Esther didn't say a word; she just cocked her head and glanced at him. Henry knew what she meant and set down his spoon. They bowed their heads and gave thanks for their food.

"*I Jesu navn gå vi til bård...*" (In Jesus name we go to the table...) Henry recited the entire table grace just as she had taught him.

The seven months had passed so quickly, and Henry had adjusted very well to life on the farm with his grandmother. The boy was not sure he was going to like it at first, but Esther was patient and like all grandmothers she seemed to know just what Henry needed to hear and when. Mostly, she was always there to hold him, and though he was growing older Henry still needed that reassurance from time to time. Henry missed his father but seemed to understand something beyond his control had pulled them apart. Henry's father had been right about one thing though—the timing of his mother's invitation could not have been better.

4

(Spring, 1939)

Ah yes, it was a fine spring morning. After the long winter, warm clear sunshine with a crisp, freshening spring breeze promised a good day and a new season. Moreover, telltale signs of improving economic trends made the future seem even brighter. It had been a rough decade since the crash in '29, but Elmer Stordal—E.A. to those close to him—had weathered the storm. He had not just kept afloat, but managed to prosper through the subtle use of his selectively refined professional skills. If it was at a cost to others, well, hard times called for hard measures. E.A. Stordal didn't make the rules, but he knew indeed how they worked. The rules were in his favor, and they showed promise for a good day.

Even the gradual return of prosperity couldn't have come at a better time in his life. E.A. had learned to recognize and appreciate the value of investing in land when the stock market and businesses floundered. Land was a safe investment, real property that would always be needed, developed or undeveloped. The old realtor's expression, "they're not making any more land," more than suggested to E.A. that there was a limited supply of a valuable resource. Owning land would not only make him wealthy, but put him securely in a position of power and influence in the area. Power and influence were fast becoming more important to E.A. than mere wealth. He was even considering entering politics.

Like everyone else, E.A. had struggled through the Depression, but as some folks said he'd come through it "not just landing on his feet, but in a pair of new shoes." As a local banker in Foster Falls, when it came to loans he was now the "only game in town." The only other lending institution in town had failed after the big run on banks at the beginning of the Depression ten years earlier. Back then, E.A. had been smart enough to lock-up and leave town for a critical period of time. It had been a close call, and a low point in his career, but he did whatever he needed to survive. Finally, time was now on his side.

Wherever he went, E.A. Stordal was preceded by his protruding belly. Once considered a sign of a successful businessman, at least in local perception, a fat paunch now in hard times suggested something quite different to many who had recently punched new holes in their own belts. E.A.'s girth was confined by a tight-fitting vest, with a heavy gold watch chain spanning its buttoned front, as if to secure his bulk. The strain on the vest buttons and chain could cause tension in those he encountered.

Through the hard times, E.A. had sought to groom a dapper professional business appearance in his three-piece suits. In his mid-forties, he kept his dark hair heavily oiled and slicked straight back, and maintained an impeccably trimmed, pencil-thin mustache along his upper lip. But the most interesting facial effect on E.A.'s flabby face was his smile. His upper lip curled back to the left, revealing a large, gleaming gold eyetooth. And E.A. smiled a lot, far too often for it to seem sincere.

The streets were still quiet as stores weren't yet open at this early hour. A large ring full of keys jingled as E.A. selected the right one and unlocked the door to the bank. Heading into his office, he hung his fedora and suit coat on the coat tree behind the door and went straight to his desk. The swivel chair groaned as it took his bulk and he selected a fat cigar from the humidor box on his desk. He clipped the end before lighting it, and then picked up a stack of manila folders, thumbing through people's names on the tabs. The glitter of gold showed in his smile as he noted names and dates on the mortgage documents, the seeds of his own crop.

They were simple-minded, these people of the soil, Stordal reflected, with stunted educations and limited understanding. E.A. was one of the few businessmen around town who possessed a college education and he was proud of it. In his mind, his education didn't just set him apart it set him above most everyone else. It gave him a vantage point from which to analyze how things worked around Foster Falls and the surrounding area. He knew which farms or businesses were doing well and which were not. These uneducated people lacked the finesse for doing business properly, and had little appreciation of the details involved. Ah, sweet details, he thought, all neat and in perfect order. Their importance had been impressed on him at the university. Details, he learned, were the key to the real objective, and that was control. Real control was contained in the details, control that moved the levers of influence and power.

To be fair, E.A. had listened condescendingly to the stories of people's various circumstances, or at least it seemed he did in the beginning. They all had sincere intentions of repaying loans, and he'd heard their pleas for just a little more time. E.A. even gave a break to some people, but that was in better times before the Depression. The drought ground away at the economy, and eroded E.A.'s sympathy as well, as he no longer listened to people's "personal problems". He told them he had problems of his own and had to consider "the big picture". He began processing foreclosures paying great attention to detail. This hard attitude had earned E.A. an unkind reputation both in town and around the rural community. But even if E.A. was losing friends, he was gaining property, which he would one day convert to influence, control, and profit.

Throughout the 1930s, with the dire conditions of the Depression, the name E.A. Stordal evoked strong feelings from people around the area. Benefactors saw him as a savior when hard times knocked on their door. Most people, by experience or by word of mouth had learned that he was a man of few favors and never forgot one owed to him. E.A. kept very accurate books, and one did not want to be in the situation of owing the man anything.

It was understood around town and especially by area farmers that Stordal's success was gained at the misfortune of others during the hard times. Asking him for a loan was considered a last desperate measure by most, and those who did were considered marked men. The countryside was dotted with vacant farms that, at least on paper, now belonged to Stordal. He had become a man of power and influence around the area, but when his name was mentioned in pleasant conversation these days it usually changed the tone. His appearance at a gathering sometimes caused certain folks in this quiet Scandinavian community to turn away muttering Norse epithets under their breath.

But E.A. wasn't in business to win popularity. He saw himself as a predator in the process of natural selection, and he was simply "culling the herd." In the stack of folders on his desk this fine spring morning, he held the futures of several individuals around the county, most of them struggling farmers. They were those whose loans would be due by the end of this year's harvest. Either he'd be paid back or he'd control more property that would convert to power and influence one day. Farming took a lot of patience, and E.A. could afford to be patient. In what seemed like a few more months, E.A. would be ready to reap his own sort of harvest.

Two folders out of the stack were of particular interest as being the most ripe for plucking. They were the files of two farmers, Oscar Halvorson and Theodore Bergstrom, both bachelors independently working their own land. Both men would have gone under several years ago, but each had borrowed money to keep operating through the Depression. E.A.'s bank had been happy to oblige, loaning each man considerable sums on very carefully arranged terms -- terms he'd written himself, with detailed legal language that promised the forfeiture of their properties if they failed to repay the total amount of their loans by a specific date following next fall's harvest.

E.A. only knew Halvorson casually, but had loaned him money in the past for the man's various farming needs, new equipment, improvements, and the regular sort of things that come up and are part of farming. Halvorson always had paid back his loans on time with the interest, but that was before the Depression. Depression economics called for different tactics, the details of which worked to E.A. Stordal's advantage. Economically there wasn't room for charity in his business these days, and any such language had been carefully eliminated from E.A.'s loan contracts.

The drought and crop failure a few years ago left Oscar Halvorson in financial trouble. Like so many other area farmers whose crops had failed, he'd come to E.A. Stordal, the only surviving bank around the area, for the financial means to keep farming.

It wasn't anything personal with Halvorson, E.A. felt as he flipped through the contents of the man's loan folder. It was strictly business. Actually, he didn't understand how the aging farmer had held onto his place this long. Without education, other than what experience had taught, the man had done all right—until now. Halvorson may be a decent fellow, but E.A. never let sentiment interfere with business. It was simple. Halvorson had come to him in need, E.A. supplied his need according to agreed terms and, according to those terms E.A. would be coming to Halvorson with his own need—the need for payment. The man must have been desperate to have made such an agreement, E.A. thought, but it wasn't his problem. It would take a miracle for Halvorson to keep his farm after this year.

Bergstrom was a different matter. E.A. didn't like Bergstrom and had never forgotten the incident in his office over fifteen years ago. The drunken farmer had forced his way into his office and roughed him up. Absolutely unacceptable, E.A. thought, and unforgivable. Moreover, the man remained suspicious about past incidents. Only suspicious, but obviously obsessed with what had happened to his wife and the crop into which he'd invested so much. Nothing had ever been found, no evidence of any sort at the field, the scene of the tragedy.

Yes, it was a tragedy. Bergstrom had lost his wife. That shouldn't have happened. Nora shouldn't have been involved with that fire, but then E.A. felt she shouldn't have been with Bergstrom at all. That shouldn't have happened either. Those two should never have come together, never have been man and wife. There are many ways to get burned when you play with fire, E.A. thought. He had his own feelings too, but had learned to cover them stoically.

That Bergstrom was crazy was of no doubt to Stordal, but the man's obsession with the past was disconcerting. The fire was long ago now, and far from people's minds and daily conversations. Bergstrom's obsession and fragile mental state eliminated him as a credible witness for his own case, but E.A. still considered him dangerous. Putting Bergstrom out of business would probably put him completely out of the way. Patience now, after waiting all these years, would come easily for E.A.

It was nothing more than fair, E.A. thought, as both men would have already lost their farms without his help. Besides, they were bachelors; single men without dependent families, so minimum personal harm would be done. These men were well aware that farming has its risks and they had entered into their respective contracts of their own accord. If things didn't work out for them, E.A. would simply be claiming what was legally his. If things went as they had for the past ten years he smirked; at least E.A. Stordal would have a good harvest. God, how he loved farming.

Of course, it was spring and the beginning of a new season and nothing was certain. But E.A. had gotten pretty good at predicting who was going to fail. He closed the Bergstrom and Halvorson folders and with a golden smile set them to the side of his desk, patting them gently. It was never anything personal of course; it wasn't his fault if these people wanted to keep pouring money into worthless efforts. They all knew that someday they would have to come back and repay E.A. Stordal what they owed. The economy was going to recover from the Depression and a feeling of optimism was returning. He could feel it, smell it in the fresh spring air this morning. Thanks to his careful attention to details E.A. owned a lot of property around Ottertrack County as well as in town, and as the economy recovered it would put him in control, make him a man of power and influence, make him wealthy. Stordal leaned back in his chair and exhaled a blue cloud of cigar smoke. Now those two folders indicated he was either going to realize a nice profit from two loan repayments this year or gain two more farms. Either way, it worked out in favor of E.A. Stordal, and that's just the way he liked it. Yes, this was a fine spring morning indeed.

5

Oscar's Model-T pickup bounced and jostled over and through the potholes, sending muddy water flying everywhere. A steady spring rain pelted the windshield, making it difficult to see and avoid the water-filled holes, let alone detect how deep they might be. The driveway to Theodore Bergstrom's farm was in terrible condition, a matter which apparently was of no concern to the man. His driveway didn't get much use, as he seldom left his farm and visitors were very rare. But Oscar's mind was not on potholes or the weather this morning. He was coming to see Bergstrom on business.

Theodore Bergstrom was another bachelor farmer, and probably for that reason alone, he and Oscar felt they shared a common bond. Though their farms lay several miles apart, whenever their paths crossed they traded thoughts on running a farm single-handed, what things worked and what didn't. Being bachelors, their independence set them apart—at least in their own minds—from other farmers in the area. They each knew the other understood what it meant to live and work alone, to struggle and survive alone, and each had an unspoken high esteem for the other's farming ability. Neither would have called it a "close" friendship, but there existed an odd sort of relationship that passed for one.

When the Depression hit, both men struggled to hold onto their farms through the drought years, mechanical breakdowns, various diseases in crops or cattle and always, always fighting off foreclosure. To Oscar it had been hard times for sure; but to Bergstrom, it was an accumulation of life's injustices, one after another over the years, and he could not, or would not let go of them. Oscar did feel a little sorry for the man, though he never expressed it in any way.

Neither man had much time or inclination for a social life, but if Oscar was reclusive, Bergstrom was antisocial, a virtual hermit. He had cut himself off from or alienated friends and neighbors except for the most patient and those he occasionally had to deal with.

But Bergstrom hadn't always been that way. Most folks around

Aasness township, particularly the older generation, could recall when Theodore Bergstrom got married. As a young man he'd been different, gregarious with youthful vigor and a positive outlook on life. But when his young wife died tragically in a fire of suspicious origin, Bergstrom's life, his entire personality, seemed to take a bitter turn. He couldn't get past the mysterious fire that took his flax and his wife, and left him cynical and pessimistic about people and life

Folks around Aasness Township were sympathetic at first, and tried to console him, tried to pull him from the grip of his despair. But Bergstrom became fervently negative about most everything, and skeptical of the potential of anything or anyone. He had little to say, but when he spoke his words were often caustic and insensitive. Consequently people who knew him, other than Oscar, avoided being around him if they could. Relationships eroded with time and he seldom had visitors, a matter that concerned him about as little as the potholes in his driveway.

In a sense, Bergstrom could have been considered a progressive farmer, as he was one of the first in the area to make the transition to farming with a tractor instead of horses. Some believed it was because the man simply did not want to maintain a relationship with anyone, including his animals. That was why instead of being a dairy farmer like nearly everyone else around Aasness township, he raised beef. Unlike Oscar, Bergstrom did not have a dog. Feral cats roamed his farm but he paid less attention to them than they did to him.

Bergstrom had been a pretty good farmer in more prosperous times and Oscar had abundant respect for the man's opinions and advice on agricultural matters. That was why he was bouncing through the muddy potholes of Bergstrom's driveway this rainy morning.

Oscar never quite felt comfortable around Bergstrom, and he suppressed a tight feeling deep in his stomach as he pulled into the farmyard. Perhaps a subliminal effect, the feeling always seemed to be there when he was around Bergstrom. There was no sign the man was around, almost no sign of life at all. Oscar parked in front of Bergstrom's machine shed, since that's where he'd most likely be working on a rainy day. Oscar got out of his pickup and squished over the soggy ground to the side door of the shop and let himself in.

"*Hei på deg*! (Hello to you)", Oscar called out cheerfully in the darkened shed as he closed the door behind him. Most everyone spoke or understood at least some Norwegian in Aasness Township. The only sound was the steady pattering of rain on the roof of the shed. Oscar strained his eyes to probe the darkness for any sign of Bergstrom.

"Bergstrom!" Oscar called out. No answer. The shop was a jumble of broken down machinery and parts in a tangled maze that made no sense. He ventured into it, stepping over and around things, peering into dark corners looking for the man and feeling a bit uneasy about finding him.

"What the hell d'you want then?" Bergstrom's voice growled right behind Oscar, startling the daylights out of him.

Bergstrom could be a dreadful sight with his wild hair and sunken eyes on a bright, sunlit day, but his silently materializing in the gloomy light of the machine shop was particularly unnerving. Oscar didn't appreciate it, but it was typical of Bergstrom, and Oscar did his best to seem unaffected as his eyes adjusted to the dark.

"So, it's you then, Halvorson," he said before Oscar could collect himself.

"Yah. Dammit, you nearly scared hell out of me. Why don't you let a guy know you're around?"

Bergstrom had been scrunched down under a planter and out of sight when Oscar came in. His ragged bib overalls were grimy with dirt, grease and oil and blended like camouflage with the chaotic pattern of mechanical shapes in the dim light. Bergstrom hadn't shaved in years, and the thick gray beard covering his face and neck was stained brown at the corners of the mouth from snoose. Haunted red eyes glared out from under the frayed brim from the dirty battered tweed cap clamped low over his brow.

"What did ya' come here for? Ain't you got anything to do at your place?"

"Sure, same as you. I'm working on it. But 'dat iss why I come to see you Bergstrom. I got somet'ings I need to talk to you about 'den."

"There's nothin' I know that you don't know already," Bergstrom said. With any other man, that's about as far as the conversation would have gone, but when it came to saving his farm Oscar would be as persistent as Bergstrom could be obstinate.

"Yah, well, I'm just lookin' for some ideas, Bergstrom. I just come to see what you t'ink. See, I got a problem an' I need to know what I should do."

Bergstrom turned to spit snoose on the dirt floor. "We all got problems Halvorson."

"Yah, but me an' you, we got the same problem. I was wondering if you had figured out what to do about it?" Oscar said.

"If you're talkin' 'bout Stordal, only one answer comes to mind," Bergstrom growled as he dug through a bucket of bolts.

Oscar just sighed. He needed real, practical answers. Bergstrom knew it and shared Oscar's frustration. They each could lose their farms after this season, if they couldn't pay off their loans at E.A. Stordal's bank. Neither man had a family, neither man had many friends, especially Bergstrom. Their farms were everything they had, everything they'd worked for their entire lives. It was home, family, security; it was how they related to the world.

The Depression had taken nearly everything but the land itself, and now Stordal was ready to claim that. Of course, they'd paid on their loans as they could over recent years, lean years, but for both men a large balance remained, and the time was soon up. Stordal wanted their land and wasn't interested in bargaining. Now was a time for real answers, and both men knew it.

"Okay then, what have you got in mind?" Bergstrom said, turning his attention back to the planter.

"Only t'ing I can t'ink of iss to grow another crop," Oscar said shaking his head. "If I could just get in a couple more crops of... of somet'ing. If I could just work it out so I could... ahh, what iss the use? I don't have the land, the equipment, or the time." He sat himself on the wheel of the planter above where Bergstrom's legs stuck out from under the machine.

Bergstrom appreciated the frustration in Oscar's voice.

"An' d'en I got to make enough profit too, or it just don't pay. I t'ink I know where I might lease a field, but at the price o' wheat it iss just not..."

"Who's got a field to lease around here?" Bergstrom inquired skeptically from under the planter.

"Well, I been t'inkin' 'bout asking that Holmvik widow if we could work out somet'ing for tilling one o' her fields."

"It wouldn't work anyhow," Bergstrom said. "Not wit' the price o' wheat. You'd need a bumper crop on at least forty acres. Shit, more'n that.

More like two farms. Too much for one man to handle, along wit' your own place.

"You talk to her yet?" Bergstrom asked.

"No, not yet. Don't know if it makes sense."

"That depends on if you're interested in th' widow or her land Halvorson,"

Oscar just shook his head at Bergstrom's teasing remark, though there had been no humor in the way it was spoken. He quietly muttered some Norse epithet under his breath. He'd anticipated there would be comments like that, and it would be just the beginning if he worked the Holmvik widow's land. There was an extended pause before Bergstrom spoke again.

"You think she'd ask a fair price to lease her land?"

"Don't know. Don't know that it matters. Even if she let me rent all her land I couldn't make enough profit. An' d'en there iss the price o' wheat. Why in hell can't we get a good price for wheat? No, no, I can't afford to rent. Even if I could work it all by myself."

"Yah, you'd need a hell of a lot better price on wheat than we'll likely ever see. No," Bergstrom said, "you'll never make enough money from wheat," his voice was muffled and strained as he pulled on something under the planter.

"I know, I know. But you're no different; we're in the same fix you an' me. What are you gonna do? Have you t'ought of that?"

"'Course I have Halvorson. Everything is ridin' on this season," Bergstrom said patronizingly. "Just like wit' you. Hand me that nine-sixteenths on the frame there, will ya. Last fall I sold off half my herd, y'know, an' I plowed under a lotta my hay so I can plant... I don't know, corn I guess. That's at about fifty cents now, so it's better'n wheat, but still... It's goin' to be close. I just don't know."

"A guy has to wonder if it iss worth it at all. I mean, to put in all the work, all season, invest all the money, the planning, an' d'en just lose it to Stordal in the end anyhow. I jus' don' know, maybe I'm getting too old for diss anymore."

There was another long pause in the conversation. Finally Bergstrom dragged himself out from under the planter.

"What do ya know 'bout that Holmvik woman?" Bergstrom asked.

"Not much. She must know somet'ing 'bout farming though," Oscar said. "She ran th' place after her husband died. 'Course she had a hired man d'en, an' her son for a while, too."

"Sounds to me like you know something 'bout her," Bergstrom groaned as his stiff joints brought him to his feet.

"No more d'en anybody else. She iss a neighbor, ya know," Oscar said sounding defensive.

"I meant, d'you think she might actually lease you a field, Halvorson?"

"Maybe. Don't know. But I sure don't t'ink that iss enough."

Bergstrom wandered over to his workbench along the wall as though deep in thought. Daylight filtered through dirty windowpanes illuminating the work surface, and he picked up delicate little device and began examining it in a distracted way. After a long pause he spoke again, in slow and distant tones, without facing Oscar.

"Maybe it could be enough Halvorson. Maybe it would be... just enough."

"What? We was just sayin' how I can't work th' whole farm along wit' mine Bergstrom. Ain't you forgettin'..."

"I ain't talkin' 'bout wheat Oscar. Twenty acres could maybe be just enough, if it was th' right crop," Bergstrom said, still examining the small object in his hand.

"Yah? Twenty acres?" Oscar said. "An' what could I grow on it d'en, money trees?" There was a pause.

"Flax," Bergstrom replied.

"Flax? Did you say flax?"

"Yah. Flax."

"Flax. Where'd you get that idea? Nobody grows flax 'round here."

"Some have," Bergstrom mumbled, clutching the thing in his hand.

Another pause. "Oh, yah, so I recall," said Oscar; suddenly conscious they'd intruded on a sensitive issue. "Okay but that was long ago. I'm serious Bergstrom," he steered back to the subject at hand. "I need a real..."

"I am serious too Halvorson," Bergstrom interrupted. "D'you know what flax is selling for now days? Three an' a half bucks a bushel. That's better than several times what you get for wheat. Think o' that a minute." He turned to face Oscar. "Three an' a half bucks a bushel! At least six, maybe seven times more'n wheat. Why, twenty acres o' flax with a decent yield would pull ya' right out of the hole and set ya' back on your feet." Bergstrom had slipped a bit from his negativism, and there was a touch of actual excitement in his voice.

"It would?" Oscar asked amazed by the potential as much as the new tone in Bergstrom's voice.

"Yah, Halvorson, it would," Bergstrom said, returning to his sullen self.

"It would huh?" Oscar said stroking his jaw and thinking. He was not impulsive about things, no matter how good they sounded. There was always a catch, that's just the way things were with farming.

"Ahh, I couldn't afford the seed. Seed would cost too much," Oscar finally suggested.

"I bet ol' Kruger'd cut you a deal on the seed, don't ya' think?" Bergstrom replied right back.

"Why would he do that d'en?"

"Why not? Kruger don't owe anything to Stordal. Stordal is puttin' a lot o' his customers out o' business. What th' hell, I bet Kruger'd be glad to work out a good deal for th' seed just to stick it to Stordal. Maybe you'd be doin' him a favor in the end by stayin' in business."

"Yah, but if I lose the crop, I'd be in debt to Kruger too, an' still lose my farm to Stordal."

"S'pose so. It's a risk all right, but your farm has been at risk all along. What have you got to lose? If it works, you'll keep your farm."

"That iss true, I guess," Oscar said, "I got nuttin' to lose, except maybe George Kruger as a friend."

"You're Kruger's customer. He ain't never done business wit' you that wasn't in his own best interest. An' if you lose the crop, you won't be doin' business wit' Kruger again anyhow. Him an' Stordal can fight over your farm."

Bergstrom was a hard man and Oscar knew it. He didn't like the idea of putting his relationship with the local feed and seed dealer on the line, but he was desperate and would do whatever he could to save his farm. Besides, Oscar reasoned, he'd present it to Kruger and let him decide. In that sense, keeping the farm would be more up to Kruger than to Stordal, and Oscar liked his chances better dealing with Kruger.

"Okay d'en, let's say Kruger iss willing to take th' risk an' sell me th' seed, an' the widow rents me th' land. You got to have 'dem special screens on th' separator to thresh flax," Oscar said, still challenging Bergstrom's idea.

"I've got 'em," Bergstrom said. "When the time comes, I've got 'em, an' you can use 'em if ya want."

Oscar stood up and took a couple steps toward Bergstrom.

"You have flax screens?" he said. "You still got d'em after all dis time? Why didn't you...?"

"None a your damn business. I said you could use 'em, ain't that good enough for ya?"

Oscar turned aside, sensing he'd blundered into personal issues again.

"Yah, well, that would be... that would be really nice, I guess," Oscar said looking away. He'd run out of arguments. Then turning to Bergstrom again he asked, "Why are you wantin' me to grow flax d'en Bergstrom? Why don't you grow flax an' save your farm?"

"Look here, it was you that came wantin' to know what to do to get your farm out o' the hole wasn't it? I'm just givin' you an idea. If ya' don't wanna do it, that's fine by me. I got work to do," Bergstrom said turning back to his bench.

"Okay, Okay, it iss a good idea. I'll t'ink about it some. But d'ere iss still the matter of the land though..."

"That's the other thing," Bergstrom turned again. "You ain't gonna get but one shot at this, Halvorson. Flax takes a lot out of the ground, leaves it weak. It takes maybe several years for a field to recover. That's why neither your fields or mine would grow a decent crop o' flax. You got to have soil that's well rested, an' that Holmvik land hasn't had a crop other'n weeds in years. Once the soil's been turned, it should be ideal for growin' flax."

"Yah, that iss true. I s'pose it wouldn't hurt to ask her."

"That's up to you," Bergstrom said turning away and fumbling with the small object in his hand again. "But..." he added quietly, "you're runnin' out of time, ya' know."

"Yah, but... What would folks say about... well, 'bout me an' her. You know how folks talk an' all. An' d'ey would, too, you know it. I just don't t'ink I want d'em sayin' t'ings 'bout me an' that widow woman. You know what I mean?"

"Halvorson, you can fertilize your field wit' what folks say. Now then, you got what ya came for." With that, Bergstrom retreated into the darkened jumble of parts and equipment toward the rear of his shed and Oscar knew their conversation was over. Whatever he decided to do was all up to him.

He inhaled a soft "yah" and headed for the door.

6

"Wine is like rain: when it falls on
the mire it but makes it the fouler,
but when it strikes good soil wakes
it to beauty and bloom."
—John Hay

As the spring sun went down, a damp chill moved over the land and fog began forming in low pockets between the hills.

After he finished milking and his other evening chores, Oscar went into his house and stoked up a fire in the kitchen range. He opened the oven door to chase the cold from the room and reheated leftover *lapskaus*, a stew from the night before. After cleaning up his dishes for the day, he sighed and plopped down on a kitchen chair, unlaced his boots and pulled them off. The cool touch of the linoleum felt good through his stockinged feet. Hektor stretched out on the floor beside him and Oscar rubbed the old fellow's ribs with his toes, as his thoughts revisited the matter of the flax.

Oscar had mulled over the problem of his debt for the past year, and realized after last fall's harvest that his situation was now more serious. When he took a hard look at what he'd made and what he owed, he was below the subsistence level and slowly losing ground. Oscar wasn't a gambler, but it seemed the idea of raising a cash crop was a risk he'd have to take.

Since Oscar's discussion with Bergstrom the day before, he had not been able to get flax off his mind. Bergstrom's logic made sense and he was now convinced that flax was the means of salvation for his farm. Other farmers might think it too risky, gambling the farm on this one crop, and they'd be watching closely to see if he was clever or a fool. Still, since he was unable to come up with another workable plan, it was a risk Oscar had to take. The one man he had to sell on it was George Kruger, owner of the feed and seed store and the one who would have to trust

Oscar for the cost of the seed. But Oscar was sure he could convince Kruger to take the risk and come up with an easy payment plan in order to keep a faithful customer.

The seed was expensive, but if a field of flax yielded well and the price remained near three and a half dollars a bushel, the profit would be far better than anything else he could grow. Bergstrom was right about the Holmvik widow's fields too. Her land hadn't been tilled in quite a few years, but once plowed and prepared the soil should be rich, exactly what a good crop of flax would need.

Of course special screens were needed in the thrasher at harvest, but Bergstrom had them and was willing to loan them to Oscar. Everything seemed to be falling into place for the plan to grow flax. First he'd get George Kruger's backing, and then the right land—the fallow fields of the Widow Holmvik's land.

"Yah," he inhaled, still rubbing Hektor's ribs with his stockinged foot. Oscar was satisfied that the plan seemed solid, that it could work.

The Holmvik woman had worked the farm with her husband years ago, and after he died she worked it with a hired man for a while. Oscar knew Esther Holmvik understood farming and realized what it took to grow a crop, the value of her land and what it could produce. He would persuade her to take a reasonable percent of the profit from the crop, if she were willing, in payment for use of her land. That was the only way he could think of to pay her. She might be willing to make a deal, but he wasn't sure how much she might want. That might take some haggling, and Oscar was not at all comfortable doing that, especially with a woman. One more thing bothered him, maybe more than he cared to admit even to himself, and that was what people might think or say.

There'd be talk for sure, he thought. Farm wives liked to gossip at any opportunity to get together. He'd heard them talk. And their husbands, other farmers, they could be worse. He could almost hear them now as he thought—him a lifelong bachelor and the Holmvik woman an available widow. Oh yes, there would be talk.

Oscar had kept to himself ever since his mother died and his brothers moved away. It wasn't a conscious choice, but in his grief and abandonment, he had turned to the land. Farming 80 acres alone and tending ten or more cows was more than enough to fill any man's life. Oscar was reserved in nature and shy around women. He never developed many social skills other than what his mother insisted on. He wasn't much of a conversationalist, being self-conscious of his lack of education. Social events consisted only of attending Eidsvold Lutheran Church at Thanksgiving, Christmas, and Easter. Oscar only went to funerals occasionally to pay respects to old men who had known his father, and never attended weddings. He knew his neighbors and they knew him, but he was considered by everyone around Aasness Township to be reclusive, and not particularly sociable even when he did attend events. Living alone most of his life had perhaps made him too independent and he held to his own ways, his own opinions without considering alternatives.

So now, if he began paying attention to the Holmvik widow, if he began to work her land, people around Aasness Township would start speculating. He knew how people were. They'd start thinking it was more than just business between him and the widow, and then they'd start having expectations. They'd have him matched with her and make a big spectacle of it all. He hated the thought and shook his head. "Uffda," he said quietly to himself.

But now it was his farm that was at risk, and Oscar knew he had to force those silly notions aside. Let people think what they will, he would remain focused on saving his farm. With that decision aside, it was time to consider what he would say to convince Widow Holmvik to let him use her land.

Oscar rose stiffly from the kitchen chair and shuffled his stockinged feet past Hektor's dozing form to a cabinet under the sink. Opening the door, he bent down and pulled out a gallon Hilex jug just under half full of a deep reddish-gold liquid. After retrieving a glass tumbler from a cupboard, Oscar pulled the cork from the big jug and poured himself a half measure of the finest, most pure, most delicate, homemade wild grape wine in the entire county. Probably in several counties, since most people in this part of the state did not consume much alcohol. Aasness Township had been a "dry" township even before prohibition, and remained so after its repeal. Around the area, wine was consumed only in church on sacramental occasions.

Making wine was a skill passed on to Oscar by his mother in his youth, while his brothers and sisters were busy in school. Late one summer when Oscar was young, he and his mother, Rakel, discovered a patch of wild grape vines. They grew thick on a secluded part of their north 20 acres, on the sunny bank of a pond in the shelter of a grove of trees. It became their little secret, and Oscar and his mother did what they could, pruning and nurturing the vines to improve on what nature provided. Over the years, the grateful vines responded prolifically, producing an abundance of sweet, plump, wild grapes.

Rakel had learned the art of making wine from a woman she worked for in the old country, where there were better fruits, and few negative associations connected with the ancient art of wine making or its consumption. Rakel and her husband, Halvor, had enjoyed a quiet glass together at special moments when her winemaking efforts had been successful.

Rakel had shown Oscar how to wrap the grapes in cloth, mash and squeeze the juice from them, and filter it repeatedly. It had taken several batches of experimenting to make their first decent wine, but each time she carefully showed Oscar how much yeast to add, and how much sugar to feed the yeast. Over the years, Oscar had refined the process on his own, keeping track of what worked and what didn't, until now it was perfected. Ah yes, Oscar's wine was indeed fit for sacramental use. Perhaps never before had anything so noble been produced from so humble a grape.

Oscar was by no means abusive or over indulgent with his wine. Besides, even in a good season, he was only able to produce three or four gallons of the righteous nectar. He carefully rationed it so the few gallons lasted until the spring, before the next season's grapes would ripen in late summer. No one knew of Oscar's wine, he never told anyone about his little hobby. It had always been a little secret between his mother and him. Like the harvest of other crops, it was an annual routine for Oscar, and making the wine became a way to maintain some sort of relationship with his mother. Its taste brought back thoughts of her, when he drank in remembrance.

Now as he contemplated the offer of his terms to the Holmvik widow, Oscar wished his parents were there for reassurance. He'd never rented land before and wasn't sure how to approach this landowner, a woman, a widow. No doubt about it, Oscar felt intimidated. Like most people of his heritage, he avoided confrontation whenever he could, and situations like this definitely felt confrontational. He tried to imagine any objections Esther Holmvik might have towards him tilling her land so he'd be prepared to discuss them. From his point of view, he couldn't think of any. To Oscar, it seemed a simple matter of how much she would want and what percent of the profit she would need to be willing to rent to him. Fifty percent was out of the question. There wouldn't be enough profit for him to pay off E.A. Stordal. Maybe twenty-five or thirty percent. No, thirty was too high. Twenty-five percent was tops, twenty sounded better, Oscar thought. After all, it would be his labor, his equipment, his fuel costs. She shouldn't need to get all that much.

Would it be a percent of the net or the gross? Would she consider the deductions for what he spent in seed, fuel and harvest costs? What if something destroyed the crop? No point in worrying about that; he'd be through farming for good if that happened. Her field was a standard twenty acres, and that was about what he thought he'd need. There would still be his other crops, wheat, corn and hay grown on his own land. All of these issues seemed complicated, and he'd have to talk to George Kruger at the feed and seed store. But first, he'd have to talk to the widow about renting her land.

Next Saturday morning he'd drop in on the Holmvik woman. It would be strictly business, not a social call. Oscar felt a little better now, having at least resolved to talk to her and see what she would say. He lifted his glass to salute his decision.

At that late hour, light from the kerosene lamp over the kitchen table set the wine in his glass aglow with warm color, releasing captured sunshine from a season long past. Oscar sipped and remembered, sipped again and dreamed.

7

Groaning in protest, the heavy door to the machine shed yawned on its hinges and Oscar propped it wide open with a fence post he kept there for the purpose. Through the doorway, a dusty column of midmorning light formed a long rectangle on the hard-packed dirt floor inside the shed, illuminating the front end of Oscar's dark green Model-T pickup truck. The air inside the shed smelled of oil and gasoline in contrast with the fresh air outside, and Oscar kind of liked the odor. Maybe it was just a change from cow manure.

As he stood in the entry letting his eyes adjust to the darkness, the cool morning breeze braced the nicks on his freshly shaved face. Oscar had awakened early to get himself ready for his meeting, and the night before he had picked out the proper clothes to wear to make the right impression. If he were going to talk business with another farmer, he would not be wearing anything other than his regular work clothes. But Mrs. Holmvik wasn't just another farmer, she was a woman, and Oscar felt somehow that called for a different approach. He had on a clean pair of bib overalls, his best chambray shirt buttoned to the neck, and an old black suit coat that had been his fathers. Topped off with his felt hat, Oscar was dressed for business.

Picking a rag from the workbench, he began wiping dust from the windshield and chrome parts of the little truck. It had been a while since he'd driven anywhere. Oscar wasn't fastidious; he was stalling, and he knew it. He tossed the rag back on the bench, reached through the truck window to set the spark, and grabbed the crank. Unlike *Gubbe* the tractor, the Model-T was much easier to start, and Oscar wasn't as intimidated by it. The engine sputtered to life in a few cranks and leaving Hektor in charge of the farm he got in the truck and chugged out of the shed and into the day. He was off to see Esther Holmvik.

It wasn't that far away, and he could have walked over the fields to the Holmvik farm, but he thought he'd look more businesslike arriving in his truck. Once out of his long driveway, Oscar turned the truck onto the county gravel road, which headed toward Eidsvold Church and the Holmvik place.

He drove past the house first to see if she was home. Freshly washed clothes were hanging on the line and he could see through the screen that the kitchen door was open. No more delaying, he told himself. It was just business and he needed to tend to it. Oscar turned the truck around and soon pulled into the Holmvik driveway.

Esther was sprinkling clothes to be ironed when she heard a vehicle in her driveway. Looking out the kitchen screen door, Esther recognized Oscar Halvorson at the wheel of the old truck as it came to a stop. "Whatever could that old hermit want?" she thought, removing her outer apron.

Oscar slid out of the seat and stood beside the old Model-T pickup with his hands tucked into the bib of his overalls, shifting his weight nervously from one leg to the other. He didn't have to wait long, as Esther stepped outside, wiping her hands on a dishtowel.

"Well Oscar Halvorson, this is sure a surprise," Esther said honestly. "Didn't I just see you at Easter services a couple weeks ago? How have you been then?"

"*G'dag* (good day) Missus Holmvik," Oscar said in the thick Scandinavian accent that tainted the speech of almost everyone in the region. He politely touched the brim of his hat as his mother had taught him to do when meeting a lady. "I guess I been gettin' by all right," he replied. "How about you?"

"Oh yah, well, I suppose I can't complain," she said.

Oscar was already starting to paw at the ground with the toe of his boot, and Esther could tell something was on his mind. There was an awkward pause in the conversation and one of Esther's hens strutted casually between them before Oscar continued with more small talk.

"So, how iss the price of eggs hold'n up d'en?" he asked, the high pitch of his voice unable to conceal anxiety.

"It's not enough to make gathering them worthwhile, but that's farming in general, I guess," answered Esther. She knew farming all right.

"Yah," Oscar inhaled while looking down the road at some vague point.

"So then, what brings you here today Mr. Halvorson?" she queried, "besides wanting to know the price of eggs." She was a little skeptical of the old bachelor, as well as curious about his showing up so unexpectedly and dressed up in his good clothes.

Oscar hadn't expected her to get to the point so boldly, but was glad to get right at what he'd come there for.

"Well d'en, I come to talk business, Missus Holmvik, that iss, if now is a good time for you to talk," Oscar said, looking squarely at her with both his feet planted on the ground.

Esther raised an eyebrow and considered his appearance. He was indeed here for some business purpose, she decided.

"You've come to talk business? Well, yah, I suppose we can do that. My house is such a mess. Wait here just a minute, please," Esther said, and quickly went inside to put away her underwear and other laundry from the table.

After primping a moment, she held the door open and asked Oscar inside.

"Okay, come in the kitchen then," she said. "You'll have to pardon the mess. I've been busy and didn't know anybody would be stopping by. Come on in, just don't look around," she said, making unnecessary excuses.

Oscar entered the kitchen and politely removed his hat, holding it in front of himself with both hands and feeling very uncomfortable. Her place was immaculate. If she felt it was a mess, he couldn't imagine what it looked like clean. Esther led him to her kitchen table and offered him a chair. Then she started talking about visitors she'd had and what had been going on with folks at the Eidsvold Church while she put the coffee pot on the stove. Oscar found himself listening to the news about his neighbors and thinking it somehow interesting when Esther was telling it. Maybe it was just her voice. She set cups and saucers on the table for each of them. Then she proceeded to set out the basic essentials that went with morning coffee: sugar lumps, a dish covered with home made doughnuts, bread and jam, and from the ice box a small block of cheese and a pitcher of cream. She did all this while carrying on a constant banter about everything from neighborhood gossip and Roosevelt's latest ideas on farm relief to what was going on in Europe with that crazy German dictator. Oscar just sat at the table, watched and listened while waiting for the coffee to boil. He began to wonder if he'd ever have a chance to bring up the business for which he'd come.

Finally the coffee was ready and Esther poured them both a cup and sat down across the table from him. She bowed her head in silence as Oscar reached for a doughnut, and a moment later she invited Oscar to help himself.

In an attempt to recover, Oscar tried to deftly open the subject. "So den Missus Holmvik, I was wondering if I could come over an'..."

"Grandma!" Henry burst through the kitchen door shouting with such excitement that Oscar nearly spilled coffee all over himself. "Grandma, Nisse had her kittens! There's four of them! They're up in the..."

Henry stopped abruptly, noting his grandmother had a visitor at the table. Setting his coffee down, Oscar turned in his chair to face the boy who, with his sudden entrance, had startled away whatever composure he had tried to establish. The boy and the man stared at each other, each at a loss for words.

"Uffda, Henry, settle down, we have company. This is Mr. Halvorson from up the road. He's a neighbor of ours. You know, when you take the short cut home from school you walk over some of his land. The part by the slough. I told you about him, remember?" Her tone was reassuring to both of them, and helped re-establish the decorum.

"Mr. Halvorson, this is my grandson Henry, my son Arthur's boy. He's been living with me since last fall," she explained. "Henry, shake hands with Mr. Halvorson," Esther said cordially.

Henry, quick to adapt to the situation, eagerly stepped forward offering his hand. Oscar, unaccustomed to having children around, stared at the boy.

"Pleased to meet ya, Mr. Halvorson," said Henry politely.

Oscar hadn't expected anyone else to be there, but managed to find his hand and engulfed the boy's with it. "Me too," was all he could manage to say.

Esther smiled at them both with approval.

"Mr. Halvorson and I were about to discuss some business Henry, so why don't you go back to the barn and see how Nisse is doing with her kittens. Maybe you can think up names for them all," she suggested. "Here, take a doughnut with you. I'll come see them later."

Henry took the doughnut but kept staring at Oscar, making the old farmer self-conscious. He turned around to his own coffee and doughnut and looked out the window, trying to ignore the boy.

"Could I stay and talk business, too?"

"No, Henry," Esther said, "business is for grownups. Besides, you've got your own business to attend to in the barn, remember?"

"Aw, all right then," Henry said with resignation as he slowly backed toward the kitchen door. "Really nice to meet ya, Mr. Halvorson."

Oscar turned again in his chair with a mouthful of doughnut, "Mmm-hum, nice to meet you too, er... young fellah."

Henry went out the door without taking his eyes off Oscar, and stood on the step awhile eating his doughnut and staring at the stranger at his Grandmother's table. When she saw he was still there, she gave Henry a scowl and motioned for him to go away. He went, but only as far as Oscar's Model-T pickup, which he started investigating from all angles.

Back at the table, Esther apologized for the interruption and refilled Oscar's cup. By now Oscar had recovered and tried to brush off the incident, saying it was nothing.

"I'm sure you're not used to having children around, Mr. Halvorson," Esther said, "but Henry's coming to stay with me now has been a real blessing. He's such a good boy, and a lot of company for me," she continued, "but I can tell he misses his father."

Oscar made no reply, but sipped his coffee.

"So then, Mr. Halvorson," Esther said after a pause, "You said you had some business to discuss with me?"

"Yah, yah, I do," Oscar replied, setting his cup down and looking hard into it as if trying to find something there. "See I was wondering if, that iss if you ain't going to use it, well, what I mean iss I need to plant a crop, see, an' I'm lookin' for some land. Good land. It's gotta be good land, an', well, if you ain't... I mean if you don't... that iss..."

"You want to plant this crop on my land, Mr. Halvorson?" Esther said.

"Yah," Oscar nodded, looking up at her across the table. "Yah, that's right. You see, I been t'inkin' how to get out of the debt I owe to Stordal at the bank, and I got it all figured out. Flax. I'd like to plant flax. I t'ink flax would do real good on your soil, Missus Holmvik, and if the price keeps as high like it's been, well I t'ink it could make a really good profit."

Esther was listening, but as Oscar spoke her own gaze passed out the window and over the fields she and her husband had worked years ago.

There were other considerations on her mind now, other dreams that she hoped might someday come to pass.

"I'd pay you fair price for the use of your land," Oscar continued. "You know I ain't got the money now, but I'd give you a share or a percent of what I make off the crop. I'm t'inkin' your sout' twenty. You just tell me what you want for letting me farm it. I don't need your answer right away, but t'ink of it, Missus Holmvik. A percent of twenty acres of flax could be a nice, easy income for you."

He paused a moment, trying to guess her answer by the expression on her face.

"An' you don't need to do a t'ing," Oscar started in again. "I'll work the land myself." He felt he was on a roll now, really selling her on the idea. "I got most everyt'ing I need to do it, and I can borrow..." Oscar was beginning to have a hard time containing his enthusiasm.

"I don't know, Mr. Halvorson," Esther finally interrupted.

"What's that, Missus Holmvik?"

"Well, since young Henry has come to live with me, I've been thinking more and more about my own son. You know, Carl and I always hoped Arthur would take over the farm some day. I'd almost given up on that after he went off to the cities and got married. But the only good thing to come out of these hard times is my grandson Henry coming to stay here with me."

"Now you see," Esther continued, "I've got my hopes up again because I know Arthur will come back for his boy. Maybe when he does he'll take over the farm. I'm not getting any younger, and I'm not sure how much longer I can live here on my own. I don't want to give up the place, not if Arthur might come back to farm it."

Oscar listened in silence, but his hopes faded as she continued.

"I'm sorry, but I hope you understand Mr. Halvorson," Esther said as she noticed a light in Oscar's eyes flicker out and he assumed his normal reserved demeanor. She explained, "If my son Arthur comes back from the CCC—and I know he will come to get his son—I want him to be able to take over the farm if he wants it. It has to be available for him."

Oscar understood, all right. He knew how much a farm meant to a family, how much his farm meant to him. He paused in silence a moment, then pushed away his coffee cup. Esther sensed his disappointment.

"Yah, well d'en," he said. "You're doin' the right t'ing for your son, Missus Holmvik. You got good land here, an' he'll do just fine with it if, I mean when he comes back."

"I'm glad you understand Mr. Halvorson," Esther said. "You do make a good business proposition but, I'm sorry, I just don't feel I can do it now."

"Yah," Oscar inhaled as he stood up to go. "I need to get back to my place. I got lots to do. It was real nice to meet your grandson, I'm glad he's good company for you. Seems like a fine boy. Hope your son Arthur comes home soon too. *Mange takk* (many thanks) for coffee Missus Holmvik. Have a good day now," Oscar said cordially as he walked to the door.

"Oh yah, it was nothing," Esther said. "I do think the flax crop is a good idea, Mr. Halvorson, and I'm sure you can find someone else with some good land to rent," she said from the steps as she watched him walk to his truck. "You must come for coffee again some time," she called, then wished she hadn't said it.

Henry was playing in the pickup box and Oscar frowned at him as he reached for the crank to start his truck.

"Are you goin' now, Mr. Halvorson? Are you gonna come back again and see us? I could show you the kittens. Maybe I could come and see you some time," Henry went on.

"Yah, maybe," Oscar replied, trying to sound friendly while struggling to conceal the disappointment in his voice. "You go help your grandmama take care of her farm now, okay?"

"Henry, come on now, get away from the truck," Esther called, "Mr. Halvorson is leaving."

Oscar started his pickup and waved once to the Holmvik woman and her grandson as he headed out their driveway.

"Good-bye, Mr. Halvorson, see you in church," Henry called after him.

8

Esther paused a moment to catch her breath as she and Henry followed a fence up a steep hill. She watched her grandson Henry, who kept up a nonstop conversation as they walked, and remembered how she used to walk these fields with as little effort as he. Heavy clouds hung low, and a cold wind reminded her that sometimes winter was reluctant to release its grip on the land. She pulled the lapels of her coat closer together. Henry seemed impervious to the clammy spring weather and she worried that he might catch a cold. Maybe this wasn't a good day to talk to Oscar, Esther thought, but circumstances had changed. Both planning and timing were critical to farmers, and she hoped it wasn't too late.

It had been just over a week since Oscar Halvorson had paid his visit to ask if he could plant a crop of flax on her land in exchange for a percentage of the profit. It wasn't that she didn't want to help him out, or that she couldn't use the money herself. Oscar's proposal had made good sense. But Esther was convinced that her son, Arthur, after working a winter in the northwoods with the C.C.C., would be ready to come home, back to the farm to join her and his son Henry. She reasoned that Arthur would need a way to make a living and Esther wanted the farm to be available. That was before the letter.

It arrived earlier that week, on a cold and rainy spring day like this one was threatening to become. After seeing the mailman's car stop, Henry had run through the rain to the mailbox. He raced back to the kitchen excited about a single letter that looked like it was from his father. Inside the envelope were two letters: one carefully printed in simple words meant just for Henry, the other in longhand, was meant for Esther's eyes only.

Arthur's letter started by saying the winter's work in the woods was nearly done and there would be a change in their assignments soon. He asked how his son was doing and how they were getting along together on the farm, but it was mostly small talk. Then, in one simple paragraph, Arthur wrote that he would not be coming to the farm for a while yet. He explained that an Army recruiter had talked to the men at the C.C.C.

camp one day, and he and his friends had decided to enlist. Army life sounded better than working in the cold north woods. There would be travel, housing, meals, a steady paycheck, and they'd wear a uniform. Besides, Arthur wrote, with world politics the way they were and Hitler on the move, Uncle Sam was building up the military forces and the offer seemed pretty good. Arthur told his mother he'd keep in touch from wherever he was sent, and promised he'd send money and come home on furlough when he got a chance. He closed by saying, "Please take care of Henry."

By the time Esther got to the last phrase, her eyes were brimming with silent tears. Henry was still sounding-out the words his father had written, but looked up when his grandmother set down her letter. Her face turned to the window and the falling rain, and Henry knew his father was not coming for him. Without words, they understood each other's disappointment, and their mutual need for compassion. Henry set down his letter and went to his grandmother's side. For a while they just held each other as the rain fell.

"He's not coming," Henry eventually said. It was a simple statement.

"Not for a while yet, Henry," Esther had replied, "but don't worry, he'll come home someday. And as long as we've got each other, you and I can get by just fine 'til then, can't we?"

Henry had learned to love and trust his grandmother, and he agreed that they could. From that moment on, Henry felt that the farm really was his home, too, and his grandmother was his family.

But that was a couple days ago. Now, holding strands of barbed wire apart for each other as they passed through the fence, Esther felt that Henry was her family, too. Life was a struggle but the two of them would manage together. They were on their way to see Oscar because it was the best thing for both of them. She had thought about Oscar's offer and now knew it was the right thing to do. For the past couple days she had considered what her terms would be, and had them worked out in her mind. Hopefully Oscar would agree, as she and Henry would need some income this season too.

After Esther Holmvik had turned down his request to farm her land, Oscar had gone home disappointed. For the rest of the day all he did was walk his land in stoic contemplation. For the past week Oscar had struggled with what to do, and searched in vain for alternatives.

He had told his friend Bergstrom about the Holmvik widow turning down his offer to grow the flax on her land. Bergstrom still thought the flax idea was good, but was unable to suggest any alternate land on which to grow it. They both knew he'd need land before he could get the seed from George Kruger. Bergstrom was a pessimist and not much support for Oscar, suggesting that it might be easier to sign the farm over to E.A. and "let that bastard try to work it." But Oscar wasn't ready to give up. Where Bergstrom felt the objective was to defeat E.A. Stordal, Oscar's only concern was saving his farm. It was a fundamental difference in thinking between the two men.

Maybe old Elof Tollerud had some land he might rent, but it was a long way from Oscar's farm and he'd heard Elof was already renting to Hjalmar Berg. Leonard Kraus and his sons were working all their available land, as were others who had sons that age to help them. Most of the nearby farmers that Oscar knew had all their land accounted for, so Oscar would have to inquire farther away, from men he didn't know as well, men who were just as desperate as he.

He considered going into town to talk to E.A. Stordal about the money he owed, but had heard of the results other farmers had in trying to reason with him. No, Oscar didn't trust Stordal. All he wanted to do was to pay what he owed to keep E.A. from claiming his land. Maybe it was time to give it up after all, he thought, but what would he do then? The farm was all he knew, it was all he had.

Immersed in these concerns, Oscar was unable to focus his mind on any single thing as he puttered away at making his equipment ready for spring planting. It just wasn't like other years when, even during these hard times, he eagerly went to work on spring preparations, anxious to get into the field. His heart just wasn't in it the way it used to be. The time for sowing was getting closer with each passing day, and though he felt an urgency, he was unable to concentrate effectively.

Oscar was struggling to replace a hitch on his tractor *Gubbe*, the temperamental iron monster he regarded with thinly veiled distrust. For the past hour he'd been puttering to remove a seized-up bolt and had only succeeded in rounding its corners. With patience wearing thin, he now resorted to using a hammer and cold chisel on the bolt head.

Straddling the hitch, hammer in one hand and chisel in the other, he bent to attack the stubborn bolt. Maybe the Holmvik woman would change her mind for a bigger percent. The second blow of the hammer glanced off the chisel, striking the base of his thumb. Oscar instantly dropped both tools. He grabbed the injured hand and spun around, gouging his shin as he stumbled over the hitch and nearly fell to the floor. Sucking air through clenched teeth until his lungs could hold no more, Oscar finally found release for his immediate pain, as well as the accumulated frustrations of the past week. In top voice he belted out fluent verses of deadly Norwegian profanity in metered rhythm which, had they been properly focused, might have loosened the frozen bolt. Hektor got up and left the shed directly.

Not until, out of breath and bent over with his aching hand clutched between his knees, did Oscar notice something blocking the light coming in the open door. He lifted his contorted face to see the Widow Holmvik and her grandson Henry silhouetted in the doorway. The only sound was the wind blustering around the eaves of the machine shed.

Oscar slowly stood upright, still holding his injured hand, still grimacing in excruciating discomfort.

"What did he say, Grandma? Did you hear that? What was that he said?" Henry finally asked with wide eyes looking up at his grandmother.

"Go find a pail and bring some cold water right away," Esther told Henry. "Mr. Halvorson seems to have injured himself. Now hurry."

Having said his piece, Oscar was now struck completely dumb with profound embarrassment despite his lingering pain, and could only stand looking at his neighbors in silence.

Norwegian was spoken as commonly as English in this part of the country, and Esther had understood all too well what Oscar said. As a woman of the church, she disapproved of profanity in any language, though she'd heard it all before. Still, unaccustomed to such dark eloquence, she approached Oscar still a little wide-eyed.

"Let's have a look at that hand," she said quietly.

Sheepishly, Oscar held out his hand like a naughty child.

"Sorry, Missus Holmvik, I didn't know you was here," he finally spoke.

"Let's just be glad the boy doesn't understand," Esther replied. "It doesn't look that bad to me, can you move it?"

Oscar pulled has hand back from hers and examined the red swollen bruise with a frown, rotated his thumb a few turns, then tucked both hands into the bib of his overalls.

"It'll be fine, thanks," he said, now more embarrassed that he'd even let her look at his injured hand.

"So d'en, Missus Holmvik, what iss it that brings you and the boy here today?" Oscar inquired, his curiosity now overcoming the previous situation. Oscar went to stand beside his workbench as though he had work to do.

Now it was Esther's turn to feel a bit awkward.

"Well, eh... Mr. Halvorson, it was just over a week ago you visited me with a business proposal," she began. "You... you said you wanted to plant a crop of flax on my land in exchange for a percent of the profit. And it was a good plan you had too, as I recall," Esther continued, struggling to maintain an attitude of business advantage. "I wanted to help you, and I'm sorry I had to turn you down at the time. But, well, it was... now it's..."

Oscar picked up a bolt from the workbench and began massaging it with a filthy, oily rag, but turned to face her to show he was listening and interested in what she might have to say.

"Yah, well you see," Esther searched for words, "things have changed since then. I just heard from my boy, Arthur, the other day, and... and I guess he won't be coming home after all." The last phrase trailed off quietly.

"Anyway," she picked up again, "if you're still interested in putting in a crop on my land, I suppose I could let you work that idle south twenty by the church. It'll be a fine piece of land once it's tilled."

Oscar stopped fumbling with the bolt and took a step in her direction.

"Oh yah?" he said, his stoic nature now betrayed by the excitement in his voice and stance.

"I have two terms though," Esther added hastily, as if to caution him. She paused when Oscar instantly returned stoic and eyed her suspiciously before nodding to indicate she should state her terms.

"I've thought about this carefully, Mr. Halvorson, and this is what I want. First, I want ten percent of this field planted in wheat."

Oscar wasn't sure he'd heard right.

"What iss that you say about wheat?" he inquired, no longer able to maintain a stoic attitude.

"I said I want ten percent planted in wheat," Esther repeated.

"Wheat?" Oscar was incredulous. "Wheat? But it iss flax I have to grow. Flax! It iss worth much more, much, much more. And I need to… wheat? Ten percent in wheat? How much iss that? That iss… That iss…"

"That is only two acres in wheat," Esther answered assertively.

"Two acres in wheat?" Oscar said. "What for?"

"Bread," Esther said simply.

"That iss a hell-of-a…" he caught himself, "that is for sure going to make a lot of bread, Missus Holmvik."

"Yah, that's right," she replied, "and if you accept my terms you might get some of it. You probably know I bake most of the bread used at the church. You see, I have an arrangement with Mr. Phillips over at the mill to grind my flour."

"That iss going to make a lot of flour," Oscar said thoughtfully. He paused before cautiously asking, "what iss your other term d'en?"

"My second term is… well, I understand the wheat will mean extra time and work for you," Esther continued, "and I know it will be an inconvenience. So, I'm only going to ask for ten percent of the profit from your flax. I don't think that's much, and it's a fair offer, Mr. Halvorson."

Oscar's expression showed relief, as he had expected the woman would want twenty to twenty-five percent. He picked up the bolt he'd dropped and began rubbing it with the rag again as he started slowly pacing back and forth, considering her offer. What would be the logistics and expense of planting and harvesting two acres of grain? What effect would it have on the profit he desperately needed? How much of his time would it take? Esther was getting nervous as she awaited his response.

"I'm sure if you take some time to consider my terms you'll find they're not so bad after all," Esther pointed out. "You will still have eighteen acres for your flax, and on that land that much should yield enough to still bring you a lot of money next fall. Anyway, those are my terms, and I have my reasons."

Oscar knew that when it came to Eidsvold Lutheran Church, Esther Holmvik would not budge. He understood that whatever her reasons were, those were her terms. It would be a nuisance to mess with two acres of wheat with his flax, but if that's what it took, he'd do it. He was in no position not to.

"Yah," Oscar inhaled in resignation to mask his satisfaction with the deal. "Eighteen acres of flax for ten percent of the profit, plus you want two acres of wheat. That's the deal d'en?"

"That's right," Esther affirmed.

"Well, if that iss what you want, I guess I will have to make it work," Oscar said. The widow had made a good and fair offer that he considered it best to accept before she decided she wanted more than ten percent. He extended a big, grimy hand.

They looked each other in the eye as they shook on the deal, her hand completely engulfed by his. It was the first actual physical contact he'd had with a woman in a long time, and he unexpectedly became aware of a delicate strength in that hand. There would be no papers to sign; none were necessary.

"So, when can you start plowing?" Esther asked.

Oscar eyed old *Gubbe* and suggested waiting until the day after tomorrow, depending on the weather and how dry the soil was.

"I checked it yesterday," Esther said, "and it should be pretty good. That south twenty always did have good drainage."

"Okay, I'll plan to be there early," Oscar said.

"Oh, there's just one more thing," Esther added.

"Yah?" he questioned.

"Please be good enough to mind your language around my grandson Henry and me."

Humbled again, Oscar shifted his feet, looked down at the dirt floor and gently rubbed his still aching hand.

"Sure t'ing, Missus Holmvik," he replied quietly.

As they finished their business, Henry showed up at the door with Hektor and a broken crockery jar with some well water in it for Oscar to soak his hand.

"I don't think Mr. Halvorson will be needing that after all Henry," Esther said, "but thank you for bringing it." Oscar nodded in affirmation, and Henry and his grandmother said their good-byes before heading across the farmyard toward the fields over which they'd come.

The clouds were thinning as he watched them go, and Oscar thought the sun might be trying to break through. He returned to his shed, humming "Nickolina" to himself as he concentrated on getting his equipment ready for the Widow Holmvik's field.

9

When Oscar was still a boy first learning about farming, his father had told him to always maintain a good relationship with the man at the feed and seed co-op on the edge of town. That was George Kruger, a big, heavyset, bald man with a round face and an easy laugh. Following his father's advice, Oscar had always done his best to keep up with his account at the co-op. George was a good-hearted man who had often extended credit to farmers over the years, helping many of them, including Oscar, through some hard times. Socializing wasn't one of Oscar's better skills, but he really tried to develop a friendship with George. Fortunately, George was an outgoing sort who enjoyed his work and his customers, and he and Oscar were on good terms.

For as long as he had owned the feed and seed co-op, George had kept closely attuned to what virtually every farmer in the county was doing. He came by the information naturally in his line of business, and it served his business interests to know.

During winter months, when farm life slowed to mostly just tending livestock, George's feed and seed co-op was a popular place for farmers. The front room had a big pot-bellied stove fired with oak and corncobs, and there was always a pot of coffee warming on top. It was a good place to get away for a while, a place where a man of the land could always count on meeting a couple of his peers sipping coffee and spitting snoose toward the ash can. Typical conversation was usually quiet and reserved, with an economy of words, as that was generally their character. Mostly they complained about things, usually the government and its lack of response to their needs. Often they swapped news about what they'd seen or heard on other farms. It was a good place to get caught up on things around Aasness Township.

George Kruger heard it all, and passed the information on to others who dropped by later. It was understood that if someone wanted to know what was going on in the area, they only had to ask George, dispenser of feed, seed and information. It was a role he enjoyed perhaps a little more than he should have, and in other societies George might have been considered a gossip. With that concern in the back of his mind, Oscar went to talk to George about his plan.

"Flax? You wanna grow flax?" George asked with a skeptical tone. "That's kinda unusual ain't it, Oscar? 'Specially for you. Seems like you're goin' out on a long, thin limb with this idea. Why flax? What you got goin' on here?"

Oscar knew George would press him for details, since it was his nature, and because he'd want some assurance he'd be getting paid for the seed some day. It was a fair question, and Oscar was prepared to explain.

"Well, I need your help on d'is here one George," Oscar began. "I went an' got myself in debt wit' E.A. Stordal a few years back."

"Yah, so who around here hasn't?" George replied, leaning over his counter with new interest at the mention of Stordal's name. George had a delicate relationship with E.A., since the bank often provided the money farmers needed to buy seed from him. Even George's business had occasionally borrowed money from Stordal on a short-term basis. But since the Depression and the collapse of other local banks, E.A. had put many of George's customers out of business. His heart was with the farmers, but he also knew where their money came from.

"Ya see, the note comes due after harvest next fall, and the way t'ings look I ain't goin' to have the money to pay him," Oscar confided. It was no surprise to George who was familiar with the financial situations of most of his customers. "Wit' the price of flax up where it iss, I t'ink I should make enough off twenty acres to get out of d'is trouble."

"Huh. Yah, I guess so. It's around three an' a half a bushel now last time I heard."

"Yah, I been talkin' it over wit' Bergstrom," Oscar replied. George winced at the mention of the name.

"That cranky ol' bastard? He sure don't show up much around here. I'd guess his wallet is about as flat as yours Oscar. Ain't he in the same situation with Stordal as you are?" George asked. "Maybe worse. You say he suggested you should plant flax?"

"Yah, he did. An' I got to say it sounds like a good plan to me."

"Uh-hmmm," George murmured considering the proposal a moment in silence. He knew Oscar had already bought seed and planted his corn and wheat, and inquired, "So then, where you plannin' to grow this flax?"

"I got that worked out too," said Oscar. "I been talkin' wit' Carl Holmvik's widow about her sout' twenty an' I got a deal worked out wit' her."

Oscar explained the arrangement with the Holmvik woman to grow two acres of wheat on her land as well, and George had a good laugh at that. Oscar laughed along to indicate he thought it amusing as well, but he didn't.

"Well, should be good land there all right. She agreed, did she? The Holmvik woman?"

Oscar nodded. "Yah, an' Bergstrom said he'd loan me the threshing screens, so all I need now iss the seed."

"Yah, he'd have the screens all right." George mulled it over a moment to himself and had to admit it probably was a good plan. He wished he'd come up with it himself. There was one problem though. The big one.

"So, how d'you plan to pay for the seed, Oscar?" George got to the point.

Oscar wasn't good with the numbers and didn't trust his own figuring, so he went over them with George, based on the price of flax. If George would take the risk to extend him credit on the seed until harvest, Oscar would pay him a slightly higher interest on the cost. That way, he explained, George could make a profit and keep a customer from going under. George laughed at the audacity of Oscar's reasoning, but he liked Oscar and sympathized with his situation. He had to admit this might just be a chance to show everyone, including ol' E.A., that there were still ways to win the game, and that farming was still a good way to make a living.

George had some very legitimate reservations about the financial risk he'd be taking. But the economy was starting to change, and for the first time in years there was growing optimism throughout the country that the Depression was coming to an end. He sat for several long moments alternately working out the numbers with pencil and paper and gazing out the window into the distance considering the possibilities. Oscar's stomach tied itself in various knots for what seemed like forever waiting for George to say something.

"Flax eh. Ya know, I'm takin' a mighty big risk if I back you on this,"

George finally said. "Flax. Shit, if it was Bergstrom asking for the seed I'd tell him to go to hell. He burnt the bridges wit' me years ago an' he knows it. That's probably why he ain't tryin' to grow flax himself, even if he could find somebody to rent him land," he said, then he considered a while longer.

"Dammit all Oscar," George finally said, "I don't know why I should take this chance wit' you, but I guess I just like the plan. Maybe I just like the idea that it might work an' you'd beat E.A. at his own game. That'd be enough for me. I'll do it. I'll even give you credit on the flax on the terms you're askin'. I'm bettin' flax on that Holmvik land should yield really well with the right weather."

"Good. Ok d'en," Oscar said with his stoic mask dropped for the moment. "Yah if we get a good summer we should come out pretty nice wit' dis."

"If we don't have a good summer, you an' me an' a lot of others ain't goin' to have to worry about our farms or this feed and seed business anymore."

Both men understood the situation very well. They shook on the deal and George filled out the paperwork. As he did, George's active mind considered something else in the business arrangement between an eligible bachelor and a widow, though he didn't mention it to Oscar.

Oscar knew George and realized it was inevitable the man would tell everyone in the area about him farming the Holmvik land. A bachelor farming the Holmvik widow's land would make pretty hot gossip in Aasness Township. Oscar hoped the men would take it all in stride, but their wives—especially certain of them—seemed to consider it their duty to see that every man was matched up with a woman, happily or otherwise.

George didn't keep flax seed on hand and told Oscar he'd have to come back to pick it up in about ten days. He drew up and explained the credit forms, and Oscar licked the tip of a pencil stub he kept in his bib overalls and signed his name with careful deliberation. The two men loaded the wheat seed into the back of Oscar's pickup truck, and he was grateful it was planting time so no farmers were loitering around the co-op. He knew George would have announced news of him farming the Widow Holmvik's land, and the thought of their teasing and badgering had him complaining to Hektor all the way back to the farm.

It was mid-May and planting was well underway on other farms by the time Oscar got around to turning over the soil on the Holmvik property. He had already sown his own land with wheat, corn and alfalfa for his cattle before taking on the flax project.

He set out for Esther Holmvik's farm with the plow hitched to old *Gubbe*. It would take some work to get that twenty acres ready to plant after it had lain idle for the last eight years.

Oscar idled-back the throttle on the Massey-Harris as it rolled down the Holmvik driveway and into the farmyard. Henry came running to meet him with whoops of exuberant joy at seeing the noisy tractor with the mass of steel machinery in tow. For Henry, this was the most exciting thing that had happened on his grandmother's farm since his arrival. It fascinated him. Though he was too young to understand why, the attraction came quite naturally. It was mechanical, it smelled, it was noisy, dirty, and oh, so... masculine. Esther noted the boy's excitement from the back steps of her house, but made no comment.

Henry ran alongside the tractor, waving his hands and shouting greetings to Oscar who was trying to ignore the boy and watch where he was going. With the exception of when his own brothers were young, Oscar had never been around children and he didn't really know how to deal with them. He wasn't comfortable having the boy around *Gubbe* either, and young Henry's lively antics beside the iron brute made Oscar nervous.

Oscar stopped the tractor but left the engine idling and set the hand brake before dismounting.

"Hi, Mr. Halvorson," said Henry, with a tone in his voice that young boys normally reserve for baseball heroes. "Did ya come to plow today? Is that what's behind yer tractor Mr. Halvorson? Is that a plowing machine?"

"Yah, that's a plow all right," Oscar replied, a little surprised by such an obvious question. "That iss, if your grandma says it's okay to plow that piece today."

Henry headed straight for the implement and climbed up on the frame before Oscar could do much more than furrow his brow in disapproval. From her back steps, Esther saw Henry climb on the machinery and before Oscar could think of what to say she called the boy back.

"Henry, get down off that and stay away from it," she shouted with a stern tone in her voice. "It's not safe to climb on machinery, you could get hurt real bad. Now get down off there right away."

Henry obediently jumped down from the plow and looked at Oscar to see what his reaction would be.

"Your grandma iss right," said Oscar. "It's not safe to climb around on machinery, 'specially when it's hitched to the tractor."

Satisfied that the boy was keeping his curiosity at a safe distance, Oscar turned and walked over to talk to Esther. Meanwhile, Henry's eyes examined every inch of the exposed tractor engine as the warm air off the radiator fan blew through his hair. He was completely absorbed by the chugging rhythm, and unconsciously his mouth formed to orally mimic the sound.

"Goo morn, Missus Holmvik," Oscar said. "I come to turn over that field so I can get it ready to plant soon—that iss if it's okay wit' you to do it now."

"Well, you've got a good day for it," Esther replied, nodding and noting the direction of the wind. Any dust would be blown away from her wash that hung on the line. "You know where to go then?" she added, nodding toward an opening in a windbreak of box elders at the far end of the yard.

"Sure t'ing. East from that corner by Holden's land and over to the church. Iss there any rocks or soft spots I should know about?"

"No, I don't think so, the field was pretty clean last time it was cultivated. You'll just have to watch for rocks in case any have come up, but there shouldn't be any big problems Mr. Halvorson. It's a good piece of land and nicely drained."

"Yah," Oscar inhaled, squinting in the bright spring sunshine under his old felt hat. With both hands deep in his pockets and gazing in the general direction of the field in question, he asked, "So d'en... when I'm ready to plant, Missus Holmvik, I was wondering where it iss that you'd like d'em two acres of wheat?"

Esther paused only a moment before answering, detecting a lingering note of skepticism in Oscar's question. Even so, she was pleased that he hadn't forgotten, and wasn't still trying to change her mind about growing the wheat. Subtly testing the demeanor of the old farmer, she looked at him and released her lovely smile before replying.

"You know, I think it would look nice over in that end of the field that adjoins the church. Don't you think so Mr. Halvorson?"

The softer tone of her voice caused Oscar to turn his gaze from the field to Esther. He was completely disarmed by her smile and quickly shifted his gaze from her face to his boots and then toward the opening in the windbreak.

"Yah, yah, over by the church there," he agreed just a little flustered. "Well, I... I better get to it d'en." With that he turned and walked away.

As he approached the tractor, Henry pointed at the spinning flywheel and asked, "What's that for, Mr. Halvorson? How come it's goin' around and not doin' anything?"

"Keep away from that, boy," Oscar said, "that can be really dangerous. Stand back now, me an' *Gubbe* got to go to work."

"*Gubbe*?" Henry asked. "Is that your tractor's name, Mr. Halvorson? Is that what you call it?"

"Yah," said Oscar as he climbed back into the seat.

"Can I come along Mr. Halvorson? Can I watch you plow?"

The engine clamored as Oscar revved-up the throttle, and he pretended not to hear. He put the tractor in gear, let out the clutch and chugged out of the farmyard off toward the field.

"Gramma, can I go watch him plow? Please, Gramma?" Henry pleaded.

"I don't see why not, just keep out of his way. Farm machinery is not safe Henry, and Mr. Halvorson is busy enough with his work. He shouldn't have to be looking out for you, too."

"I'll be safe, Gramma," Henry assured her. "I won't be in the way." His words drifted off as he was already running to catch up with *Gubbe* and Mr. Halvorson.

Esther watched her grandson joyfully chase after the tractor as it turned through the opening in the trees at the edge of the farmyard and headed into the chosen field. She watched until she could no longer see them, but her thoughts followed the tractor too.

Oscar was in his element. If it weren't for the noisy iron monster he rode he'd have felt completely at home with the land. When he drove onto the field where he was to break the idle soil, he stopped the tractor and turned to drop the plowshares to the ground and set their depth.

"Hi, Mr. Halvorson," Henry called as he came running up beside the big wheel of the tractor. "I've come to watch you plow. Gramma said it was okay."

"Yah sure," he replied with a frown. "Just keep back and stay where I can see you. I don't want something bad to happen, you understand?" Oscar shouted over the engine. The boy was going to be a bother, he just knew it.

"Okay, I'll just watch from here," Henry answered.

With that, Oscar climbed into the seat, revved the engine and let out the clutch. *Gubbe's* voice changed timbre and dropped an octave as it lurched ahead and the plowshares sank into the soil like mechanical claws. Henry's young eyes took it all in with boyish wonder. Each blade of the plow sliced cleanly through the earth, cutting, scooping and lifting a deep layer of sod, then rolling it over neatly. The grassy ground was like a carpet, and the plow steadily cut through the pile in continuous strips and turned them over to reveal the backing. As the tractor moved on, the moist, black soil in its wake gave off a rich scent of the earth, a seductive aroma to certain men. Even at his young age, Henry sensed it in the open furrows.

He knelt beside a black furrow and grabbed the soil in his small hands, squeezing the moist clumps, crumbling them to bits. There were earthworms, bugs, and interesting stones to be found among the clods. The plow had uncovered a new world for Henry. Every now and then he looked up to see where the tractor was, how far it had gone. When it reached the end of the field, he watched Oscar make a looping turn and head back toward him, and the strip of black earth grew wider.

It was a perfect spring day with bright blue sky and puffy white clouds. The grass was green and wildflowers bloomed everywhere along the fencerows. Meadow lark and cricket songs carried on the gentle breeze. Soon, white gulls floating above the black earth behind the plow, added their cries to the celebration of the season. Despite Oscar and Henry being far apart in age, both felt their own sense of contentment just being on the land, and at that moment there was no where else either one of them would rather be.

10

The plow took to the soil well, and though an occasional rock had worked its way to the surface, the field was as nice a piece of land as Esther had said it was. Whenever the plow would unearth a rock, Oscar stopped to pick it up and set it on the plow frame. A rock pile had been established near the center of the field under a stunted burr oak, a common practice among farmers. Over the years rocks had been tossed on the pile until it was now of considerable size, and each time Oscar passed with the plow, he added the rocks he'd collected.

The week after the plowing was done, Oscar came back with a disk and drag hitched to the tractor to get the soil ready for the seed. The disk cut up the furrows left by the plow, and the drag worked like a big garden rake, breaking up the clumps and leveling the soil. Each piece of machinery was of new interest to Henry, and he followed it to the field to see how it worked. Though Oscar knew he would be late getting the flax planted, the soil was in good condition, warm and just moist enough. But it was still spring, and a rainy spell could come any time causing delays. He worked with the weather-regulated sense of urgency that determines so much of a farmer's schedule. These were long days, caring for his farm as well as the extra work of the flax project, and his aging body felt the strain at the end of each day.

Whenever Oscar worked the Holmvik field, Henry tagged along and watched from the rock pile. It became his island fortress in the midst of the dark sea of soil that surrounded it. The little tree gave some shade, and from on top of the pile he watched Oscar traverse the field on *Gubbe*, like a ship tacking to and fro. Whenever the tractor came close, Henry stood and waved, calling to Oscar, who gave little if any acknowledgment.

After a couple days of working the soil with the disk and drag, it was finally ready to plant. Henry watched as Oscar stopped the tractor mid-field, climbed down and started walking toward the edge of the field near the church. Henry raced across the field to join him.

"Whatcha' doin' now, Mr. Halvorson?" Henry called out as he got closer.

Oscar didn't respond. His mind seemed fixed on something else at the moment. When he reached the edge of the field he turned, and concentrating on a measured pace, walked back into the field at a perpendicular angle to the edge. His careful count carried him past the tractor well into the open field, where he dragged the heel of his boot on the ground to mark an "X." Henry was right behind him watching every move. After Oscar made the "X" mark, he headed off in a ninety-degree direction, toward the edge of the field by the road that went past the church. Once he got to the fence, he turned and in the same carefully measured gait, walked back again just as he had done before, carefully measuring out the two acres he would plant in wheat. The widow would get her two acres of wheat, no more and no less.

Concentrating on counting his paces, Oscar kept his eyes to the ground until he came back to the "X" he'd marked, but something wasn't right. He was sure it wasn't where he'd made the mark. Confused, he looked around to see "X's" in the dirt all around him. There was no way of knowing which one was his original mark, they were all careful duplicates of his own. Oscar became aware of young Henry off to his side, busily scribing yet one more mark in the dirt with his heel. There was no way to figure out which of all the "X's" was the right one, the one he'd originally made.

Oscar looked away mumbling a couple Norwegian epithets, which Henry's keen young ears didn't miss.

"Are you sayin' those bad words again Mr. Halvorson? Can you teach me some of those words?"

"What? Oh, uh, no, no," Oscar said, fixing a cold blue eye on the offending boy. "I ahh… ahh… I was yust t'inkin'," he said in a moment of inspiration. "Maybe you could help me out here, you bein' such a clever young fellah an' all."

"You bet, Mr. Halvorson, what do ya' need me to do? Should I drive *Gubbe* for ya or make more Xs'?"

"Well, what I'd like iss for you to go over there an get me a good long stick," Oscar said pointing to a grove of trees behind the outhouse on the church property. "A good long, straight one."

"How long?" asked Henry innocently.

"Well, if you could get one about as long as me, that would really be swell," Oscar said. "T'ink you can do that?"

"What are you gonna do with it?"

"I'll show you when you bring it, that iss if you t'ink you can do it," said Oscar, still eyeing the boy. "You sure you can?"

"You bet I can Mr. Halvorson!" and Henry turned and started running full-speed toward the trees by the church.

"Wait!" Oscar called. "You'll maybe need to cut it down. Have you got a pocket knife?"

"Nope, I'll just break it off," Henry replied confidently.

Oscar nodded, then dug in the pocket of his overalls and pulled out his worn old pocketknife and handed it to the boy.

"You may need this," he said.

Henry beamed with pride at being trusted with handling a tool, a knife at that, and he took off again for the trees. Oscar, pleased with himself at how neatly the little task got the kid out of his way, set about re-pacing the measurements of the two-acre plot.

By the time he was done, Henry was heading back with a sapling that still had a few leafy branches on it. It wasn't as long as Oscar had asked for, but it didn't matter. Oscar had his coordinates measured and was standing at the inside corner of the two acre plot where the widow's wheat would be planted. When Henry presented him with the sapling, Oscar placed the thick end between his feet and pushed it deep into the soil so it stood on its own.

"D'ere now," he said. "D'is here marks the corner of your gramma's wheat field, boy, you understand?"

Henry gave him a blank look, so Oscar explained, pointing in ninety-degree angles from the sapling toward the edges of the field. This area, he said, would be planted in wheat for Henry's grandmother. Henry was not to move the sapling from where it was stuck in the ground. Henry understood; but more important, in his understanding he began to feel like he was included in something grown up, something that was part of a man's world.

"Here's yer knife back, Mr. Halvorson," he said, offering it back to Oscar.

Oscar reached to accept it, then withdrew his hand.

"You keep it," he said. "A boy should have a pocket knife."

Henry's face beamed. "Wow, you mean it, Mr. Halvorson? I can keep it?"

Oscar nodded.

"Forever?, Gee, thanks. Thanks a lot," he gushed. It wasn't much, just an old Barlow knife, polished by wear and its single blade ground down from use, but it was a treasure to Henry. He turned and ran off to the grove of trees to find something else to cut, and Oscar wished he'd thought to give the knife to the boy long ago. He climbed back on the idling tractor and headed off the field and toward home for evening chores.

That evening, when Henry came in to clean up for supper, he proudly showed his grandmother the knife, explaining that Mr. Halvorson had given it to him for helping mark the field. He explained where the plot of wheat was going to be, and how the corner was marked with the sapling he'd cut. Esther considered whether it was safe for the boy to have the knife, but realized its significance to him. She told Henry to be careful with it and let it go at that, but was touched by Oscar's small act of kindness to the boy.

The next day Oscar showed up in his pickup truck with the sacks of seed. He unloaded them in a granary between the Holmvik's barn and machine shed, then drove off without stopping to talk. Henry and Esther had their own planting to do, and were off working in her big garden and didn't see him come or go.

A couple days later, just before the Memorial Day weekend, Oscar and *Gubbe* rolled into the Holmvik driveway again, this time with his seeder on the hitch. Esther was baking bread again, and saw him pull up to the granary from her kitchen window. Henry had already joined him at the granary to see what was going to happen today.

It was overcast and cool and looked like rain was on the way, so Oscar's timing for planting was great, if the rain would just hold off until he was done. Esther went out to talk to him as he hauled the sacks of seed from the granary.

"Good morning Mr. Halvorson," she called out over the idling tractor as she approached. Oscar looked up from one of the dual hoppers on the seeder.

"*God dag* (Good day,)" said Oscar cheerfully as he worked the linkage back and forth that opened the seed chutes, and checked the settings.

"It looks like rain is on the way," Esther said, "it certainly would be good to get that seed in the ground today."

"I t'ought the same, Missus Holmvik," said Oscar as he turned to pick up a sack of flax seed.

"Oh, I was hoping you would plant the wheat first Mr. Halvorson. Would you mind?" She couldn't resist testing him a bit further.

Oscar looked up at her and she smiled her disarming smile again. He clenched his jaw, but carried the flax back into the granary and emerged with the wheat seed. As he poured the seed into the hopper, Oscar noticed Esther Holmvik's bowed head and folded hands from the corner of his eye, as she prayed over the seed. "Couldn't hurt," he thought to himself, and he silently said a little prayer of his own as he went for another sack of wheat.

As soon as the hoppers were filled, Oscar climbed aboard Gubbe, revved the throttle of the Massey-Harris and, after tipping his hat to Mrs. Holmvik, headed off to the field. Henry followed close behind and Esther watched them thoughtfully until they were out of the yard.

Over the past week, as Oscar had been working the soil, Henry had practically taken up residence on the rock pile in the middle of the field. The boy had a rich imagination and made his own entertainment there on his little island. But sometimes Henry just sat there on the pile of stones. Like each of the stones, he'd been removed for being in the way, and cast off to the side of life. It was then he wondered about his own mother and father, where they were, what they were doing and when he would see them again. Today was one of those days and Henry just sat on the pile of stones, quietly whittling on a stick.

Soon Oscar was finished planting Esther's two-acre plot of wheat and he headed back to the granary to re-set the nozzles on the seeder and load the hoppers with flax seed. Henry followed the tractor back to the farmyard, but when Oscar headed back to the field to plant the flax, he went into his grandmother's house instead. After a few trips over the field, Oscar noticed with some relief that the boy was not on the rock pile. When the seeder was empty again, Oscar headed back to re-fill the hoppers. Before long he was back in the field and making good progress with the seeding. It looked like the impending rain was going to hold off just long enough.

After making a turn at the end of the field and heading back toward the middle, he noticed Henry and his grandmother standing on the rock pile waving and motioning to him. Oscar kept the tractor on course until he was near them, then stopped, climbed down and headed over to see what they wanted.

"We brought lunch for you!" Henry shouted as he approached.

Oscar stopped in his tracks. In all his years of farming, since his mother died, no one had been there to bring him lunch in the field. This was totally unexpected and the surprise stunned him. It was midday. He hadn't eaten since before sun up and suddenly realized he was hungry. Oscar acknowledged with a nod and walked back to the tractor to shut it off before joining Esther and Henry on the rock pile under the scrubby little burr oak.

Esther had brought the lunch in a pail, and had a Mason jar of coffee tied up and carried in a dishtowel. By the time Oscar joined them, she had things spread out and ready for him to eat. He pushed back his hat and bent down to seat himself on the rocks, letting out a great sigh as he looked over the food Esther had brought.

There were sandwiches, egg salad on fresh baked bread, a jar of ground cherry sauce, a tin of sardines, and a big piece of cake; all that and fresh, warm, delicious coffee.

"This iss really swell, Missus Holmvik," Oscar said as he seized a sandwich and took a huge bite. He stopped chewing abruptly when Esther interrupted with a hasty blessing, and then sheepishly continued to eat. Henry took a sandwich and headed for the grove of trees by the church to hunt phantom tigers.

"Ain't you goin' to eat?" Oscar said to Esther with his mouth full.

"Oh no," she replied. "I ate before fixing this for you." It wasn't true, but she could see how hungry the man was and was afraid she hadn't prepared enough.

It was wonderful for Oscar to eat food he hadn't had to prepare himself, and it tasted much better too. With his busy schedule, he survived on a bachelor's fare, which was unimaginative at best, and he'd gotten skinny. Esther's bread was so good it tasted heavenly. Oscar indulged himself, and was so engrossed in filling his stomach that he could barely respond when Esther spoke.

She talked about her husband working this field years before, and about how she and a hired man and Arthur had worked it after her husband died. Oscar wasn't paying close attention, but vaguely knew about it all anyway. Everyone in the area did. She spoke of what they had grown on this field, and how well it had produced. Soon the food was gone, and he leaned back luxuriously on the rocks with a full belly and a cup of good coffee.

"*Mange tusen takk for matten*, Missus Holmvik, (Many thanks for the food)," Oscar said.

"*Velkommen*...(You're welcome...)" Esther said, pleased by his appreciation and impressed by his appetite.

"This was really good. I didn't know I was so hungry and I didn't bring no lunch today. You are sure kind to do this."

"Well, I know a man's got to eat when he's working," said Esther with gratification. "Glad you enjoyed it."

"I ain't had good bread like d'at since my mother used to make it," Oscar mused as he finished the coffee. He was not accustomed to giving compliments, and was probably just thinking out loud, but it was the nicest thing he could say about her baking. Esther understood and felt pleased.

Her mind flashed back to the early years, when she had brought lunch to her husband, Carl, when he worked in the field. They had worked hard together then, struggling to build up the farm. She and Carl loved each other deeply, and she still missed him. After Carl's death, their son Arthur had been a comfort and a companion until he left home. Now his son Henry's coming was a blessing and he was great company.

Esther knew how much Henry missed his father, and she shared many of the same questions about him. She and Henry comforted and supported each other, but Esther understood the boy was missing something important in his young life that she couldn't provide. She was beginning to realize that perhaps she was missing something too.

A light breeze sighed in the budding branches of the little oak on the rock pile as Esther sat on the stones watching Oscar. Reclining on the rocks, he had dozed off quickly after his lunch and probably hadn't heard much. She knew how hard he had been working, and let him have his nap.

Esther had known Oscar Halvorson since they were both young. Or at least she knew of him. He had always been that reclusive bachelor who kept to himself, immersed in his farm work. She knew her other farm neighbors well, but realized she didn't really know Oscar Halvorson. She supposed no one did. Now as he dozed, she wondered what he was actually like.

He was a rough old cob for sure, but he seemed to have a good, kind heart. He wasn't at his best just then, with his mouth sagging open as he softly snored, which made her smile a bit. His face and clothing were dirty with the media of his trade. Several days' growth of hoary stubble bristled his jaw, but his features were not unpleasant. His eyes, now closed, she considered to be his most unique attribute. They were a clear, light blue, the color sometimes held in blocks of ice cut from the lake. She wondered if he ever felt lonely.

Henry's calls as he came across the field broke the silence, and Oscar awoke abruptly.

"*Uffda, jeg hadde litten høne blund, tror jeg,* (I think I had a little cat nap)" said Oscar with a groan, and he stiffly drew himself up to his feet. "Sorry for being so rude Missus Holmvik, especially after that fine lunch you brought."

"That's okay," Esther replied. "I know you don't get much rest this time of year. You shouldn't push yourself so hard, Mr. Halvorson. Neither of us is getting any younger. Come along Henry," she called, "I'll need your help getting the wash off the line before it rains."

"Yah, an' I better hurry an' get this seeding done before the rain, too," Oscar said. They hurried off in opposite directions to finish their work, but as they went, they were each thinking of the other in a different way.

11

The rain came, but not until Oscar finished seeding the flax and Esther got her washing off the line. It was a good rain, a slow, steady soaker that spoiled holiday plans for fishing and picnics, but none of the farmers complained. It started raining Friday evening and continued most of Saturday. Sunday morning brought a few more showers but by Monday morning, Memorial Day, the rain had moved on, leaving a humid overcast. Parades and events were held in area communities as scheduled, and people were able to go to cemeteries to tend graves. Around Aasness Township, the dead were remembered.

Memorial Day morning Esther put on her straw gardening hat with the big broad brim, remembering that Carl had liked how she looked in it when it was still new. She took a trowel and dug a lily from her flower garden and cut a few fresh blooming irises as well. Then she explained to Henry that this was the day each year when people remember those who died in past wars, and loved ones who are no longer with us.

"You mean like my dad and mom?" Henry inquired. "I think about 'em on lots of days."

"Of course you do Henry, and so do I," she replied, "and that's good. But we'll see them again some time. Memorial Day is to remember those who have died, those we won't see anymore in this life."

To help him understand, Esther told Henry that each Memorial Day she visited the grave of her husband Carl to plant flowers, and she'd like him to come along. She sent Henry to fetch an old pail from the barn. When he brought it, she placed the flowers, earth and all, in the pail with the trowel. Then together they walked out the driveway and then the short distance to Eidsvold Lutheran Church.

A couple cars were parked on the gravel apron along the road in front of the church, and people were already busy in the cemetery sprucing up the graves and laying their flowers. Esther greeted them and exchanged small talk about the rain and the condition of the cemetery before making her way among the head stones to a small, simple slab on the ground that marked the grave of her husband, Carl A. Holmvik. Henry was checking out the different stones, trying to read what some of them said or make out the ornamental designs on the few fancier stones. Esther sat beside Carl's grave and plucked grass away from the headstone and pulled weeds around the plot. With the trowel, she dug a little hole above the head stone and planted the lily she'd brought.

"Henry," she called, "you can help. Bring me a pail of water from the pump over there." Henry grabbed the pail and trotted off dutifully.

Esther soaked the earth around the lily and washed the headstone before arranging the irises at its base. When she was satisfied that everything looked proper, she removed her hat and sat next to the grave. Then she called Henry over to sit beside her, and she began to introduce Henry to his grandfather.

Henry had barely gotten to know his mother's father in Minneapolis before the man died just a few years ago, and he remembered his mother's mother there as well. Now, living with Esther, he understood she was his other grandmother, but he hadn't quite made the connection to having another grandfather.

"Was he your dad?" Henry asked.

"No, Henry, he was your father's father," she explained, "just as I am your father's mother."

She told him about how she had first met young Carl Holmvik many years ago, when he had come to her parent's farm with a thrashing crew.

"He was young and handsome," Esther said, "just like your father." Henry pretended to grimace at the romantic-sounding words.

"You would have loved him Henry," she said. "The two of you would have had so much fun together. He was quick-witted and could make me laugh even when I tried to be serious."

She told about going on hayrides with other young couples their first fall together, and sleigh rides that winter. After about a year of seeing each other, Carl asked to marry her and she accepted. He had a small piece of land that his father gave him to start farming, and he later inherited his father's farm, which was the custom.

"Is that your farm now?" Henry asked.

"Yes, that's right," she said.

"In the early years, Carl and I worked from first light until after dark. It was really hard then. But after a few years things got better. Then we had a baby. A boy we named Arthur. That's your father," she explained.

In wistful phrases Esther talked about what his father was like as a boy, where he played, what he liked to do.

"We were so happy together then Henry, but that was before the accident."

"What happened Gramma? Did something happen to Grampa Carl?" Henry asked.

"Well, one day Carl bought a fine pair of young stallions from a dray man in town," she went on. "They were a big, beautiful team, and oh, they were so strong. It seemed there was no load they couldn't pull. But the drayman wanted to sell them because, being stallions, they were too difficult to control in town. Carl loved horses and was good at handling them, but it was always difficult trying to manage those two. That's what probably led to the accident."

"How did it happen Gramma?" asked Henry.

"It was during the corn harvest, when Arthur was just a little older than you," Esther continued.

"Carl was on his way back from Phillips Mill with an empty wagon. Those stallions were no doubt feeling frisky with the light load. No one knows for sure what happened, no one saw it. Maybe Carl let them run, or maybe he lost control and they just started to run on their own."

Henry listened intently as the scene played out in his active imagination.

"That forenoon a neighbor, Mr. Tollerud, found the team walking on the road about a mile past the bridge. They were all sweaty and still breathing hard," Esther said, "and they were still dragging the wrecked wagon. But there was no sign of Carl."

It had happened many years ago. She had relived the story many times, but even after all this time her voice became strained and her eyes welled with tears. Henry was a sensitive boy, and the effect on him was evident as he sat up and took his grandmother's hand.

"Mr. Tollerud unhitched the team," Esther continued, "and secured them to a fence post before heading down the road to look for the driver. He found Carl, your grandfather, lying on the bridge over the river," she gestured to the south, "just down the road from the church here. The wagon had crashed into a steel girder on the bridge trestle and Carl got hit really hard on his head."

Esther paused a moment, but soon went on.

"Mr. Tollerud went for help and they brought Carl home and sent for a doctor, but it was no use. Carl died two days later."

She told Henry that this was where they buried Carl's body those many years ago, and that friends and neighbors came from all around to attend the funeral. It had been very difficult for her, and she had been sad for a long time.

"Are you still sad Gramma?" asked Henry.

"Sometimes I am." she said. "If I'm alone and think about it, I still get very sad. I've been lonely for so long Henry, I miss Carl terribly."

Henry was too young to understand it all, but his grandmother's eyes welling with tears as she spoke told him far more to him than her words. He opened his arms wide and they held each other there among the gravestones.

"It's okay, Gramma, you've got me now," Henry finally said, "I'll take care of you. I'll make you happy again."

"Oh, God bless you child," Esther replied, her voice heavy with emotion. "That you do. That you do for sure. Now put all those weeds I pulled in the pail and dump them over the fence while I wash up the trowel."

"Sure thing Gramma," Henry said, and off he went on his errand while Esther lingered a while longer in thought beside the grave of her husband.

"He's a fine boy, Carl. How I wish you could have been together. He's brought me new life, it seems."

"We're farming again. I've let out the south twenty by the church to Oscar Halvorson. You remember him. He lives all alone. He's a good man, and Henry enjoys being with him. It's good to have a man around again, but I wish it were you he was getting to know. I miss you so much, Carl."

Esther got up, and with her eyes to the ground, turned and made her way to the pump to clean the trowel. Neither she nor Henry had been aware that they were being watched as they sat by her husband's grave, or that even now she was being observed from another part of the cemetery.

Henry joined her at the pump and worked the handle vigorously. After rinsing the pail they walked toward the front of the cemetery to leave.

"My hat! I forgot my hat," Esther said when she reached the parking lot, but Henry had run ahead and was talking to school friends.

She went back to retrieve her hat from beside the grave. When she stooped to pick it up, a cluster of yellow lay inside the straw crown. It was a bouquet of little wild marsh marigolds. 'How sweet' it struck her. She loved wild marigolds and Carl knew it. He enjoyed their rich, bright color too. '*Ringblomster*, he'd called them in Norwegian. Sometimes he brought them home for her from marshy areas in the pasture when they were in season. But there were no such wet areas near the church. She looked around but there was no one near who might have placed the flowers in her hat. Esther mused for a moment on the possibility they could have been a gift from beyond the grave, but she was too rational for that. No, Henry must have found the flowers and put them in her hat while she was at the pump. But how could he have known she liked them? Where and when did he find marigolds?

Holding the flowers to her cheek, she felt deeply touched in her heart as she walked out of the cemetery to rejoin Henry. She would be sure to reward the boy's thoughtfulness when they got home. But as she approached the corner near the front of the church Esther stopped abruptly, her attention focused on the small bouquets of marigolds adorning each of the graves on the Halvorson family plots.

12

Elof Tollerud was found face down in the manure on the barn floor where he'd just released the cattle from their stanchions. He'd gone back to check for mastitis in the udder of a remaining cow, and hadn't returned to the house for morning coffee. The cow had been lowing for over an hour before Tollerud's son decided to investigate and found his father. To those who knew him best, the way the old farmer met his end seemed inevitable, if not somehow appropriate.

No autopsy or medical tests were performed, no questions were asked. It was just assumed Tollerud's heart finally gave out. If he'd been having heart problems, no one ever knew since he never mentioned it. Typical. The man was dead now, and no medical test would change that. His son had taken over the farm years ago, but even at the age of 86 the old man couldn't completely give it up. The younger Tollerud didn't run the place to Elof's satisfaction, but that was a family matter.

Old Tollerud wasn't one of the original immigrants to the area. Though born in Norway, he was quite a bit younger than those who first came over, but had been their contemporary. That alone had made him venerable among the people of Aasness Township.

Tollerud had belonged to Eidsvold Lutheran Church practically his entire life. Some folks knew him better than others, but everyone in Aasness Township at least knew of him. Word traveled quickly and hasty preparations were made for what would surely be a well-attended funeral.

When she got the news, Esther went through her music and selected a few appropriate hymns. "Rock of Ages," "The Old Rugged Cross," and "Blest Be The Tie That Binds," all standard favorites. She went to the church to practice the music on the old pump organ, and made sure everything was tidied up around the altar and pulpit. Then she polished the cross, put new candles in the holders and gathered up the altar cloth to bring it home for a careful washing.

Between weddings and funerals over the years, the preparations had become fairly customary for Esther, and she personally enjoyed the interruption in her regular routine to participate in the spiritual as well as social aspect of rural fellowship. While carefully washing the altar cloth by hand, she considered what she would bring for the luncheon afterward.

Lunch after these affairs was more than tradition, it was a necessity. The seasonal and daily routine of farming determined the order of events in people's lives, as well as how they dealt with death. Events outside of farming, including funerals, had to be scheduled midday, between the daily needs of livestock.

Sometimes people would come from a long way over poor roads, and it wouldn't be proper for them to return without a good meal. Distance between rural friends and neighbors made folks appreciate each other, so even funerals constituted a social event. In any case, a midday meal was not to be missed.

The Depression greatly affected what was served, and everyone simply brought what they could to the church to share in the "pot luck". For some, it meant bringing a few potatoes to boil, for others it meant they just brought their appetites. Whatever was in season from the garden, fruits or vegetables, was converted into delightfully creative concoctions through variations of shared recipes. This "lunch" became a challenge among farm wives who dug deep into their canned larders to provide the best of what they could, and "lunch" inevitably became an extraordinary bill of fare.

Some women were known for a trademark dish they made, like Emma Berg's irresistible "postlude" pork and beans, the refrains of which were rehearsed all the way home; or Sonja Halland's *kjøtt kaker* (meat balls), a wonderful example of the very subtle art of Scandinavian seasoning applied to fresh-ground pork and beef. Of course the Depression had forced Sonja to alter her recipe to conserve meat and extend portions, but everyone understood and ate the *kjøtt kaker*, recalling what they tasted like before these "hard times". The creative alterations in recipes were shared and the efforts of all the women were always praised and appreciated by everyone in attendance.

Esther Holmvik's specialty was her bread. All the farm women baked bread of course, but Esther's was considered to be distinctive. Not that it was a big issue, it was just accepted by virtually everyone in the congregation. First of all, it really was especially good in flavor and texture. But more significantly, because she baked the bread for Communion at Eidsvold Lutheran Church, and people perhaps somehow thought it "holy." Perhaps it was because the charitable Mr. Phillips donated the flour from his mill for the bread. Whatever the reason, Esther's bread was the bread consumed at Eidsvold Church. She was self-effacing and remained humble about it, but in her heart she was pleased.

The day of the funeral, Esther was at the church long before anyone else. She rehearsed the hymns on the organ one more time and scurried around checking details.

A full hour before the service the first car pulled up and parked on the gravel apron out front. Esther looked out the church door and saw it was Mr. and Mrs. Thorvald. As they got out of the car, she heard them arguing in loud Norwegian about whose funeral they were attending today. Mr. Thorvald was convinced that if it wasn't Arne Gullerud's funeral, it ought to be. Mrs. Thorvald staunchly suggested that Mr. Thorvald should just keep quiet and be darned happy it wasn't his own. Such disputes were typical between the Thorvalds. Esther called out a greeting, which abruptly ended the discussion.

"Sure glad you came early," Esther said as she walked toward their car. "I was just going to start getting things ready in the kitchen."

"Oh yah," said Mrs. Thorvald, "I thought we should come early to help get set up. Is there anyone else here then?" Her Ladies Aide group was serving.

"Not yet, just us so far. Can I help you carry anything downstairs?"

"Oh, I think we can manage. Gus, bring the basket and be careful with it. And don't forget the bars," Mrs. Thorvald said to her husband.

He didn't say a word, but with an expression on his face that suggested he'd rather be mucking out his barn, Gus Thorvald drew a large picnic basket from the backseat and retrieved the pan of bars before following the two women toward the church.

"I made a rice pudding," said Mrs. Thorvald, "and a pan of bars in case we didn't have enough desserts." There were always more desserts than needed.

"Oh yah, that sounds good," said Esther. "I made a rhubarb cake, too, just in case. Had a bumper crop of it already."

The two women began setting up the tables in the crowded church basement and putting food where it would be ready after the service. Soon others began arriving and the kitchen was bustling with activity, carried out with a business-like, somber demeanor meant to imply the women weren't actually enjoying all the preparation. This was a funeral after all.

Young Henry arrived at the church on his own, looking for his grandmother. He found her in the basement and was quickly put to work outside working the pump to fill several large cream cans with water. There was no running water inside the church and they needed gallons of it for cooking, making coffee, and of course cleaning up. Once Henry had pumped the cream cans full of water, one of the men carried them into the basement and quickly retreated from the estrogen-ladened atmosphere. In the kitchen, the sturdy farm wives muscled the heavy cream cans around just as well as the men.

The men congregated outside the church, watching over the cars like idle parking valets, a holdover from when most arrived by horse and buggy. Some men, perhaps half-a-dozen or more, looked uncomfortable in ill-fitting, double-breasted dark suits and ties. Most simply wore a dark suit coat over a clean chambray shirt and bib overalls, topped by a felt hat or tweed cap—the formal attire of the farming man of the '30s. Standing side by side in small clusters with hands deep in their pockets or clasped inside the bibs of their overalls, they focused their gazes quietly on some distant object rather than each other. Some of them hadn't seen each other in weeks, so there was news to catch up on. Sofus Grunvald and Carl Swenson spoke typically:

"So, *har du komm idag også*?" (So, have you come today also?)

"*Yah*." (The affirming word is inhaled while spoken and infers a multitude of meanings, depending on the context. A long pause follows as both men scan the horizon.)

"*Yah*," again in resignation. (Again the word is inhaled.)

"*Yah*." (Inhaled reply by the other man, after another significant pause.)

Eventually, Sofus turns his gaze to his boots, launches a stream of Copenhagen at the ground, then speaks again:

"You hear about Hoffmier's new bull, d'en?"

(Carl frowns, indicating that he has not heard.)

"Got into Torgerson's alfalfa." (This is potentially bad. The animal eats green alfalfa which causes severe gas and bloating, possibly death.)

There's a significant pause.

"Dead?" Carl asks.

(Sofus shakes his head to say no, then adds:)

"Gunderson had to come an' stick 'im." (This refers to the art of driving a pocketknife deep into a spot on the side of the animal to release the gas. It's a critical spot found by counting ribs, measuring and guessing. If the spot is missed, the animal might be killed. Without the treatment, the animal would die anyway.)

"He iss good at it," Carl replies.

"*Yah*." (Inhaled agreement from Sofus.)

"*Yah*." (Inhaled confirmation from Carl.)

The first strains of music from the pump organ indicated to the men it was time to enter the church and they did so in reverent silence.

Friends and neighbors from all around filed by the open casket to pay last respects to the departed, as Esther pumped out a medley of old hymns. Once everyone was satisfied that Elof Tollerud "looked good," that he "looked at peace", they took their places in the pews for opening prayers. Reverend Ellerby took to the pulpit and confronted a congregation of somber faces, the women with their cheeks flushed from recent efforts in the kitchen, and the two-tone, sunbaked faces of the men without their hats.

Ellerby was a young fellow in his mid-thirties, considered by most to be progressive, since he gave the entire service in English. Some remained skeptical, believing Norwegian to be the "language of the Lord." Ellerby was handsome, tall, and blond, and ladies of the church all doted on him, wishing he were single so they could match him up. He was not.

Esther would always remember it was Elof Tollerud who had found her husband Carl's body on the bridge after the accident. How helpful he had tried to be in his clumsy way. Everyone had their own recollections of him, and Elof had indeed been a decent, if imperfect man. Today everyone had come to remember only good things about him.

Alone at the end of a pew in the back of the church sat Oscar Halvorson. He had timed his arrival for a minimum of socializing before the service, and would slip away quickly afterward. Oscar came because of a sense of responsibility to his own mother and father, who had known

Elof Tollerud well. He came representing his own family, paying respects to the deceased on their behalf. He was not a regular church attendee, and though he knew everyone there and they knew him, Oscar felt uncomfortable around so many people.

Reverend Ellerby spoke encouraging words of comfort to the family and of the "many mansions" that were prepared for the faithful, the basic funeral stuff. But he did a very nice job eulogizing old Tollerud as a son of the pioneers, a good farmer, a decent and honorable man of faith, a loving husband and father. As he spoke, everyone had time to reflect not only on memories of old Tollerud, but on their own mortality as well.

The church was warm and stuffy, causing Gus Thorvald to nod off a few times, which might have gone unnoticed, except when he began to snore prodigiously. That prompted his wife to deliver a swift, sharp elbow to his ribs, from which the lingering discomfort allowed Gus to remain alert throughout the rest of the service.

The funeral ended with Esther pumping out the final hymn as the pallbearers came forward and walked the casket back down the aisle and out of the church to the cemetery for interment. With handkerchief to her nose and tears rolling down her face, Tollerud's widow followed the casket with the oldest son beside her, arm around her shoulder. Another son and daughter and grandchildren followed close behind, and then the congregation.

Everyone filed past Oscar, who waited in the last pew to join the congregation as they headed for the grave. When Esther finished playing she came down from the organ and met Henry, who had sat in the front row waiting for her.

Henry had never been to a funeral before, had never seen a dead body. He'd been too young to attend his grandfather's funeral in Minneapolis over two years before, and still had a child's vague concept of death. Until now, it had been a shadowy subject, dark and distant, less real than Santa Claus. Death was something adults dealt with, a subject not part of his child's world. The funeral gave Henry a harsh feel of real life and a new sense of real death. He felt the familiar loneliness of the rock pile there among the headstones in the cemetery, and it left him reaching for the reassurance of his grandmother's hand.

Esther and Henry walked down the aisle and joined the last of the exiting congregation. Henry saw Oscar standing alone in the last pew, and reached out his other hand for him to come join them. Oscar hesitated, looked at Esther, then took the boy's hand and together they followed the congregation to the grave.

After Reverend Ellerby's final prayer and benediction, each family member took a turn tossing a handful of earth on the coffin. As they did, a warbling soprano voice lifted spontaneously from the crowd in poignant song. It was Tollerud's widow, Hannah, singing in Norwegian, "*Tryggare kan ingen vara*" (Children Of The Heavenly Father). It was one of Elof's favorite hymns, sung in final tribute by his dear companion in life. The old woman's children clung to each other with somber tear-stained faces and the congregation stood in stoic silence as the verses lifted over them on a breath of summer breeze. Relatives, friends and neighbors gathered around the family, offering comfort, sympathy and support. Then it was over.

With Tollerud laid to rest, the crowd disbursed to reassemble in the church basement where the luncheon was being served. After expressing condolences, Oscar started to head for his truck, but for some reason he didn't want to leave. Seeing the last of his father's old friends lowered into the ground was a sobering reminder of his own lonely mortality, and he felt a rare need to be with others. On the parking apron his pace was slow and heavy, his eyes to the ground.

"Mr. Halvorson, ain't ya' gonna have some lunch?" Henry's voice reached out to him, and he turned and saw the boy standing by the church steps, still holding his grandmother's hand.

"Yes, come on, Oscar," Esther said, "you can take time for lunch. Join us."

Oscar hesitated, then a voice spoke quietly from behind him.

"What're you waiting for?" It was Theodore Bergstrom, getting into his own truck. What was he doing here, Oscar thought; he never came out for these things. "Go wit' them, Halvorson," Bergstrom said, "it's gettin' late." Then he closed the door and started his truck.

"Yah sure, I suppose I could eat something then," Oscar said, and his smile expressed relief as he followed Esther and Henry into the church. This did not go unnoticed by those farmers lingering outside the church, who by now knew Oscar was working the Widow Holmvik's land. George Kruger, gossipmonger of the feed and seed store, noticed it in particular.

It was hot in the church basement. When he was young, Oscar's father had advised him that: "Horses sweat, men perspire, but ladies 'glow.'" Oscar noticed many of the Ladies Aide women who were serving the lunch were "glowing" profusely. Mrs. Gunderson was "glowing" with particular intensity, and her round face was framed by moist curls of hair. Still, she smiled and chatted pleasantly while maneuvering her bulk between the tables, filling cups with hot coffee and glasses with cool lemonade.

Smells of hot dishes, breads, cakes and coffee hung deliciously on the damp basement air, and Oscar knew right away staying to eat lunch was a good decision. The three of them made their way through the serving line together and took places at a table that others were vacating.

"So d'en, Esther," said Kordula Hanson getting up from her seat, "I see you got two men with you today. I know young Henry, but who iss this new comer?"

Kordula's voice wasn't loud, but its pitch carried well in the noisy church basement, and several heads turned toward them. Henry was more interested in getting through his food so he could get in some play time with the other kids who had come and he barely looked up, but Oscar's discomfort was immediately apparent. He had foreseen dreaded moments like this and knew they were inevitable. Esther sensed his distress.

"Oh, Kordula, you know Oscar as well as any of us. Don't make him feel uncomfortable here now," Esther chided.

"Oh yah, I know him, but not as well as you I guess," Kordula replied with a wink. "It was so nice of you to come today, Mr. Halvorson. I hope we see you here more often," she added, looking back at Esther as if there was something else going on. "Don't forget to try that rhubarb cake, Mr. Halvorson, it iss really good."

With that, Kordula Hanson headed toward the kitchen window carrying her dirty dishes. A number of the women nearby couldn't help smirking a bit knowing Esther had made the rhubarb cake. Even a couple of the men had to smile at Oscar's discomfort, though they would have felt no different.

"Uffda!" Esther said in disgust as she sat down. "Sometimes women act like a bunch of school girls."

Oscar smiled as he nodded in agreement, pretending it didn't bother him.

As they ate, a few people came by to greet Oscar and tell him they were glad to see him there, which made him feel better. The delicious hot dishes, sauces, and cakes were well worth staying for, Oscar decided, even worth putting up with a little discomfort. He ate like he hadn't eaten in days, and it was wonderful to taste good foods that contrasted drastically with his own cooking. Even Henry was impressed with Oscar's appetite. He watched Oscar eat and fed him questions with each mouthful.

"Are ya planting any more fields Mr. Halvorson?"

"What are you goin' to plant now?"

"When does the flax come out?"

"How do cows make milk?"

"Shush Henry, let Mr. Halvorson eat," Esther said, but the questions kept coming, random and nonstop. Oscar replied in barely understandable one-word answers, usually with his mouth full. Finally, breathing a contented sigh, he stopped to just slurp hot coffee from his saucer.

"Can I come help ya again some time Mr. Halvorson?" Henry asked.

"Well, I uh..." Oscar looked at Esther, "I don't know if that iss a good idea.. I'm not sure that would..."

"Oh, I guess it's all right," Esther said. "Just be sure you're not in Mr. Halvorson's way, and keep out of trouble."

"Oh, Gramma, we'll be workin', I won't be in the way," Henry assured her in his best manly voice. "Right, Mr. Halvorson?"

"Well, uh... yah sure, I guess so."

"Say, Mr. Halvorson, maybe you could come with us to the picnic. Could Mr. Halvorson come to the picnic with us, Gramma?"

Oscar's brow furrowed as he again looked at the Widow Holmvik. He had no idea what the boy was talking about.

"Well... sure," said Esther, looking at Henry, and then at Oscar. "Sure, why not? I think that's a swell idea Henry. Won't you join us, Mr. Halvorson?"

"What iss that you say?" Oscar replied. He had no social calendar and no idea of any picnic plans.

"It's the Fourth of July picnic. Haven't you ever been to it?" Esther said in mild disbelief. "It's held at Ottertrack Lake. Lots of fun, and there's fireworks at the fairgrounds that night. You should join us Mr. Halvorson, you'd enjoy it."

"Yah, well, I got hay to put up an' the cows and...," the look on Henry's face stopped him from going further. He hadn't been to a Fourth of July picnic since he was a young man. For an instant, his mind flashed to Tollerud's casket recently lowered into the ground. Bergstrom was right, he wasn't getting any younger.

"Oh, what the heck d'en. Why not? Yah, sure, I guess I could go," he said.

Henry beamed and ran off to play with the other children while he could.

"I'll fix a chicken for the picnic if you'll drive us there," Esther said.

Oscar agreed.

13

The warm, damp breath of summer sighed through the kitchen window screen as Oscar sat in his underwear, watching the deepening dusk. The only sound carried on the dense, muggy air was the ratcheting of crickets as he pondered the day's events in the amber glow of kerosene light.

"*Hva tro du det min gammel venn*?" (What do you think, my old friend), Oscar asked Hektor as he massaged the old dog's ribs with his stockinged foot. Hektor exhaled a long, contented sigh and thumped his tail on the linoleum a couple times to say he was listening. Oscar sighed too, but not with contentment.

He had only planned to attend Tollerud's funeral, which would have been fine if he'd stuck with just that. Why had he joined Mrs. Holmvik and the boy for the luncheon? He had anticipated the comments of the ladies in the church basement, as well as the winks he got from some of the men as he left, and yet he had joined them. What had he gotten himself into? Sure, the food was wonderful, but he shouldn't have stayed, shouldn't have been with the Holmvik woman and her grandson. By now the gossip mill was working overtime, and Oscar wondered what rumors were being churned out.

Considering the situation, he pulled the stopper from the jug that held the last of his wild grape wine, a final taste of the past. Fortunately, another crop of grapes was on the way Oscar thought while pouring the garnet liquid into a glass, and it looked like it was going to be a good year for wine making.

If only he hadn't agreed to go with them to the Fourth of July picnic. How was that going to work, he thought. How would his chores get done? What would people say if they saw him with the Holmvik woman at the picnic, too?

Oscar took a sip of the wine and held it in his mouth, savoring its rich, sweet satin texture before it warmed his heart. For some reason, the sensation of the wine brought Esther Holmvik's image to his mind, and he allowed himself a smile as he thought of her.

It wasn't as awkward being around the Holmvik woman as it had been at first. It was... different now. In spite of his skeptical Scandinavian nature, Oscar realized there was something special about her. She understood the business part of farming and appreciated how much work it involved. She was strong and independent, just like him. Esther Holmvik was a no-nonsense, practical woman, with a good, kind heart. After all, she had taken in her grandson and given him a proper home, hadn't she? And she worked hard to scratch out a living for herself and the boy, and managed to do it from practically nothing, too.

"Yah," he inhaled, she was a good woman. But there was something else about the Holmvik woman other than just her good-natured character. Something about her he didn't quite understand. Or maybe it was him. Maybe he had discovered something about himself that, even at his age, he had not encountered before. That was more disturbing. Whatever it was, it was something he couldn't quite comprehend. It was new to him, and for the first time Oscar felt skeptical of his own feelings.

His chair creaked constantly as he squirmed with the discomfort of these new emotions. Oscar tried to dismiss the mental image of the Holmvik woman. He hadn't meant to be thinking of her; he had intended to dwell on rumor control and how to get out of going on the Fourth of July picnic with the widow and her grandson. But the soft summer breeze subtly carried off his will, as a spring day lures a schoolboy from his books. Tonight the early summer air sifting through the screen reminded him of the scent of her, clean and fresh, the way she smelled that day she was hanging out her wash.

Time had been kind to Esther Holmvik and she was still an attractive woman. With her clear, bright eyes she seemed to look deep inside him in a way that made him think she might know what was on his mind before he spoke. And that smile of hers, it made him feel young inside and his problems seem insignificant. It made him want to do things for her just so he could see her smile again. When she smiled at him he couldn't help but smile in return.

Another swish of the breeze reminded Oscar of how elusive strands of her hair, silvery in the sunlight, blew delicately across her cheek that day she brought lunch to him in the field. He wondered what her cheek felt like.

Noting his own dim reflection in the pane of the raised window, it occurred to Oscar that time had not been as benevolent to him. The sun and wind, heat and cold had worked their effects on his face, leaving deep creases and spots of broken veins on each cheek. His hair, gray and thin on top, stood in a messy swirl, and the stubble of his beard showed he needed to shave again.

"Uff da," Oscar said to himself. "*Du gammel tosk*" (You old fool.) What was he thinking? They were both getting on in years, too old for such silly thoughts. And then of course there was the boy. The mental image of her dissipated. With that he stood up and swallowed the last of the wine in his glass before heading off for bed. But again, with the lingering taste of the wine, thoughts of Esther Holmvik returned. She would not leave his dreams this night.

Throughout the evening and into the night, the soft summer breeze flowed over the ponds and hillsides, through woods and pastures around the countryside. As it drifted over the land, the air gently stirred new life awakening in the dark fields; shoots of corn and tender blades of wheat... new sprouts of flax. In a certain area of bottomland, between a grove of trees and an isolated pond, the breeze rustled quietly through a thick tangle of vines, carefully caressing the leaves and the buds of new fruit yet to come.

The same breeze waved the curtains on the upstairs window of Henry's bedroom where his grandmother had just finished reading a chapter from Treasure Island to her grandson. Esther put down the book and pulled the sheet up over the boy, but he pushed them back, complaining that it was too warm.

After listening to his prayers, together they asked God to bless and watch after Henry's father, Arthur, and the boy's mother. Then Esther kissed Henry on the forehead and blew out the lamp on the dresser.

"Goodnight, Henry," she said, "tomorrow's another day."

"G'night, Gramma," Henry said. "I had fun at the funeral today."

Esther smiled, closed the door behind her, and headed back down the narrow stairway. In the little parlor room off the kitchen she lit another lamp on a stand beside a rocking chair and sat down to read her Bible. As she opened it, a badly worn old photograph of a young Carl Holmvik slipped out from inside the cover and dropped into her lap.

She picked up the faded picture and looked at it fondly, but the softly whispering wind slipping through the parlor window distracted her.

Esther turned to look out at the moonlit farmyard as the breeze gently turned the pages of her Bible. Her hand still held the photo of a young man, but her thoughts were of another.

He was a good man, Esther thought, and relatively well mannered for one who had been a life-long bachelor. Though far from perfect, he must have had someone who cared about him, who showed him proper ways at some time in his life. He was polite, and respectful, though inclined to profanity if things weren't going his way. He was a simple, uneducated man, she reasoned, but Oscar had managed his farm well all his life, and held onto it during the worst of this dreadful Depression. That spoke very well for his intelligence and work ethic.

Physically, he was healthy and limber, moving around well considering his life on the land. He stood straight and somewhat taller than Carl had been, she recalled. He wasn't particularly well groomed, but Esther understood that a bachelor with a farm wasn't apt to have time for vanity. She knew Oscar was a couple years older, but it was hard to guess how many because farming aged a man beyond his years. Still, the strong lines of his face remained intact, and without too much imagination she could consider him handsome, in a way. Mostly it was his eyes that truly fascinated Esther. Clear and pale blue, their gaze was intense and honest, always searching for something.

Then there was the matter of the marigolds in her hat at the cemetery on Memorial Day. They must have come from Oscar, since she had noticed each of the Halvorson graves were decorated with bouquets of marigolds. Besides, Henry had mentioned marigolds growing in a pasture on Oscar's land. For some reason, she wanted the flowers to have come from Oscar. But why had he put them there? Did he feel something for her?

Esther had been alone for a long time after Carl died. Of course there were her friends and neighbors, and she'd had Arthur's company while he was growing up. She wouldn't have made it without him. His presence and dependence on her held her life together through those difficult times. It had been so hard when Arthur left the farm to make a new life in Minneapolis.

Now she was blessed with caring for her grandson, Henry. But Arthur would come back for Henry one day, and she was sure he would not stay on the farm. She had always given help, comfort, and care to others in times of crisis, especially in recent years as the Depression took its toll. Now, with the passing of each year, Esther felt the chronically growing emptiness within.

She had briefly known the passionate love of a man with whom she toiled to make a life and start a family. But she'd been cheated of the happiness of seeing their love grow beyond passion and dreams, to mature into the profound relationship it was meant to be. Other people had someone to share their life, and she missed having a dear companion to grow old with.

Now, as she stared through the gently swaying lace curtains at the moonlit trees in her yard, her thoughts centered on Oscar. Did she love him? No, it felt... different. She remembered the love she had with Carl, and this was definitely not that. That had been the love of young couples, exciting and sensuous. The kind of love that produces families and grows to become... what she should have now, but something was missing. Carl. No one could take his place.

But things had changed in her life, and that was the reality of things now. She was aware that over the past few months as she had come to know Oscar better, she'd begun to care about him. Care a great deal. Maybe it was the idea of a companion in her life that she really cared about. But that meant a certain level of intimacy, a certain level of sharing that she wasn't sure existed yet. Was Oscar even interested in such a relationship? Esther couldn't be sure.

But then there were the marigolds.

And so her thoughts of Oscar continued while the hour grew late and the gentle wind persisted. Sleep would be elusive for Esther that night as the soothing summer breeze brought a restlessness that's familiar to those in love, and disconcerting to those who want to be.

14

The Fourth of July dawned impeccably on Ottertrack Lake. Surface ripples blinked in the sunrise as a soft breeze blew the misty blanket off the water. It was a morning that promised a clear if hot and humid day for a picnic. It was also the first day of a week-long heat wave that would remind people around Aasness Township of the terrible drought not so many years before.

Ottertrack Lake is easily the biggest of many lakes in the area, and a perfect Minnesota recreational lake. Its clean, clear water with shallow, sandy bottom extending far into the lake along much of the shoreline made it popular for both swimming and fishing. Hardwood forest bordered the lake, sheltering numerous family cabins and several resorts. The county picnic grounds were carved out of the same woods along the shore, and included a swimming beach, boat dock, baseball diamond and horseshoe pits. Beyond the tree perimeter lay the rolling hills, fields and farms that characterized the land, and farther off, the small towns.

Everything was as it should be in this quiet, stable land of routine. People everywhere were beginning to feel positive about the future again. It looked like the economy had turned the corner and the Depression was fading. Corn had hit the "knee-high by the Fourth of July" point, and with a promising season of crops well underway, farmers and townspeople felt they could afford to relax and enjoy the beautiful summer day. Oh, that crazy German dictator was causing trouble a world away, but that was only a concern for the few who cared to discuss such vague political issues on a fine Independence Day like this.

The dew wasn't off the grass at the county park on Ottertrack Lake when cars started showing up. First were some folks from town and then, as morning chores were finished, farm families began arriving. Bird songs and the rustle of leaves in the breeze gave way to the random pops, bangs and staccato of firecrackers, and the whoops and shrieks of children getting wet in the lake.

Food appeared on picnic tables and blankets were spread on the grass. Soon the smell of smoke drifted over the picnic area as fires were kindled for roasting hot dogs and keeping bean pots warm. As conversations arose between families, the women soon settled into chat groups at shaded picnic tables. When someone arrived with a bat and ball, teams were quickly chosen for a baseball game. Some of the men pitched horseshoes while the older men tried matching wits at checkers.

It was late morning by the time Oscar's Model-T pickup pulled into the Holmvik driveway, with Hektor riding in back. Though he didn't say it, he had always felt attending events like picnics was for city people with time on their hands, or those who weren't as serious about farming as he. Anything not work-related he pretty much considered a waste of valuable time, and running his farm required all the time he had. That was the regimen that ran his life.

This morning, their late arrival at the park was Oscar's fault. He blamed it on his chores and how much he had to do at home. He was nervous about going to the picnic with Esther and Henry, and had stalled throughout his chores.

Esther suspected this was why he was late. She realized he had been uncomfortable at the reception after the funeral, but she remained patient. She was a very social person and knew nearly everyone in Aasness Township, whether they attended Eidsvold Church or not. Running the farm on her own had made that happen. But she was also aware of Oscar's reclusive nature.

She sat waiting on her doorstep as he pulled up near her house, and Henry scrambled down from his lookout in a favorite climbing tree. Oscar noticed the marigold she'd placed in the band of her straw hat as he got out of his truck, but said nothing about it.

"Sorry I'm so late to get you," he said, "but you know I shouldn't really be here. I got so much to do, and..."

"Nonsense," Esther cut him off with her delightful smile. "No one was meant to work all the time Mr. Halvorson. It will be good for you to get away from that farm awhile. This is going to be fun. You'll see. The farm can do without you for a few hours. Now we'd better get going."

A resigned "Yah," was his only response, and he loaded the picnic basket, blanket, a jug of lemon water and another of ice tea into the back where Henry already sat with an arm around Hektor.

When they got to the county park, Oscar stopped his truck behind some trees, away from the picnic area, thinking people wouldn't notice their arriving—or leaving. Henry was so excited, both about riding in the back of the truck and about going to the picnic, that he could hardly contain himself. He bounded from the truck before Oscar shut off the engine, and ran toward the lake with old Hektor following at a more leisurely trot.

Henry wore a pair of old pants that had belonged to his father when he was young. Esther had hastily cut them off and hemmed them to make suitable swimming trunks. A length of cord ran through the belt loops to cinch them around Henry's scrawny waist. When the boy saw the other kids swimming, he shouted and ran full speed, not stopping until he splashed headlong into Ottertrack Lake. He came up sputtering, coughing and laughing. Henry didn't know how to swim, but neither did most of the others. He knew a couple kids there from attending the country school, and after quickly renewing acquaintances he was absorbed by the lake and his peers. Hektor was content to just wade in to shoulder depth and simply stand in the cooling waters, watching the wildly splashing children.

While Henry and the dog enjoyed the lake, Oscar and Esther carried their picnic items from the back of the truck to a shady spot by the woods, just at the fringe of the other picnickers. Esther spread an old blanket on the grass as all the tables were taken, and Oscar set the basket and the big jars of ice tea and lemon water beside it.

"Hi Esther!" a woman called out as she approached. It was Irene Haugen, a pretty young woman whose family attended the Eidsvold church. "Good to see you could make it here today."

"Oh, hi Irene, yah we wouldn't want to miss this. What a perfect day. Where are you set up?"

"We got here about an hour ago and took a table over by the playground," said Irene. "You can just see my daughters playing on the swings there. Say, isn't that your grandson I saw with my boy in the water?"

"Probably," Esther nodded. "He couldn't wait to get here and play with other children.

"Say, Irene, do you know Mr. Halvorson?" Esther added, rather sure that she knew who he was.

"I don't believe we've actually met," said Irene, extending her hand.

Oscar carefully shook the Haugen woman's hand and tipped his hat politely as Esther explained that she'd invited him to the picnic to get him away from his farm for a while. Most women are adept at reading between the lines, and Irene smiled, somehow understanding something else might be going on.

This pleasant encounter set a tone for the day, as other folks passing by them said hi or introduced themselves.

"Let's go for a walk and see who's here," Esther suggested after placing their things in a good spot. "I think you probably know a lot of these people. C'mon, it'll be good for both of us."

Oscar silently complied, but was less than eager. After they walked together a while, Oscar soon noted he was recognized in a friendlier, more casual way while in Esther's company. He usually didn't have much to say unless he knew a person, but he listened intently to Esther's conversations. He was amazed and impressed at how she seemed to know so many people and they knew her. They spoke together in a comfortable way with people Oscar had known for years, but only on a business or farming basis. Esther introduced him to new people, mostly younger couples like Irene and her husband. As they socialized together, Oscar began to feel better about being at the picnic.

He no longer thought about people associating him with Esther, or if they saw their relationship as something other than just business. He lost his concern about rumors and began to feel that Esther cared about him, actually cared about him as a person. Oscar had no idea where this was leading but thought to himself there was something special going on between him and Esther. He didn't know whether or not others could tell it that hot, sunny Fourth of July, but Oscar now realized he felt something for the Holmvik woman. It was a new feeling, totally foreign, like a new kind of energy flowing through him, and he liked it. He didn't understand it, but it felt like he was young again. Maybe it was happiness. He wasn't sure, but it felt good—so good that he could barely suppress it.

The feeling found an outlet in his becoming congenial. Little by little he opened up to people more than he ever had before, listening and talking while strolling around the park with Esther at his side and a smile on his face. To people who had known Oscar for years it was like meeting a new man. Being with her gave him the same feeling, and made everything seem right. If people saw them together as a couple, Oscar decided he didn't mind. He didn't mind it one bit.

They made their way around the picnic area, accepting a taste of salad from the Swensons, a drink of lemonade from the Bergs, and friendly greetings along the way. By the beach they paused to watch children splashing in the lake or playing in the sand. There Oscar noticed a young adult couple sitting close together on a blanket, the young man's arm around the woman and her head resting on his shoulder. Their intimacy was intriguing and he stared a bit too long.

"Oh look," Esther said distracting him, "there's Henry with the Haugen boy at the end of the dock. Isn't it deep there? Henry can't swim. I wish he..."

Henry and his friend leaped with abandon, splashing into the lake and out of sight beneath the surface. For an instant, Esther caught her breath, but the two boys' heads popped up laughing in water that was up to their chests.

"Uffda. Boys" Esther said with exasperation. "Henry! That's too deep! You come in closer or you could drown. Come on right now," Esther insisted in her most authoritative voice.

"Aww Gramma," but his protests were in vain, and he moved reluctantly toward shallower water until Esther seemed satisfied.

"The boy should learn to swim Missus Holmvik," said Oscar, though he himself did not know how. "It's the only way to be safe around water."

Esther shot him a stern glance for interfering, and Oscar winced a bit.

"That boy is my responsibility," she declared, "and I'll not have him learning to swim so he can go off somewhere and drown when I'm not there watching out for him. What would my Arthur say? What would I tell him?"

Oscar just shrugged, realizing she took the boy's safety very seriously.

They watched the boys play in the water a while, and Esther considered in silence what Oscar had said. Not that she changed her mind about Henry learning to swim, but that in his way Oscar had shown concern for him and his wellbeing.

"Henry," she called again, "come have some lunch now!" She and Oscar headed back toward where they'd left the picnic basket and blanket.

Oscar lowered himself to the blanket with a strain-relieving groan as Esther pulled out dishes, glasses, and food from the basket. She'd packed fried chicken, her fresh homemade bread, pickles, potato salad, ground cherry sauce, and radishes from her garden. She also had coffee in a mason jar wrapped in dishcloths to keep it warm, and another jar of cool water and lemon slices. A nice rhubarb pie topped off the meal. Simple farm fare, but a real feast considering her economic situation and the Depression. Oscar knew only that everything she prepared was delicious and he was already anticipating the first mouthful.

Henry came towards them with his wet hair plastered over his head and water beads glistening on his skinny body. He smelled of the lake, aquatic and fresh. Somewhere he'd found an old baseball with the cover completely ripped off. "Wanna play catch?" he asked Oscar.

Oscar wasn't sure how to respond. The truth was, he had never played catch, never played ball as a kid, never actually played much at all. His boyhood was spent learning to farm beside his father. Oscar was young when his father died, and he had taken over the work full-time and done it ever since.

"Uh, yah, sure... sure," Oscar said uncertainly, as he roused himself from the blanket and awkwardly extended his thick, heavy hands to receive the ball.

"Here," Henry said, and tossed the ball to Oscar, who bobbled it and dropped it in the grass. Henry quickly backed away to increase the throwing distance between them. Oscar picked up the ball and as he examined it, recalled an outfielder in the ball game who put all he had into a long throw to home plate to put the runner out. His team cheered him. Oscar looked at the round, foreign object in his hand, then gave it a mighty heave in Henry's general direction.

Thrown with great power but no control, the ball arched high over Henry's head, bounced off someone's picnic table and through the midst of a family before rolling to a stop in the tall grass at the edge of the trees.

"Wow!" shouted Henry as he chased after the ball. "You can really throw far, Mr. Halvorson."

Esther laughed, and apologized to the surprised family as Oscar hung his head sheepishly.

"I think you should come eat something Henry. You can play catch with Mr. Halvorson later," Esther said, the diversion intended more for Oscar's benefit.

They sat together on the blanket under the shade of an overhanging oak, the boy, the widow and the old farmer, while dappled sunlight danced lacy patterns around them to the music of the summer breeze in the treetops.

"*I Jesu navn gå vi til bord...*" (in Jesus name we go to table... etc.), Esther prayed the blessing in Norwegian for Oscar's indulgence. He didn't notice. Henry did, but was growing accustomed to hearing the "other" language. More hungry than curious, he grabbed a chicken leg and began to eat. Oscar followed suit.

"I see you're getting along well with Eldon Haugen then," Esther said to Henry as she dished up some potato salad for him.

"Yah, hum an' meh'r goo frensh fra skawl."

"Don't talk with your mouth full. Slow down and eat normally. There's plenty of time to play, yet," Esther said.

"What are you going to do after lunch?" she continued. "You know you can't go back swimming for an hour after you eat or you'll get cramps."

Henry slumped and looked pleadingly at his grandmother a moment, but knew there was no contesting the matter.

"There's plenty of things to do here other than swimming with Eldon. Maybe you could just rest awhile," she suggested. "It's going to be a late night with the fireworks show."

"I think me an' him will play catch awhile. Maybe we'll get in the game over at the ballfield."

"He and I," Esther corrected.

Henry and Oscar shot each other a confused glance that said neither understood what she was talking about but thought it best not to ask.

"You want to come along Mr. Halvorson? They might need somebody in the outfield an' you can throw really far," suggested the boy.

Oscar was careful to stop chewing and swallow before he answered.

"Well, yah, sure, I s'pose I could come an' see how it iss done anyway.

"That's a good idea, Mr. Halvorson. When you and Henry have finished eating, go ahead to the ballfield. I'll clean up here and come over there later."

"Don't wear yourself out, Henry," she said. "You'll want to be awake for the fireworks show tonight."

"Oh, don't worry, Gramma, I'm not gonna get tired today."

When they'd eaten their fill, Oscar and Henry got up and headed for the ballfield. Many of the men were dozing off the mid-day meal and it was mostly kids playing ball after lunch. Henry soon connected with Eldon and together they began inquiring about getting on a team. With his belly full and no knowledge of the game, Oscar was content to watch the action. Henry came back to Oscar soon to report that he and Eldon had gotten picked for the same team, and that they could rotate innings so Oscar would have a chance to play, too. After assuring them he'd rather watch, Oscar stood at the end of the bleachers to see if he could figure out how the game was played.

Before long, he took a seat and leaned back on the bench behind him. He tipped his hat to shade his eyes and soon nodded off. The boys woke him up after a couple innings, and asked him if he wanted to take a turn playing in the outfield. Oscar could hear some farmers talking with George Kruger from the feed and seed store about market prices, so he told the boys they'd better play for him. Casually, he made his way toward the group of farmers.

"Hi there Halvorson," George said amiably as he approached. "How's that flax comin' along?"

"Well, not as good as I hoped d'en," Oscar lied. His flax was just fine, but no farmer in the area would admit his crop looked good or couldn't be better.

"Could use some rain I s'pose."

A number of heads bobbed in mute agreement. He knew the other farmers were interested in his flax, as it was not a common crop in the area. This was a game all farmers understood, and he played it a little longer.

"Yah, I don't expect it to yield much anyway," he added. No man would let his hopes get too high. It was always best to be cautious in speculation, especially if things didn't come out well.

"Besides, the price probably issn't going to hold into fall." This was an invitation for George to submit his reply with a forecast price.

George was pretty good at making an educated guess at market futures, and everyone took his estimates into serious consideration, applying them hopefully to their own crops. But today George was enjoying his attention in the spotlight, and he decided to have some fun at Oscar's expense.

"Yeah, guess I wouldn't count on takin' too much to the bank from that flax if I was you Halvorson," George said with a serious tone. Oscar's unexpected double-take caught everyone's attention, suggesting George knew something.

"Why iss dat?" Oscar asked, now with sober naiveté.

"Well, 'cause you ain't the only one workin' the Holmvik farm, if ya know what I mean," George said with a wink and a grin aside to the other men.

There was no laughter, but eyebrows went up and smirks appeared on the faces of the other farmers, indicating they understood. Even in the heat of the day, Oscar felt himself flush at being the brunt of a joke that the others all seemed in on. Mercifully, another man asked George a question, diverting attention from Oscar and he took the opportunity to sneak away.

Embarrassed and confused, Oscar tried to figure out what was so amusing, what George had meant. There was no one else farming the Holmvik woman's land. What did they all find so amusing?

Suddenly he felt very uncomfortable among the crowd at the picnic grounds, and he headed back to where he'd left Esther on the blanket. As he approached the place, he could see from a distance she was not alone. There was a man with her on the blanket. It was Martin Phillips, owner of the flourmill. They sat close together, laughing and talking in a very friendly way that gave Oscar a strange, queasy feeling in the pit of his stomach. Now he understood all too well George Kruger's remark and the amusement of the other men. He turned abruptly and walked off in another direction before the two of them saw him.

Oscar knew Phillips, as did every farmer in the area, since they all brought grain to his mill. Phillips was a prosperous businessman, a couple years younger than Oscar, educated, well groomed and a widower. It was obvious that Esther and the miller were very well acquainted. A picture was coming together in Oscar's mind, and he did not see himself in it.

What a fool he'd been. Of course the Holmvik woman would know Phillips. He ground the flour for her for bread and had done it for years. It was natural that she would be interested in him; he had a lot to offer a woman like Esther Holmvik. Oscar had nothing. He wasn't much to look at, he was uneducated and didn't have anything but his farm and that was in debt. Now he began feeling old as well. What a fool he'd been.

Oscar wandered around the picnic grounds for a while, but without the same sociable feeling he'd had just a few hours before. Other couples walked by with arms around each other or holding hands, and he became aware of his own hands hanging at his side, heavy with emptiness. His mind was full of questions, but every one came with a bad answer. Had she been leading him on? No, he didn't think so; he'd just jumped to the conclusion that she cared about him. Was she using him? Growing wheat for her to bring to the miller so she could see more of him? Possibly, he just wasn't sure. Maybe she thought of him as a sort of Christian charity case. How could he have been so stupid?

As he walked and pondered the whole mess, his heart grew heavy. He wanted desperately to leave, to get back to his farm, but couldn't. He had to bring the Holmvik woman and her grandson home. That was why he was there after all, wasn't it? Transportation? Oscar determined not to mention that he'd seen her with Phillips, not to show that he'd been foolish enough to allow himself to have feelings for her. He had to preserve what was left of his dignity. He wandered around in a very unfamiliar emotional state, his mind sorting through a variety of strange conclusions.

"Mr. Halvorson! Mr. Halvorson!" It was Henry running up behind him.

"Mr. Halvorson, we've been looking for you. We're going to have a bit more to eat and then you know what Mr. Halvorson? Everybody'll go to the fairgrounds for the fireworks show. Won't it be great? C'mon, let's go!" At his age, Henry still had the notion that somehow time could be hurried away to get to the good part. Oscar followed at his own pace, somehow frozen in time. He was not in a hurry to see Esther just now.

That evening, Oscar sat with Henry and his grandmother on the blanket at the fairgrounds, watching the fiery showers of skyrockets as the band played one Sousa march after another. It was a glorious finale to a glorious day, for everyone but Oscar. He thought the music was nice, and the fireworks were just fine, but his day had fizzled out like a dud. His fragile psyche was badly shaken, and he no longer wanted to be part of all the festivities. Especially, he no longer wanted to be with Mrs. Holmvik and her grandson.

The ride home was quiet. Henry and Hektor slept in the back end of the pick up, wrapped in the picnic blanket, and Esther thought Oscar was probably just tired. He dropped them off at the door to their house, and after exchanging rather formal thanks and goodnights, drove off into the darkness with Hektor in the seat beside him.

15

"The wind blows where it wills, and you
hear the sound of it, but you do not know
whence it comes or whither it goes..."
—John 3:8, RSV

Oscar didn't like it. He'd seen heat and humidity like this before and he knew sooner or later it had to break. It had been nearly a week since the picnic, and each sultry day since seemed more uncomfortable than the previous one. Like the other farmers, Oscar knew that this hot, muggy weather wouldn't last, and inevitably a storm would mark the pivotal change in conditions. The resulting storm and its potential for destruction was usually in proportion to the duration and intensity of the heat and humidity. Cooler, drier air would be a relief, but Oscar didn't like storms.

He straightened upright, removed his hat and ran a rolled-up shirt sleeve across his sweaty brow. Heat shimmered in the haze over the slough, and if any air was moving the trees on the bank above him blocked it. Only the insects liked this weather, and their incessant buzzing seemed a part of the air itself. Oscar stooped to his work again, clearing back unwanted weeds and growth from his grapes, lifting vines and checking the leaves for blight or insect damage. He checked the progress of the little green orbs budding in thick, numerous bunches. His mother would have been pleased. It looked like a bumper crop and he felt good knowing he'd have wine for the winter. In a few weeks when the grapes began to ripen, he would come back and cover the vines with nets to keep the birds from devouring them, but the fruit was safe for now.

He took the two pails he'd brought and walked through the weeds to the edge of the slough. Hektor was standing up to his neck in the water, grinning his dog grin at Oscar with tongue lolling to one side to indicate the relief he'd found in the slough. The old mongrel seemed to be suggesting that the man should quit laboring in the heat and join him.

"*Ja, du har det godt i vannet for sikkert* (yes, you certainly have it good in the lake)," Oscar said to his friend, "*men mellom oss, en må arbiede vite du* (but between us, one must do the work you know)." The old dog just swished his tail back and forth in the water, suggesting he liked the arrangement just as it was. Besides, Oscar had other things on his mind.

Tending the vines as she had taught him always brought fond memories of his mother, making him feel she was there with him as he worked, and that brought him comfort. Ever since she died, Oscar would come to this place when he wished to be close to his mother again. This was one of those times, and as he carried the pails of water to the vines, his spirit sought to her out.

If these recent events had happened when he was a young man, Oscar was sure his mother would have known how to advise him. Now thoughts of the Holmvik woman would give him no peace. He could no longer function without her eventually intruding on his consciousness. But he and his mother had not quite gotten to matters of the heart. Now, though advanced in years, his heart reached out to his mother for some hint of guidance in these unfamiliar matters, but he sensed none.

"D'is iss nonsense," he muttered aloud to the vines, "t'inking like a schoolboy at my age. I'm too old for d'is sort of t'ing!"

The only ears that heard him were Hektor's. Hektor always listened.

"*Oh mamma, derres hjalp nå kunne jeg brukke så mye.* (I could use your help so much now.)" He always thought she heard him better in the old tongue.

"*Aach, jeg er bare et gammel tosk.* (I'm just an old fool.)" He sat himself on a big rock near the shore of the slough and Hektor put his head in Oscar's lap and whined sympathetically.

"*Oh ja min gammel venn, kanskje bare du kan forstå* (my old friend, perhaps only you can understand,)" he sighed stroking the dog's head. Together they sat in quiet contemplation. "*Jeg ønske du kunne prate til meg* (I wish you could talk to me,)" Oscar mused.

Were these the feelings of a frustrated boy that had come to taunt him so late in life? No, Oscar knew this was deeper, issuing from an unfamiliar place inside of himself that he'd not visited before. He had ventured into a small wilderness within him, uncharted, unexplored, a secret place hidden away behind thick barriers all his life, a place of deep feelings for another. He had been poised, perhaps, to enter that place and risk what lay inside himself in spite of doubts and fears. He'd been ready to leave the lonely rock pile that he knew all too well and discover this new place inside himself.

But all Oscar understood now was the familiar safety of his loneliness, even though it felt empty, cold inside despite the heat of the muggy day. Had his life been a waste? Had he been wrong to live alone so long? Was his small farm all there was for him in this world, the only result of his life's labors and his only satisfaction? In the end, was there not to be at least someone to share his remaining days, a deferred comfort after life's effort? Bergstrom was right, Oscar thought, it is "getting late." But it was so hard to have these questions now and these feelings for the Holmvik woman when she was apparently interested in someone else.

It was likely she'd been interested in Martin Phillips for a long time; they obviously were very close acquaintances. Cautious now, Oscar was beginning to realize she didn't have the same feelings for him. They were just business partners. That was, after all, how he'd presented the flax proposal to her. Their relationship was a business deal and nothing more. Whatever could have happened to change that?

After washing his face and neck in the slough, he picked up his pails, called Hektor, and headed back toward his house.

They followed a cow path that led up over the bank and back to the barnyard. As Oscar reached the top of the bank, a gust of wind from a new direction met his face. It was still hot and humid, but not stagnant like the air down by the slough, and he noted the contrast.

Tomorrow would be Sunday. He didn't attend church often, but this time he would go. The Holmvik woman would be there, she always went to church. It would be an opportunity to see her, maybe get a chance to talk to her, maybe learn how she felt about him. Maybe he'd find out if there was a chance of… he didn't know what. It would be a bold move, certainly George Kruger's remark at the picnic about someone else "working the Holmvik land" would have gotten around to everyone by now. Oscar knew he would be exposing himself to further humiliation, but he was sure he'd felt something special with the Holmvik woman when he was with her, and it was good. He wasn't getting any younger and it was the only way he'd find peace with the matter. He'd have to muster his courage and take the risk.

That night Oscar bathed and made sure his good clothes looked presentable for church, then he went to bed. He lay in his underwear on top of the bed sheets in the muggy night air with the insects reveling outside. Normally he didn't mind their night music, but tonight the constant buzzing and ratcheting contributed to his anxiousness, and sleep would not come. Over and over he tried to think of what he would say to Esther Holmvik. He had to know whether their relationship was just a business arrangement or if, just maybe, she had feelings for him as he had for her. At Eidsvold church he'd find the truth. Maybe a little prayer wouldn't hurt. That was his last thought as Oscar at last fell into a restless, sticky slumber.

He awoke earlier than usual, and Sunday morning was only slightly cooler, bringing no relief from the uncomfortable weather and no idea of what he would say to the Holmvik woman. He wished he could just talk to her alone for a while, if he could just think of what to say. Being in church meant being around people, and of course the boy was always around. Still, he felt confronting her at the church would be appropriate. Maybe, he reasoned, she'd be more... understanding there.

Oscar shaved, dressed, ate a couple leftover pancakes he'd wrapped in waxed paper the day before, and washed them down with cold coffee. Leaving Hektor in charge of the farm, Oscar headed off on foot for church, hoping it would give him more time to think.

He arrived at the church early, still with no idea of what he hoped to say to Esther Holmvik. By now, he was thinking that maybe just seeing her would be helpful, or maybe she would say something that would settle his mind. Oscar took a seat in a back pew and, as people began arriving, he pretended to be engrossed in a book that he thought looked like a Bible.

People began filing in and the pews were filling up quickly. It remained quiet in the church except for occasional whispers. Esther took her place at the organ and began pumping out music. Then Reverend Ellerby prayed, read scriptures between hymns, prayed some more, and delivered a sermon which, along with the heat, had the effect of a hypnotist's chant on the congregation. The plate was passed, and after a final wake-up hymn and benediction, God's sweaty people were sent forth into the world of Aasness Township.

Oscar was among the first out of the stuffy church and into the slightly less stuffy air outside. Inside, Esther was glistening from her efforts on the organ, but she kept playing as people exited the church. Oscar walked around outside and the other men greeted him, some with a sly "knowing" grin and a comment about how his flax was coming along. Oscar was uncomfortable and kept moving around to avoid too much contact. He was only waiting for the music to stop so he could talk to her.

He didn't have to wait long. Almost as soon as she stopped playing, Oscar watched Esther emerge from the church, her face flushed and beaming and arm in arm with the miller, Martin Phillips. They were talking and laughing about something, and neither of them saw Oscar. But Oscar had seen all he needed to see, and turned and walked home alone.

He walked along the road past the Holmvik farm and the patch of wheat he'd planted beside his field of flax. Both crops were flourishing, but Oscar didn't even see them as he passed. A short distance further up the road, he cut through the ditch and walked a fence line that led toward his hay field and home. Home was where he needed to be, it was where he wanted to be, where he felt he belonged.

He'd been trapped there all his life, never gone anywhere or done anything else, never known anything else. Other than his dog, he hadn't even really known or cared about anyone else—until now. Now, after all these years, he realized his farm was, in fact, the sum total of his existence. Without the farm he didn't exist. It was what he was born to, it was his legacy, and it would be his tombstone. One more rock on the pile. Over time, he had somehow allowed himself to not exist as a person. The Holmvik woman and their time together at the picnic had been a glimpse of what he'd missed, but he had been alone too many years. It was no use, Oscar felt, he was what he was. His farm.

The remainder of the day he spent walking his land with Hektor. It was a time of introspection and getting reacquainted with himself and the farm. In truth, he took a good deal of familiar comfort from the land, and eventually as he walked the rolling fields and looked over the little lakes and sloughs, Oscar found solace with the land again. At his age, he felt it was perhaps too late to start a new life. But if the farm was his life, well, at least he knew how to live with it. It was safe and comfortable and where he was meant to be. His relationship with the Holmvik woman had been just a business deal, nothing more. Yet a peculiar aching emptiness lingered inside him.

As he headed over a hilltop back toward the barn to do the same chores he'd done his entire life, he noticed anvil-topped clouds building on the far western horizon. Finally, he thought, a change is coming.

Oscar finished the milking and fed his cattle before making the rounds to prepare for the possibility of bad weather. By the time he'd finished, the clouds had moved up from the horizon enough so he could see their boiling thunderheads. "Now comes a good storm," Oscar said to Hektor as he went inside to fix his supper.

Supper consisted of *knakke brod* (a dry rye cracker) and cheese with sausage he kept in his icebox, and some produce from his garden. It was too hot to cook and he was tired. Heat and lack of good sleep in recent days had caught up to him. The sun soon ducked behind the mass of towering clouds and it got dark earlier than usual. Oscar stayed up to observe the advancing clouds in the waning light of day, and watched the flicker of lightning in them. The air was dead still and birds darted quietly from tree to tree; seeking shelter in anticipation of what they knew was coming. As darkness became complete, Oscar went to bed to await the storm. What would be would be, and there was nothing he could do.

The wind woke him later in the night, blustering in the bedroom window, hissing through the screen and knocking over a picture of Rakel and Halvor on a chest of drawers. Oscar sat up on the edge of his bed and looked out the window. A brilliant flash of lightning lit up the whole outdoors, showing trees thrashing about in the wind. Thunder exploded violently and a few big drops began splattering on the roof as Oscar stood up half asleep, closed the window and fumbled with matches to light a lamp. Hektor's dark form followed nervously from room to room as together they closed the rest of the windows. The storm broke in full fury outside and rain came so hard against the windows that he couldn't see out. He went to the back door on the lee side of the house and looked out the window. Hektor stood beside him and let out a soft whine.

"*Ja, riktig Hektor*, (yes, that's right Hektor)," Oscar said to the dog, "*det var for skrekkelig vær inat* (it is terrible weather tonight)." The house creaked with the wind and windows rattled in their frames with each blast of thunder. In the lightning's brilliance, he saw sheets of rain washing over the yard forming pools in the low spots.

Suddenly with the rain lashing the house, came a loud "tap" sound. Before Oscar could figure out what it was, there was another "tap" then another and another, becoming a loud, sustained rattle all over the house. Oscar knew it was hail. Looking out the window again, he saw the bouncing white balls of ice dancing all over the ground in the strobes of lightning. He suddenly felt weak and queasy. It was every farmer's nightmare. Heavy rain could wash out or drown crops or lodge standing grain. But hail, if large and enough of it, would literally pummel crops into the earth, destroying in a few moments everything a farmer worked for. The sickening feeling he had wasn't just for himself but for other farmers in the same financial situation he was in. If it destroyed his crops, he'd lose the farm and all that he was. Simple as that. Oscar watched the white pellets collecting on his yard along with leaves and small branches stripped from the trees. Totally helpless, he had no recourse, no back up plan for hail.

Oscar returned to his bedroom as the sounds of the hail tapered off, leaving only a soft, steady rain. Without consciously thinking about it, he knelt at his bedside but could form no words to pray in English or Norwegian. There was only deep desperation in his heart. Sometimes, no matter the attitude of the body, the soul is on its knees.

He didn't know how long he'd knelt there, and it didn't matter. "What's the use now," he eventually said to himself, and he got up to look out at the darkness. Lightning still flickered in the distance but the rain had slacked to a steady sprinkle. The passing front that brought the hail had also brought low humidity and a much cooler temperature. Oscar lifted the window wide to let the fresh air into his stuffy bedroom. Carried on the soothing breeze was the sweet scent of the earth Oscar had tended and loved so well. Of the relationships in his life, it was the only one that remained. He sank into his bed and pulled the blanket over him as new clean air filled his bedroom. In resignation he sank into a peaceful, dreamless sleep.

Oscar overslept the next morning. He hadn't done that since he was in his teens and his mother had to wake him for morning chores. Now he lay on his bed feeling like he'd sunk deep into the mattress and was too heavy to rise. Finally, with great effort, he sat up on the edge of his bed and looked out at a bright, innocent morning sky that held no sign of the storm that had passed.

On the ground, signs of the storm were everywhere. Leaves and branches stripped from trees by the hail covered the yard, and puddles of water stood on the saturated earth. The evidence quickly removed any doubts about the violence of the previous night.

Like all farmers, doing chores was so ingrained into Oscar's life that even if his crops were destroyed, he would care for his cows. He couldn't conceive of not tending to them, and did so before seeing to any of his personal needs. The barn and other buildings seemed to be fine, but he was in no hurry to check the damage to his fields. That could wait until after milking and feeding.

When finished with the cattle, Oscar was making his way across the farmyard when a beat-up muddy pickup truck came splashing through the puddles on his driveway. He recognized it was Theodore Bergstrom and waited until the truck drove up beside him.

Bergstrom operated on the brink of disaster for the past eight or nine years of the Depression, and the stress of it showed in every outward facet of his character. He had been a hearty, vigorous man when he was young, but had grown lean. His eyes had acquired a desperate look, and his face seemed always tense and haggard to those who knew him best. This morning though, that tension was completely gone.

"Morn' Bergstrom," Oscar greeted him cautiously. A visit from another farmer always brought news, good or bad, but Bergstrom never visited anyone.

There was no reply from inside the truck, and the man's thoughts seemed focused somewhere beyond the horizon. Oscar watched him a moment, looked off in the same direction and sensing a dark void, turned his eyes to the ground.

"I'm all done," Bergstrom finally said. Oscar looked up at him and frowned, but did not speak. He knew what Bergstrom meant. There was an aching long pause.

"Hail?" Oscar quietly stated the obvious question.

Bergstrom nodded. "Cleaned me out," he replied quietly. It was spoken with resignation about his life in general as much as about farming.

"Nut'n left to do now but give it all over to Stordal," he continued with a great sigh. The words came slowly, like fingers releasing their grip, letting go one by one. They were the words of a man who had nothing left to give, and Oscar sensed it. He stood silently absorbing what Bergstrom had said, his empty hands hanging heavy and useless, the wrong tools for the job. The man's way of life was over. Oscar knew full well what Bergstrom had put into his farm over the years, and he could not comprehend a life beyond farming. After last night Oscar knew he might be through farming too. He felt sorry for Bergstrom, but could find no words to express the breadth and depth of it. Across the silent void, both men somehow sensed and understood the unspoken message.

"Just so you know, Oscar. There's a lot of crops down all around. Your corn don't look too bad comin' in your driveway though, but the hail was spotty," Bergstrom continued as though somehow removed. "Seems the wind lodged a lot of grain too, but I 'spect some o' that may come back." He paused, and then added quietly, "Not mine though."

"You been sou't o' here?" Oscar asked.

"No," Bergstrom replied. Then he turned to face Oscar and said, "You need to walk your fields and see for yourself what kinda shape they're in. Hope they fared better than mine."

"Bergstrom, I uh... I just..." Oscar quietly tried to put some words together to express his sympathy, but the man cut him off.

"Well, I gotta be gettin' into town, gotta see Stordal y'know," Bergstrom said. Oscar nodded and offered his hand. They exchanged firm grips and the eyes of the man in the truck brimmed. He turned his head with an inhaled "yah," put the truck in gear and headed out Oscar's driveway.

"It may be all over for me too d'en," Oscar said to Hektor as they watched Bergstrom's truck drive off. He'd been afraid to look, but knew it was time to check his own crops for damage.

The twenty acres of corn had battered leaves that would no doubt limit the yield, but Oscar figured he'd still get a crop. From the cornfield, he headed east to the back twenty where he'd planted wheat. There the picture looked less hopeful. The grain lay flat in broad patches, lodged by the wind the way Bergstrom had described other fields. It could come back, but to what extent Oscar wasn't sure. In any case, Oscar knew the yield would probably be affected as well, but couldn't guess how much. A lot depended on drying weather now.

Walking along the perimeter of his wheat field, Oscar headed south and then west, toward the alfalfa field that lay just south of his farmhouse. It wasn't as critical, since he could get more than one crop of hay in a season and alfalfa usually could take a lot of abuse from the elements. Overall, Oscar realized he'd been extremely lucky; damage was relatively light on his fields. Still, a knot of concern remained in his stomach, keeping him uneasy.

His remaining land was twenty acres of woods and pasture, including the large slough where the grapes were. The grapes were sheltered and too small and green to be affected by hail or wind at this point, and they were not critical crops. He'd survived winters without wine before, though winters without wine seemed longer and colder than those with. There remained only one more field for Oscar to check, perhaps the most important one.

With steps weighted with anxiety Oscar headed out across his hayfield and up the high hill that gave a distant view of Eidsvold Church, the Holmvik farm and his field of flax. The view from the hilltop would tell his future in farming, whether he'd make it in the long run or end up like Bergstrom, destroyed by the storm.

On gaining the hilltop, Oscar gazed out over the land as the cool breeze shimmered over distant fields, caressing the earth with its healing touch, even as he surveyed the tracks of the storm. Here and there trees lay toppled by the wind and great pools of water stood in some fields and across roadways. Numerous patches of grain lay flattened, lodged by the wind, and more evident were areas damaged by hail.

Corn was stripped in some fields, leaving naked stalks sticking up at odd angles from the soil. The crazy, random path of the storm made no sense from Oscar's vantage point, but the destruction seemed distinctly interrupted in the area around the church, Esther Holmvik's house, and the field of flax. Even the two acres of wheat he'd planted for the Holmvik woman appeared unharmed. There was damage to crops on all sides, but the flax somehow had been spared, untouched it appeared other than by quenching rain. Of course it was a long way off, and he'd have to make a closer inspection, but his crop and the future of his farm seemed to be intact for now. For now, at least, it looked as if his farm might still belong to him and not E.A. Stordal.

Oscar stood a long time on the sunny hilltop, all wrapped in the soothing breeze. In the distance he noticed the tiny white flecks of the Widow Holmvik's wash swaying on the line. Beyond lay the staggering track of storm damage over the land that was so much a part of him. Gratitude filled his heart as he stood on the sunny hilltop, yet it seemed so odd the random way some are spared and others destroyed.

16

Radiant heat from the oven made Esther's kitchen uncomfortably warm even with all the windows open, and her forehead still glistened from the exertion of punching down the dough earlier. The bread was needed for Holy Communion in church the next morning, so she'd risen well before dawn to get the baking done before the heat of day. Morning's first light brightened the kitchen windows, and after placing the loaves in the oven she blew out the lamps to save kerosene.

The whole process was routine, a ritual repeated at least once or twice a week to provide bread not only for Henry and herself, but also for a friend or a bake sale or for church. This morning she had baked an extra loaf, thinking she and Henry would bring it to Mr. Halvorson and encourage him to come to church for communion.

It had been several weeks since Esther had seen Oscar Halvorson. As far as she knew, he hadn't even come to check his flax after the storm four weeks ago, and that she thought was rather strange. Considering the importance of the crop and how much damage the storm had caused around Aasness Township, she felt he would have come by to see how his flax fared. Perhaps he had, she thought, and she just hadn't seen him. Oscar Halvorson wasn't much for social visits.

Before, during, and after the storm, Esther had prayed for Oscar's flax. She also prayed for those whose crops were damaged or destroyed, and whose farms and fortunes were now uncertain. Oscar hadn't even come to church after the storm, but Esther hoped he had found a way to express gratitude to God that his flax had been spared. Perhaps he was just too busy with haying or some other project to stop for a visit.

Esther poured a cup of coffee and sat by the open window at the kitchen table, letting the morning air refresh her as it mingled with the aroma of her bread. It felt good. Birds were singing their wake up calls and her roosters were crowing at the bleary sun just blinking over the horizon. To Esther, it was the best time of the day.

As usual at these quiet hours, she reflected on her son, Arthur. It had been several weeks since he'd last written. The last she'd heard he was training with the Army down south somewhere in Louisiana. It was so far away it might as well have been in another country. His last letter suggested to Esther that it was rather rough business, but he was enjoying it and doing fine. It helped a lot to know that. Arthur always included a note to Henry, and asked Esther how his son was doing, what he was up to, and how he was growing. Esther responded with long letters telling him that Henry was much taller than last fall, perhaps only a slight exaggeration. She wrote that the boy had taken a strong interest in Mr. Halvorson and was learning a lot about farming. She did not mention that Henry wasn't the only one who had taken an interest in Mr. Halvorson.

Since one of her loaves today was for Mr. Halvorson, she thought it would make a good excuse to pay a social call and maybe find out why she hadn't seen him lately. Esther envisioned him at his table with the bread before him. For a moment she demurely considered whether he would think of her as he ate it. Would he make a meal of the loaf, devouring it in one sitting, or enjoy it one slice at a time, savoring each bite? What sort of man was he?

"Uffda!" Esther said, the sudden flush in her face brought her back to the reality of her kitchen. Oscar Halvorson had been on her mind often the past few weeks, and lately he seemed to be invading her thoughts whenever she wasn't concentrating. She had become accustomed to his visits as he prepared the field, and now she missed the strong presence of this shy, quiet man.

Henry was good company, but it had been nice to have an adult around the farm again. An adult male. She recalled bringing lunch to Oscar the day he planted his flax, and how he fell asleep on the pile of stones after he'd eaten. The image of him lying there, like one of the rocks on the pile, made Esther uncomfortable.

He smelled of the earth that day, and of sweat and gasoline from his tractor too. She could tell he was a gentle man with a sensitive way, but he still seemed distant and uncomfortable around Henry. Not surprising for a man who lived alone and was unaccustomed to children. Still, he was patient with the boy, and he was honest and good. If Oscar was shy and naive for his age, she understood it was due to a lack of social exposure and education. There were other men like him in Aasness Township; not that Esther felt sophisticated or superior by comparison, they were all products of their times. She saw a vulnerability in Oscar that made his independent survival all these years a real testament to his character. She liked the thought of being his friend and advocate, but wanted more than that. They could work well together, Esther felt. If only he could understand that. If only he could know how she felt. If only she could tell him.

In her heart she knew she cared for the aging bachelor. There was no doubt any more. As to when or how the relationship had transformed from a neighborly business acquaintance to… whatever it was now, she wasn't sure, but her interest in Oscar continued to grow. Maybe it started with the marigolds, or maybe with the man she saw blossom at the picnic, but somehow she just woke up one morning with Oscar Halvorson in her heart. Thoughts of him remained in the back of her mind constantly since she'd acquired this new feeling for him. Esther didn't know how to explain it, didn't care to. It simply made her feel happy to be with him. But where had he been lately? Why hadn't he come to visit?

She wanted him to care, too, of course, so it was disconcerting that she hadn't seen him for several weeks. Before long it would be harvest time and like all farmers, Oscar Halvorson would be very busy and he wouldn't have time to spend with her. After harvest would he return to his reclusive life and not include her? But perhaps he was lonely too. Oh, she hoped so. Yes it would be good to bring him a loaf of bread today and see how he was doing, Esther thought.

A creaking came from the stairway and her groggy grandson yawned his way into the kitchen.

"Well, good morning then, Henry, it's about time you get up," she said.

"Morning Gramma," he replied, sounding only half awake. "M-m-m, sure smells good. Can I have some?"

"Yah, soon as it's ready. But first, where's my big morning hug?" Esther said, and the bleary-eyed boy happily obliged. "Okay, now go wash your face and I'll set a place and get you something to eat. The bread is soon done."

While Henry washed the sleep from his eyes, Esther put out some butter and milk and a jar of her homemade strawberry-rhubarb jam.

"Will you have coffee this morning Henry?" she asked.

"Yah, if there's cream," he replied. That's the way they liked Esther's bread the best, fresh from the oven with coffee.

"I'd like to can another batch of ground cherry sauce today. After you eat, can you run up to the garden and see if there are any more for us to pick?"

"Sure, Gramma," Henry said between gulps of milk. "Can we go to see Mr. Halvorson again some day?"

"Yah, sure, I was thinking we should do that this morning. I made an extra loaf and we can bring it to him. Maybe we should see if you could help him at harvest time. What do you think?" She was reaching for possibilities.

"Can I Gramma? Can you ask him? I bet I could be a big help. Maybe I could drive the tractor. He calls it *Gubbe* ya' know. When is harvest gonna be Gramma?"

"Oh, it should be starting in a couple more weeks I think," Esther replied. "Grain is turning and it won't be long 'til it's ready. We can talk to Mr. Halvorson about it when we see him."

She sliced generous pieces from a loaf that was ready and they ate together, relishing the taste of the warm, fresh bread and each other's company as the morning sun filled the kitchen.

"If you're done eating, go finish getting dressed and go check on those ground cherries for me while I clean up," Esther finally said.

"Okay, Gramma," he said, snatching one more slice of bread before bolting back upstairs. Humming a medley of hymns, Esther proceeded to clean up the baking mess and wash the dishes.

When she was finished, the remaining loaves of bread were cooled and ready to be put away. She took the one intended for communion, said her customary little blessing over it, and reverently wrapped it in a towel before placing it in the breadbox. The loaf for Oscar she wrapped in another towel and placed it and a jar of her strawberry jam in a basket for the walk to his farm.

"Gramma! Gramma! Come quick!" Henry's distant call came through the open window in urgent tones. Looking out the window Esther saw the boy running toward the house from the direction of the garden. Was he hurt? Wiping her hands on her outer apron, she went to meet him at the kitchen door.

"Gramma! You gotta come an' see!" he shouted breathlessly. "It's... it's Mr. Halvorson's field! His field is all... it's all blue!" the boy exclaimed.

In a moment Esther realized what had happened, and was relieved that Henry brought good news. The flax had bloomed. She had seen flax in flower before, but it had been many years and she had forgotten the timing as well as the striking impression it could have. Eager for his grandmother to see it, Henry seized her hand and towed her around the house toward Oscar's field.

"Slow down, Henry, I'm coming!" Esther laughed. "Uffda! Be careful! You're going to pull me over." They hurried along the thick grove of scrub oak and box elders that separated the backyard from the field, toward a gap that provided access through the trees. When the flax suddenly came into full view, Esther stopped abruptly and let go of Henry's hand. With a sense of awe, she slowly walked to the edge of the field.

The precise combination of sunlight, moisture and time had been met according to some formula imbedded in each seed Oscar planted. Morning sun had finally coaxed open the little azure flowers that grew in such abundant glory it seemed the sky had spilled its brilliant blue over the surface of Oscar's flax. The entire field looked as if a piece of the heavens, for some unknowable reason, had settled on this small patch of earth. For a long moment, Esther just looked at the mass of tiny blooms shimmering on the softly rustling breeze.

"Oh," she said at last, "oh my." She expressed it quietly, reverently, not with Henry's unrestrained joy but with a sense of awe. It was like she just realized something, like she'd just seen the field from a perspective she'd not had before. With it came a new understanding of Oscar Halvorson, the man. The flax not only held his future in farming, it was his past. It was a tribute to his involvement with the land and the cycles of perpetual re-creation with the rhythm of the seasons. The flax was the color of his hope, a fleeting shade of beauty that would be quickly reclaimed by the earth.

"Oh Henry! This is... so special," Esther finally said, mostly to herself. Henry was running along the edge of the field. He knew better than to run through a crop and trample it down, though it was hard to resist plunging into the sea of little flowers. She plucked a sprig of the little flowers and tucked the stem into a buttonhole in the bosom of her house dress, then picked herself a small bouquet for her kitchen table.

"Henry!" Esther called, "I think we should bring Mr. Halvorson the loaf of bread and then have him come back with us to see his field."

"Yeah! That's a good idea. He's probably never seen so many flowers. Let's go get him!"

"Wait, we've got to get the bread first!" Esther said, and they stopped by the house to grab the basket and her straw hat before setting off down the road and over the fields.

Oscar was returning from covering his grapes with netting to keep the birds from reaping the harvest before they fully ripened. Along the way he stopped to check his wheat, which itself was nearly ready and mostly recovered from the storm. It was mid-morning, as he stepped through the barbed wires of the fence around the barnyard and walked among the cow pies toward the machine shed. Time to start tuning up the machinery for threshing. He was just opening the doors to the shed when he heard someone calling his name.

"Mr. Halvorson! Mr. Halvorson!" It was the Holmvik woman's grandson, and she was with him. They came around the corner of his house and Henry seemed excited about something as he ran towards Oscar.

"Your field is all blue, Mr. Halvorson!" shouted the boy. "You should see it! It's really pretty. Hey, is that *Gubbe* in there?" Henry asked, distracted by the tractor resting in the darkness of the machine shed. "Are you gonna work on the tractor now? Can I help?" the boy asked.

"Henry, don't be a pest," Esther said as she caught up. She was out of breath from trying to keep up with her grandson, and she removed her straw hat to wipe her brow with the back of her slender wrist.

Henry was already inside the machine shop investigating equipment when Esther spoke again.

"We've brought you a loaf of bread Mr. Halvorson, fresh baked this morning," she said. Her chest was still heaving from the exertion of trying to follow Henry and silver-blond strands were blowing across her face the way it did whenever Oscar thought of her. With her hand she drew the errant strands from her face and flashed her enchanting smile. She looked radiant to him.

"D'is iss really a surprise Missus Holmvik. I sure wasn't expecting to see you," Oscar replied, caught completely off-guard and a little uncomfortable. "I mean for you to come here an,'" He eyed the basket hanging from her arm. "I mean, it iss nice to see you again, Missus Holmvik. Iss that bread for me then? "

"Well, yes it is, and we're also here to ask you to come to church," Esther said, thinking he looked thinner and tired since she'd last seen him. "We haven't seen you there in a while and it's communion Sunday tomorrow, you know, and, well, we just thought maybe you might come."

"Yah, well, I'll see. I got to get things ready for threshing you know," he replied tentatively. There was a pause, as the obvious question on Oscar's mind concerned her relationship with Martin Phillips. He just couldn't quite bring himself to ask it. Not just yet.

"So what was the boy saying about the flax d'en?" Oscar said changing the subject. "Has it flowered?"

"Oh, yes it has, Oscar. You really must come and see for yourself what you and God have done," Esther said. "It's so beautiful! I've never seen such color and so thick a crop."

"Yeah, Mr. Halvorson," Henry said from inside the machine shed, "it's really pretty. You've just got to come an' see it."

Oscar turned and looked at the boy on the tractor seat, then rubbing his stubbled chin, he looked down at the ground before turning to Esther.

"Come on," she said again. "It's worth taking the time to see it. It's your crop, your work, Oscar. Come and see your flax."

"Yah, okay d'en, I suppose I really should," Oscar said with a grin he couldn't suppress. He was deeply pleased with the turn of events; the Holmvik woman coming to see him and now the news about his flax.

"I'll just take an' put d'is bread in the house. Come along an' you can get a drink of water before we go. We'll take my truck."

A short time later Oscar's pickup rolled to a stop at the side of the road between Esther's farm and Eidsvold Church. The elevation of the road gave them a view of the field, glowing bright blue and rising as it sloped up in the distance. They got out of Oscar's truck and he walked around it for a better look.

"What do ya think, Mr. Halvorson? Isn't it really pretty?" Henry said. But Oscar said nothing. Esther and Henry watched as the man walked down through the ditch and out into the field until the sky blue sea of flowers surrounded him. For a long while he stood there scanning the field, then his hand reached out and brushed over the top of the flax. Bergstrom had been right. Finally Oscar turned and walked back out to join the boy and his grandmother.

"It is beautiful, don't you think, Oscar?" Esther said.

After a long pause, an inhaled "yah," was his only reply, but Esther noticed a glistening, moist track had recently descended from the corner of his eye. In that moment, Esther realized she loved the man.

"It's going to be a good crop," Oscar finally said. "A really good crop." Then he added, "Looks like your wheat is soon ready, Missus Holmvik. What are you going to do with it?"

17

"What am I going to do with it?" Esther said. "That's all figured out, Oscar, but it's become a long story." They got into the truck and drove into her farmyard and she began to explain.

"I'm sure you must know I bake a lot of bread for church functions, right?"

Oscar nodded.

"Well, I've got a pretty nice little arrangement with Martin Phillips over at the mill," she said.

"Here it comes," Oscar thought to himself, the explanation he'd been waiting for. He braced himself for the news of Esther and Martin Phillips.

"You see, years ago when Carl needed cattle feed," Esther continued, "he'd have it ground over at Phillips Mill, same as everyone else. Whenever we needed flour, Carl would pick up a sack when he was there. After Carl died, I went to Elof Tollerud to see if he could bring me a sack of flour whenever he came back from the mill, since I don't have a way to get there myself. I'd pay him when he dropped it off. Finding the money became difficult after awhile, so I told Tollerud I'd pay on credit at the mill if he'd just continue bringing the flour. It was an arrangement that worked out well enough, since I don't drive. But baking for the church bake sales, my own needs and the needs of others, I was going through a lot of flour. Before I knew it, I realized I was in debt to Mr. Phillips for several hundredweight of flour.

"So, oh some years ago, it's been quite a few years back now, I went to the mill to see Martin and pay him something on my account. I felt I owed him an explanation."

Oscar mentally noted she was on a first-name basis with the miller.

"When I got ready to pay him, he told me I didn't owe anything. I told him I wasn't ready to accept charity, but he said 'no', my account was already 'paid in full'.

"I didn't understand, but he showed me his ledger and there it was. I didn't understand and asked who was paying? He told me he couldn't tell me that, it just happened and I should accept it.

"It's been a secret for all these years, and I just accepted it as, well, you know, as God's grace. It wasn't 'til this summer, after Elof Tollerud's funeral, that I learned from Martin what was happening," Esther continued.

"Elof Tollerud had worked out an arrangement with Martin. Whenever he'd come with feed to be ground, he'd pick up a couple sacks of flour. Martin said it seemed like an awful lot for one family, but never said anything. Finally he asked Tollerud, and the old guy said he was getting it for me, but to keep it secret."

"Ol' Tollerud did that?" Oscar asked skeptically.

"Yah, he did Oscar. Said it was just a little contribution to the church," Esther continued. "Martin said he was happy to do it, too, so the secret kept on going, and I kept getting flour for free.

"Don't think that didn't bother me some Oscar, never knowing where the flour came from. But then, as years went by, I accepted the charity as grace. Still it was my curiosity that troubled me. Wasn't until after old Tollerud died this summer that I found out who was buying all the flour for me. It fact, Martin just told me about it when we were at the picnic. I guess I should have known, but still, I can't tell you how pleased I was to finally put my curiosity to rest. It was a relief! Yah, we spent some time laughing and talking together about it all then. You know, Tollerud was really a pretty good man, I must say."

"You an' Martin Phillips are just good friends d'en." Oscar spoke the words flatly, like a simple statement or casual observation, but wrapped in them was the question in Oscar's heart.

"Yah well, he and Carl were old school friends," Esther said. "Martin has been good to me over the years since Carl died, so I'd say he's become an old friend to me as well." Then she turned to him with a curious look and said, "He's just an old friend, Oscar."

There it was. Her explanation brought everything together for Oscar, illuminating the situation like the sun breaking through dark clouds. Esther Holmvik's conversations with Martin Phillips were just about how she got her flour from Tollerud. It all made sense now. Oscar sat quietly behind the wheel as the significance of her words seeped into his heart like a balm. How foolish he'd been. He was glad he hadn't said anything about her interest in Martin Phillips, how embarrassed he would have felt. Now, sitting beside her in his truck, Oscar felt a great burden lifting from him and an almost giddy feeling rising inside. Perhaps he still had a chance... a chance with her.

"So, the wheat I had you plant was to be my tribute for the grace shown to me, since I have no money. That's why I wanted you to plant ten percent—a tithe—in wheat. It's for the church, you know," Esther pointed out.

Esther began talking about his flax again, how thick the crop had come in and how much money he might make from it, but Oscar was no longer listening. He was watching the expressions of her face as she spoke, memorizing the way she looked in the morning sun just then. When she turned to him and smiled, it broke the spell and brought him back into the moment.

Oscar thanked her profusely for getting him to come and see the flax. It was a surely beautiful sight, one he assured her he'd never forget, and he meant it. It looked like it would be a bumper crop for sure, one that would keep E.A. Stordal's hands off Oscar's land once he got it harvested.

Esther invited him in for coffee, but Oscar declined, saying that he needed to stop by Fritz Hoffmeier's place and confirm threshing arrangements. With that, he turned the truck around and headed out the driveway, feeling like he was riding on air. Hoffmeier had a threshing machine, and Oscar had a standing arrangement with him to thresh his grain each year, as did several other farmers. Now that it was soon ready, he had to schedule a time for Hoffmeier to bring his rig over and thresh his wheat and Esther Holmvik's, as well.

The Hoffmeier farm wasn't far, and the man's wife sent Oscar off to a field where her husband was already cutting his grain. After a brief conversation with Hoffmeier followed by a handshake, Oscar was soon on his way home again.

Oscar's own wheat was ready and would be harvested first, because he had planted it before the arrangements for Esther's wheat. It had recovered remarkably from the storm, though Oscar knew the yield would be less than he'd hoped. Still, some farmers wouldn't be harvesting a wheat crop this season, and Oscar knew he was very lucky. Based on the planting time, when he finished harvesting his wheat, Esther Holmvik's should be ready, so long as the hot dry weather held out.

It would be well into September before his corn was ready to pick, except for that which had received the most damage from the hail. That he would take early and chop up for cattle fodder. He had just finished cutting and putting-up another crop of hay, and somewhere in his busy schedule, after they were ready, he had to get his grapes picked and make wine. Maybe after the wheat was threshed.

As for the flax, well, that crop was different. Flax matured much later than other crops and wouldn't be ready to harvest until late fall, about mid to late October, well after hard frosts had killed off other plant life. The oily content of flax seeds made them impervious to damage from frost, so it was safe to leave the flax to mature until after everything else was safely harvested and in the granary. By that time, Hoffmeier would be done threshing everyone's grain and he'd have time to modify his thresher with the flax screens Bergstrom had offered Oscar. But for now and over the next few weeks, Oscar and every other farmer in the area would be very busy.

The next morning Henry showed up at the machine shed with a cheerful, "Hi, Mr. Halvorson!" He approached somewhat tentatively.

Oscar was busy filing the toothy blades on the sickle bar of his old McCormick reaper as Henry slowly approached him. Oscar looked up expecting to see Esther Holmvik as well, but the boy was alone.

"Yah, hello d'er, boy," Oscar replied, going back to filing. "What iss it that brings you here today d'en?"

"Well, ya see, gramma said you probably needed help in the field now that it's time to cut the wheat, so I came t'help."

Oscar stopped again and stood upright, eyeing the boy skeptically. He was probably about the same age when he started helping his own father. It was around harvest time, too, as well as he could remember.

"She said I needed help, did she?"

"That's right Mr. Halvorson, an' I'm a good helper. Gramma said so."

"So d'en, what can you do?"

Henry looked at him with an enthusiastic grin, "Anything you want me to do, Mr. Halvorson, I can do anything."

Oscar's intuitive resistance was softening as images of he and his father working together surfaced from his subconscious. Maybe the boy could be of some use, he thought. It would take some training and patience but maybe his learning to help with the harvest could pay off in the long run. How should he handle this?

"Well, I suppose we could give it a try," Oscar finally said. "Let's see,

...eh..., d'er has got to be somet'ing..., hmmm," there was a long pause, followed by an inhaled, "yah," as he looked around his machine shop. At last he came up with an idea.

"Let's start wit' tools," he said. "It iss important you know tools so you can bring them to me when I need them, okay d'en?"

"Oh, sure thing Mr. Halvorson." The boy moved in close.

"First you've got to learn what they're called. That's a wrench down there on that block of wood, it's used to turn a nut or a bolt like these," Oscar explained pointing to a part on the reaper. "An' d'is here that I'm using to sharpen the teeth on the cutter," he said holding up the tool in his hand, "d'is iss a bastard file."

The boy's face turned serious.

"Mr. Halvorson, Gramma said I was to come home if you started sayin' those words again."

Oscar's eyebrows shot up. "Oh, no, you see, that iss what it's called, that iss the name of d'is here file," Oscar reassured him. Henry nodded, making the connection, then looked around at the profusion of tools for something he recognized.

"Is that the goddamn hammer you hit your hand with that time we..."

"No, no," Oscar cut him off, "you see that was... that was something different then. I was eh... you see I eh... here, come take a look at what I'm doing on this sickle bar. Be careful now, these edges are sharp."

Throughout the morning, Oscar continued to work on the reaper, oiling moving parts, tightening loose fittings, adjusting the canvas conveyor and greasing the gears of the big paddle wheel. It wasn't easy and it took much longer than if he'd been working alone, as he had to explain everything he did to Henry and name every tool he used.

Whenever he'd set a tool down for a moment and go to pick it back up, it was gone. He soon found that Henry would take whatever tool he was using and start "working" on another part of the reaper. Henry discovered that a wrench not only took nuts on and off, but with a little extra effort could round its corners nicely.

"What's this for, Mr. Halvorson? Why are ya doin' that? Can I do that for a while? How does this thing work? What are ya doin' now, Mr. Halvorson?" The old bachelor had never been bombarded by so many questions. Working alone most of his life, Oscar wasn't accustomed to having "help" around or having to talk to someone as he worked.

Every time he stood up or turned around Henry was there in his way, always with a question, always wanting to "help". Once Oscar accidentally knocked the boy over when he suddenly stood up. Later he backed up and tripped over Henry, who was "working" on his hands and knees just behind him. The onerous morning passed slowly, and being inexperienced with children, Oscar struggled to maintain a patient demeanor. Several times his patience began to boil over but he never let it erupt. Eventually, he tried to ignore the boy, pretending not to hear him.

Finally the machine was set to go. Oscar gassed up the tractor, backed it into the shed, and connected the reaper to the hitch.

"What are ya doin' now? Where are ya goin'?"

"Now is when the work begins, boy," Oscar said. "I'm goin' to the field to cut my wheat."

"Can I come, Mr. Halvorson? Can I help?"

"Yah, well," he considered the consequences of leaving the boy alone in his shop. "Yah, I guess so. First fill d'is jar with water at the well over d'er," He said, dumping out the cold coffee that was in it. The wheat was in his north twenty to the back of his farm and some distance away. As the boy filled the water jar, Oscar set the controls on the tractor, inserted the crank, and gave a few brisk, powerful turns, stirring the silent beast to life. He climbed onto the tractor and considered the wisdom of letting the boy come along as he waited.

"Here's your water, Mr. Halvorson," Henry said, handing the jar up to Oscar. He wrapped it in a gunnysack and put it in the toolbox under the seat as *Gubbe* idled indifferently. Oscar paused a moment, shook his head with reservation, then turning in the seat, reached his hand down to the boy.

Henry grabbed Oscar's hand without hesitation and was lifted up effortlessly and placed between the farmer's knees.

"Now d'en, you hang on tight so you don't fall off, and don't touch anyt'ing, okay?" Oscar said in solemn warning. "D'is iss not really safe, so we both must be careful up here, you understand?"

The boy was thrilled. "Sure thing Mr. Halvorson, I'll hang on. I'll be careful."

Henry braced against Oscar's thigh and held on as he put the tractor in gear and together they headed off to the wheat field. He was careful not to touch any of the many levers, handles, and knobs, but inquired nonstop about the purpose of every control as the tractor lumbered along. Speaking loudly over the sound of the engine, Oscar did his best to explain, but the distraction made him a little nervous as they jostled over rough ground. Henry felt he had found his element.

The raw power of the mechanical beast carrying them exhilarated the boy, and he was totally absorbed in the joy of the moment. Hot August sun burned down on them and a light breeze sometimes carried the smelly exhaust back in their faces. Together they lurched over ruts and potholes, down through a ditch and up the other side; nothing stopped *Gubbe's* slow, steady progress. It was wonderful.

All too soon they reached the wheat field and Oscar brought, *Gubbe* to a halt at the edge and set the brake. They both climbed down and Oscar went straight back to the reaper to lower the sickle blades and make final adjustments before starting to cut the grain.

"You'll have to stay here now, I can't have you riding while I'm working the machine," Oscar said. A look of disappointment shaded the boy's face, but he understood it would be unsafe. Oscar started to climb back onto the seat, then reached into the toolbox and took out the water jug.

"Can you take care of the water for me, boy? I don't want the jar to break."

Henry nodded his assurance.

"I'll wave you over when I'm thirsty," Oscar said, then climbed aboard *Gubbe*, moved some levers and started into the field.

The clattering sickle blades, thumping paddle wheel and rattling conveyer joined the roar of the tractor in a raucous symphony of mechanical sound, music to Henry's ears. He walked along side, watching as the reaper cut into the standing wheat, mowing it down in a continuous mat that was swept onto the conveyor, pulled into bunches and finally tossed out the back in bundles. The man and machinery gradually pulled ahead, leaving Henry trudging behind in the straw stubble. Soon Henry came to one of the omnipresent rock piles that accumulate over time in the midst or at the edge of the fields, and there he took his place among the stones. Without taking his eyes off the diminishing tractor, he opened the jar of water and took a big drink.

Somehow the water was gone by the time Oscar waved for a drink, but it was okay. He kept working the field and by the end of the afternoon it was about half done. Wheat lay in bundles scattered over the field, ready for threshing. Oscar got down and disengaged the levers on the reaper and raised the sickle blades.

"Where is all the wheat, Mr. Halvorson?" Henry inquired. He understood that the small kernels of grain were the object of farming and was expecting to see some results other than a field of stubble with bundles of straw everywhere.

"We got to thresh it," Oscar said. "I got Hoffmeier coming wit' his thresher next week."

"What is that? What does a thresher do?" Henry asked. Oscar gave the boy a short course in how they brought the threshing machine to the field, hooked it to the flywheel of the tractor, and pitched the bundles of wheat into it. The threshing machine separated the grains of wheat from the straw stalks, and the grain went into a wagon, the straw into a pile. That was when they'd see the kernels of grain as Henry recognized them.

"Let me show you something boy," Oscar said, and they walked over to a bundle of wheat. He drew a stalk of wheat through his thumb and forefinger, stripping off the grains in the palm of his hand as Henry watched intently. Then he rubbed the grains between the palms of his hands, removing the feathery husks or chaff. He showed the grains and chaff in the palm of his hand to Henry.

"That's threshing," Oscar said, and he blew the chaff off the palm of his hand, leaving only the kernels of grain.

"That's what a threshing machine does?"

"Yah, that's what it does. That there in my hand iss wheat, that iss what I sell. It iss what makes the bread that you eat. Now watch this."

Oscar popped the grain in the palm of his hand into his mouth and began to chew.

"You can eat grain?" Henry asked. "Don't you have to cook it?"

"You chew it," Oscar said. "It makes something to chew in your mouth. It's good when you're thirsty and you don't have any water."

"I wanna try it," Henry said, and they repeated the process in Henry's hand. He popped the grain into his mouth and began to chew.

"It doesn't taste very..." he began to say, "it's... it's not so bad, I guess. It doesn't taste like Gramma's bread, though." Henry kept chewing as the wheat became more pliable in his mouth. "It's almost like chewing gum," he said. "It's pretty good. Do cows like it? What happens if you swallow it?"

"Yah, cows would like it all right, but we don't give them wheat. It gives them a bellyache. You shouldn't eat much either, it could give you a bellyache too if you eat too much. It's just for chewing when you're thirsty."

"Okay Mr. Halvorson, I think it's pretty neat. I'm gonna show Gramma."

"Well, I'll have to finish this field tomorrow. Maybe you could come and help me shock the bundles."

"Sure thing. What's that mean?" Henry asked, feeling involved with the process now and glad to be included.

"That's just gathering all the bundles of wheat you see scattered around the field an' stacking them together to keep them dry. I'll show you. Go grab a couple bundles and bring them here," Oscar said. He quickly demonstrated how to set the bundles together in a way that the heads of grain stayed off the ground and kept dry. Henry caught on quickly, but it was enough for one day.

After the demonstration, Oscar gave Henry a hand back up on the tractor and together they headed back to the machine shed. Along the way, Henry resumed his line of questioning, asking about all the controls again.

Henry was watching Oscar back the reaper into the machine shed when he noticed his grandmother approaching across the farmyard. He ran to meet her, telling all about the things he'd experienced that day. It came in erratic waves of disjointed information, requiring re-telling and explanation, but the best part was riding on the tractor. That and chewing the grains of wheat.

"Well, you and Mr. Halvorson have had quite a day then, haven't you," she said. The rumbling tractor became silent and Oscar momentarily emerged from the dark interior of his machine shed into the late afternoon sunshine. Henry went inside, still talking to his grandmother, only now he was telling about tools.

"Hallo d'en Missus Holmvik. Sorry if I kept the boy away too long. He has been learning to farm..." Oscar said with a wink and an all too rare smile.

"Yah, so I've just heard. That's good, Oscar. It's really nice of you to let him be with you. Hope he hasn't been too much trouble. He's a good boy, just very curious."

"Oh, he was okay. We got along fine. I let him ride wit' me on *Gub*... on the tractor." Oscar was a bit self-conscious about having anyone know he actually had a name for his tractor. "Hope you don't mind."

"I don't know, Oscar," she said. "I guess I'd prefer he doesn't ride up there with you anymore. I just don't think it's safe. I've heard of too many accidents..."

"Yah, I suppose you're right, Missus Holmvik I guess I won't let him ride with me if you don't think it's a good idea."

"Oh no, that's not right. He likes being included and I suppose he should learn about machines somehow. It's just that I don't know what I'd do if anything happened to Henry," she said. "It seems he's all I've got now and..." her voice trailed off.

"We'll be careful, I promise."

There was an uncomfortable pause and Oscar thought it best to change the subject.

"It was nice of you to come get the boy to bring him home," he said looking at the ground between them. "I should have got him back earlier, I s'pose, but I didn't know it was getting so late."

"Oh it's not that late, Oscar. That's not the reason I came."

Oscar noted a different tone in her voice, something he'd not heard before.

"It's Bergstrom," she paused, and he looked up at her.

"Bergstrom... he's dead, Oscar. Hung himself in his barn yesterday. Hoffmeier found him. He stopped by to offer him a job helping out during threshing season, and..."

Oscar turned his gaze in the direction of Bergstrom's farm beyond the horizon. He heard Esther speaking, but the words were just background noise from another dimension, muffled by a gust of hot summer wind in his ear. Bergstrom. It was late in the day, and though earth and air retained the August sun's heat, Oscar felt suddenly chilled by an all too familiar loneliness.

18

The funeral was not well attended. It was a busy time of year, with harvest in progress, but Bergstrom's years of pessimism and bitter outlook on life had not endeared him to his peers around Aasness Township. He had dropped all socializing after losing his wife and although everyone thought it sad the man had come to this end, he hadn't made it easy for people to feel close to him. Those who attended were mostly farmers who had known Bergstrom all their lives and perhaps understood him better than others. Some of them had been in or were going through similar financial circumstances, and though Bergstrom's funeral could hardly be considered a sentimental farewell, there were many who empathized with his struggles in life.

They were the same individuals who considered it callous of E.A. Stordal to attend. To his harshest critics, his presence suggested that E.A. would pursue debtors to the grave.

"I see Stordal has come to close Bergstrom's account then," Gus Thorvald coldly remarked.

Nonetheless, the banker came and not only sat through the church service but attended the graveside interment as well. Perhaps E.A.'s conscience compelled him to be there, or perhaps he was trying to show people he was not insensitive. No one was sure of his motives. Other than formal greetings, E.A. spoke only to George Kruger, the feed and seed dealer, and Fritz Hoffmeier, the only other man of any prominence in attendance. He left discretely, not staying for the luncheon. Farmers in the parking lot watched him light up a big cigar before he got into his car and drove back to town, chased by a cloud of Aasness Township dust.

The light attendance and lack of sentiment at the bachelor's funeral did not go unnoticed by Oscar. A soft, late-summer wind rustled the dry cottonwood leaves overhead as Bergstrom was lowered into the waiting earth beside his wife's grave. Oscar felt something good in that Bergstrom was now with his Nora in peace at last. The movement of the air helped refresh mourners that hot August day, but Oscar could not escape that lonely feeling again.

Standing by the open grave, Oscar felt every year, every day of his age. Would he be found dead in his barn someday? What would his own funeral be like, he thought, and who would attend? Would they have to search for kind words to say about him? Would anyone be around who knew or remembered him, or cared? Would Esther Holmvik pump out a dirge on the organ for him as well? Would she mourn his passing? Would he end up just another rock on the pile?

Bergstrom's death troubled Oscar, and he did not wait to be talked into staying for the luncheon this time. His head was reeling with thoughts and emotions, reflections on his past and considerations of his present and future that needed to be sorted out. Oscar slipped away before the graveside service ended and returned to his farm. Hektor met him and together they walked to the solitude of his vineyard, where he sat among the rocks beside the pond. There as he often did when loneliness closed in on the advancing years of his life, he sought solace again from his mother.

Why now, after all this time, should being alone be a problem? Hadn't he survived all these years on his own? And weren't some of the recent years the hardest times anyone had ever had to deal with? He'd made it. He'd done it all along the way, and by himself. Since his parents died and his brothers left the farm, he hadn't needed anything from anyone, except that loan from E.A. Stordal of course. Now, if the flax harvest went like it should, it looked like he was going to beat E.A., too. He'd keep his farm. He'd done it all with careful planning and the work of his own hands. After this season, he'd be free and clear, completely independent. He didn't need anyone. If that wasn't success, then what was? How proud his parents would be if they could see how well he'd done with the farm.

Why then did this damned lonely feeling have to come around every now and then? Bergstrom's life had been lonely, too, after the death of his wife. There was no one here for him, no one else in the man's life. Why now did Oscar have this desire to be liked, to be remembered...? It was more than that, he felt, but he couldn't quite grasp it.

It had to be that Holmvik woman. She was the one who started these feelings. Now he not only cared about her, but cared what she thought of him. Why did he want her to care about him? Why did he feel so drawn to her? They were both getting old, and yet he felt like he wanted this relationship to... become something. She was calling him by his first name now. When did that start? This was a crazy thing to be happening at this point in his life, but... no. He had a farm to run. He didn't need anyone, he ran it by himself. Alone. Like Bergstrom.

Then, of course, there was the boy. Was that the way all kids are? He couldn't recall his own childhood behavior, couldn't really recall being much like a child. The Holmvik boy was into everything, losing tools, upsetting his work routine and getting in the way. There was always a concern that the boy might get hurt and Esther would hold him responsible, or Oscar might curse around the boy and he'd be in trouble with her for that. And the questions -- there was no end to them. It took twice as long to get anything done with that boy around.

"Oh mamma, *hva skulle jeg gjøre nå*? (What should I do now?)" Oscar spoke aloud, hoping to somehow exhort a reply. The silence only reminded him of how lonely his life was, and how he wished things were different. At least he had Hektor. Silent, faithful old Hektor. Oscar stroked the aging dog beside him as they watched the afternoon shadows lengthen. Soon the grapes would be ready to harvest.

Later that week Oscar drove his tractor and reaper to Esther's farm, and in a few hours had the two acres of wheat cut and bundled. Henry helped him shock the bundles to dry while waiting for threshing. Hoffmeier was bringing his separator to thresh Oscar's wheat next week, and Oscar was ready for him. It was a very busy time of year but he loved it. It was the season that made everything a farmer did worthwhile. Working the land, planting the crops, tending and worrying over them throughout the summer until harvest. In west central Minnesota, harvest was like a payday that came just once a year. To a great extent, it determined the coming year's budget for a farmer, and throughout the Depression budgets had been meager. Except for areas of storm damage, this was going to be a good year for most farmers in Aasness Township.

Oscar cut and stacked another crop of hay while waiting for the day Hoffmeier would come to thresh his wheat. When that day came, Henry showed up at Oscar's wheat field as Hoffmeier and his son and a hired man arrived with the separator in tow. With the grain wagons and equipment, it was like watching a circus Henry had seen setting up in

Minneapolis. He had a lot of questions of course, but the men quickly put him to work carrying bundles of wheat from the shocks stacked around the field. Henry had to learn a lot from observation.

They positioned the threshing machine and rigged a long belt between its flywheel and the one on Hoffmeier's big tractor. Oscar had *Gubbe* hitched to a high-sided grain wagon, which he maneuvered into position beneath the spout of the separator. When all the adjustments were made and the dew was gone, Hoffmeier's tractor was started up and the flywheels engaged. Henry was sternly cautioned to keep away from the dangerous belt. They all began hauling bundles to be pitched into the hopper of the thresher, where the grain would be separated from the stalks and chaff. Soon, grain was pouring into Oscar's wagon, as chopped straw was blown into a pile at the rear of the threshing machine.

Hoffmeier's wife, a stout, ruddy-faced woman with thick braided dark-blond hair, brought a hearty lunch into the field, and Henry ate like he'd never eaten before. Then it was back to work.

When Oscar's grain wagon was full, he towed it with his tractor to a granary building on his farm and Henry helped him scoop the grain into the bin. It was hot, dusty, dirty work, and Henry was exhausted by mid-afternoon when he dragged himself home. The men worked on until late evening when they went home to eat and sleep until early morning brought them back again to continue the process.

Oscar was sure the boy would not show up the next day after being exposed to the hard work of threshing. It was tiring for grown men who were used to long days and hard work, but Henry wasn't quite 10 years old. When he got tired, he'd climb up on a wagon and watch the grain pour from the spout, slowly filling the hopper. At times Henry was both a nuisance and a concern around all the equipment, but he managed to not cause problems or get hurt.

It was nearly mid-morning the following day before the dew was gone and they were ready to start threshing again. As they began, Henry came walking over the field carrying his school lunch pail and a jar of water. Oscar watched the boy approach over the stubble field and though he would never come out and say it, he was both pleased and impressed.

Henry started right away, carrying bundles for the men to pitch into the hopper of the machine. Hoffmeier and his hired man knew the boy was Esther Holmvik's grandson, and they praised his efforts while giving

Oscar a wink of the eye. Their comments made Henry feel appreciated and accepted. They not only knew the boy, but they knew of Oscar's arrangement with the boy's grandmother. Under different circumstances, Hoffmeier and his helper might have been inclined to tease Oscar a bit with personal questions suggesting a romance with Esther Holmvik, but the boy's presence and the hard, dusty, hot work of threshing kept such talk to a minimum.

When Oscar's wheat was threshed and safely stored and the straw put up in his barn, they moved the equipment to Esther Holmvik's little two acre plot of wheat which was all shocked and waiting. They easily finished the job in less than a day, and loaded the grain in an old wagon Esther kept in a shed. Oscar agreed to haul the wagon to Phillips Mill within a few days.

When their wheat was safely in storage, Oscar spoke again with Hoffmeier about threshing his flax.

"I t'ink the flax can wait 'til late October," Oscar told Hoffmeier.

"Yah, we're all gonna be pretty busy getting ready for the corn once the wheat is done," Hoffmeier agreed. "Remember I told you I don't have flax screens for the separator Halvorson. You said you'd get 'em. You got 'em yet?"

"They're Bergstrom's," Oscar said. "He told me I could use them months ago. I don't t'ink he changed his mind." Hoffmeier grinned and nodded.

"Well, I hope you got them before he died, 'cause if they're still at Bergstrom's place, ol' Stordal will have put the clamps on that property by now. An' he may not be so willing to loan them to you, unless you got some legal okay from Bergstrom in writing."

Hoffmeier's words got Oscar's attention immediately. The man was right. He should have thought of that before. He should have gotten the screens from Bergstrom when he first offered them, but how could he have known Bergstrom was going to kill himself? Oscar had to have those screens, and he determined to get them on the way home that evening.

The sun was low when he stopped at Bergstrom's farm. At the driveway entrance stood an advertisement for an auction to be held in October, and official-looking notices were already posted on each of the buildings. Oscar disregarded the notices; he never learned to read well, anyway. Probably no trespassing signs, he reasoned, put there by the sheriff at the request of E.A. Stordal. His being there had nothing to do with Stordal or the law, he reasoned. He was simply acting on a personal offer made to him by a deceased friend.

Stordal might think the flax screens for the separator belonged to him now that he'd foreclosed on Bergstrom's property, but Bergstrom had told Oscar he could use the screens long before he died. The fact that the man was now dead made no difference to Oscar. Besides, he didn't know if there were any other flax screens in the whole county and he couldn't afford to buy them anyway. Oscar was not about to go to Stordal to ask for the screens. He could imagine the schemes Stordal might come up with to bargain with Oscar, and his farm could likely be at risk again if the banker had his way. Without the screens he couldn't harvest his flax. If he couldn't harvest his flax, he'd lose his farm to Stordal. No, from the beginning of the season, Oscar had counted on the profit from his flax to save his farm. Neither Bergstrom's death nor E.A. Stordal nor anything so minor as a piece of paper tacked on the sides of Bergstrom's buildings was going to stand in the way of Oscar harvesting his flax.

Now, just where Bergstrom kept the screens was another issue. Oscar pulled his truck up close to the machine shed, since it seemed the most likely place to start looking. That was where Oscar would store them if they were his, so it seemed the logical place to start looking. A new padlock had been installed to secure the big wide main doors, but Oscar knew there was a side entrance. It too was locked, but only with a hook latch on the inside. Applying a little brute force with his shoulder, Oscar managed to gain entry.

The low sun made poor light inside the shop with the main doors closed. In the dim light Oscar found a kerosene lantern and lit it. It dawned on him that for the first time in his life, he might be doing something illegal. He dismissed it, reminding himself that he had Bergstrom's permission. Still, he couldn't help feeling like an intruder who was being watched. The man was dead, yet the place seemed filled with his presence and gave Oscar a creepy feeling.

Bergstrom had not run a well-organized operation. Tools and junk lay everywhere and the place was a mess, a metaphor for the man's life. A hay rake and reaper were both in various states of disassembly, just the way Bergstrom left them. It looked like he had just walked away and would be back momentarily to finish the repairs, and it gave Oscar an eerie sort of feeling. He hoped he could find the screens soon and be out of there.

He headed toward the back of the shop, reasoning they would be tucked away, as they were not something Bergstrom—or any farmer—would normally use or even have around where they'd be handy. He lifted the lantern and looked in the rafters, which seemed to hold scrap lumber, coils of ropes and hoses, an old hay sling and other odd parts, but no threshing screens. He stepped carefully over dark obstructions and between equipment in the shadows, barely able to see anything in the dim light. Oscar tried to be quiet for some crazy reason, as if someone might hear him rifling going through the shed and come bursting in and catch him in the act. Not that it mattered, but he was no good at being stealthy.

"Where in hell did you leave d'em screens, Bergstrom?" he said out loud, partly to himself and partly to Bergstrom. Oscar half hoped the dead man might somehow tell him where they were, and the other half was afraid his ghost might actually appear and show him. Going to search another corner, he gouged his shin on the corner of a protruding steel beam, which elicited a spontaneous stream of Norse profanity through clenched teeth, which unsettled his nerves even more.

The cursing did not relieve his frustration, either, and continuing to stumble and probe the darkness with the lantern light produced no threshing screens. He felt sure that the machine shed was where they would be, but maybe Bergstrom had kept them in the barn. On his way through the jumble back toward the side door where he'd entered, he knocked over a cream can full of long metal rods, setting off a metallic explosion of clang and clatter.

While passing the workbench along the wall adjacent the side door, the dusky sunset glowed through a window illuminating the work surface and its array of worn tools and grimy, disassembled parts. The orange sunlight glinted off something bright and shiny hanging beside the window, unexpected among the grease and dirt. It was a woman's heart-shaped gold locket hanging on a fine chain. Its brilliance in the dim light surprised Oscar and attracted him. Simply made but skillfully crafted, it was a thing of delicate beauty, conspicuously out of place amidst the crude and dirty mechanical implements. The engraved designs were black against the gold, either from grime or charred residue Oscar couldn't tell.

Oscar took the locket carefully from its place and fumbled it open. Inside, though singed by heat around the edges, were tiny old sepia pictures of a young man and woman, perpetually facing each other whenever the locket was closed. The man was a young Theodore Bergstrom in happier times, bearing little resemblance to the lately deceased Bergstrom. The woman, Oscar recognized, was his young wife Nora. He had only met her a few times, but her young, pretty face with dark hair and large dark eyes even an old farmer couldn't forget. Their pictures seemed to be looking into each other's eyes, silently communicating something that Oscar was just recently struggling to comprehend inside himself.

The outside of the locket was smudged by grimy hands but polished from frequent handling, not covered with dirt and dust like everything else. Oscar realized he held a tender part of Bergstrom's past, a fond memory locked in gold, revealed only in the solitude of the man's workshop. Alone in this place, Bergstrom had allowed his heart to soften with memories of his dear companion. Oscar felt he had somehow intruded by opening the locket, and clicked it shut again.

The loss of his wife had changed Bergstrom, leaving his world void and dismal. Oscar sensed this, and the emptiness he'd become aware of in his own life came into focus again. Even if he kept his farm, so what? Everything he did was for himself. There was nothing to share, no legacy, no purpose to his life other than self-serving. If he harvested the flax and saved his farm, what difference would it make to anyone but himself? He felt old and vulnerable. A sense of something, someone missing in his life settled over him, bringing that too familiar loneliness with it. In the dingy darkness of Bergstrom's machine shed, he seemed to feel the dead man's presence closer than ever.

"*What're you waitin' for?... Go wit' them, Halvorson... it's gettin' late...*" The memory of Bergstrom's words intruded on his thoughts like a ghost. Bergstrom had urged Oscar to join Esther and her grandson after Tollerud's funeral. Unnerved, Oscar felt an urgent need to get out of there. Without thinking, he stuffed the locket in his pocket and headed for the door.

The corner of something propped at the end of the workbench caught his pant leg and started to fall. With quick reflexes, Oscar caught the object and only then noticed what it was. The screens. They'd been propped there waiting for him all along. Oscar recognized his own name scrawled by Bergstrom on a brown scrap of paper stuck in the frame. He hadn't forgotten.

"*Tusen takk, min gammel venn. Takk for alt,*" (A thousand thanks my old friend, thanks for everything,) Oscar whispered. Gathering up the screens, he headed out the door, placed them in the back of his truck and set out for home.

19

Never before had there been so many grapes in Oscar's vineyard. Plump, dark and juicy, they'd produce more wine than he'd ever made before. He was going to need more jugs and would need to adjust his recipe portions to accommodate the greater volume.

Threshing was still going on around Aasness Township but Oscar was not only done with his, he'd helped Hoffmeier with his threshing as well, as partial payment to the man who owned the machinery. Oscar had also given the flax screens for the separator to Hoffmeier for later use when the time came to thresh his flax. Hoffmeier asked no questions about how he'd gotten them from Bergstrom's place. Oscar realized that if Stordal knew Bergstrom's flax screens were missing he'd be the prime suspect, being the only one in Aasness Township growing flax that year. He wasn't worried about it, still feeling completely justified by Bergstrom's permission to use the screens prior to his death. If anyone at all was aware that Bergstrom's machine shed had been broken into, they weren't saying anything about it.

Now, Oscar turned his attention to picking grapes as fast as he could, and his pails were filling quickly. He'd have to make a trip back to the house to empty them soon. Hektor was not interested in grapes or wine and was off conducting a low-key investigation of what other creatures might have visited the little vineyard by the pond over the past several days. Before long, Hektor heard his name called and together they both headed back to the house, Oscar ladened with two cream cans of grapes.

After dumping them into a big galvanized washtub, he rinsed them clean with buckets of water near his pump. He was about to go pick more grapes when he heard someone calling.

"Mr. Halvorson! Mr. Halvorson!" it was Henry. Oscar didn't want him to even know about the grapes, let alone help harvest them. His wine making was a very private little hobby. He set down his cream cans and went to the house.

"Hey, hello d'er young man. What brings you here today d'en?" Oscar said, trying not to let on that he was suspiciously preoccupied.

"Well, I was just lookin' for something to do so I thought I'd come and help ya' with somethin'," the boy said. "What are ya workin' on today?"

"I er… I'm eh… well, not too much actually, that iss I ahhh… let's see now, what am I ahh…"

"Well, maybe you an' me could just do stuff together or somethin'," the boy suggested. "Ya wanna go fishin'?"

"Yah, well, I ahh, you see I'm uh… I'm kinda busy right now boy."

"What are ya doin'? Can I help?" Henry pressed.

"Well, it iss nothin' you want to do really," Oscar desperately searched for something, any excuse at all to get rid of the lad. "You see I'm ahh… I'm… I'm cleaning, that's what I'm doin'. Yah, I'm cleaning in here, an' that's nothin' a fellah like you wants to get into. Cleaning. There's no fun in that."

The boy's face fell, and Oscar took satisfaction knowing his little lie had created the right effect.

"Yah, that's right, I'm cleaning," he repeated. "Uffda, it ain't no fun either," Oscar added, sounding glum as he could. "But it's got to be done," he sighed. Referring to his house, that part was absolute truth.

"I suppose I could help ya, an' then we could do somethin' else later," Henry said without enthusiasm.

"Oh no, no, I don't t'ink so, it's a one-man kind of job. Anyhow, I don't t'ink you'd like it much," Oscar followed through with the approach, "but t'anks for the offer." He turned as if to go back to his "cleaning", and the boy started to leave by way of the hay field. Then Oscar suddenly had an idea.

"Hold on d'ere boy!" he called, and Henry stopped with an expression of hope flashing across his face.

"D'ere iss one t'ing you could maybe help me with," he offered.

"What's that Mr. Halvorson?"

"Well d'en, eh… do you suppose you could ask your grandma if she has any empty Hilex jugs she could give me?"

"Empty? Sure, I guess so. How many do ya need?" Henry asked.

"Oh, just two or t'ree would be fine."

"What do you need empty Hilex bottles for?" the boy asked innocently.

Here came the constant questions again, Oscar thought. No one knew about his wine making, and he didn't want anyone to know. Especially the boy and Esther Holmvik. What if she didn't think wine making was proper? What she thought now mattered a great deal to Oscar.

"I ahh... I need d'em for... ahh... to carry water in d'em, that iss all. That iss why I need d'em. Now, you ask her for me d'en, okay?" Oscar said. "You can bring d'em to me tomorrow afternoon. Can you do that?"

"Yeah, I guess so," said Henry, disappointment registering in his voice, as he was still looking for something more interesting to do. He said good-bye, and headed back home.

Oscar watched him go to be sure the boy was gone, then he picked up his cream cans and headed back toward his vineyard. He made several trips that day, bringing back cans filled with grapes until the wash tub overflowed with them, and then he piled grapes on his kitchen table.

He started the wine making process that afternoon, crushing the grapes in a large pickling crock with a heavy pestle. Then Oscar put the grapes into a cloth, which hung suspended by the corners. He twisted the cloth to squeeze more juice from the grapes and let them drip into another crock. All the juice was filtered through another cloth and collected into another waiting crock. The process was repeated for all the grapes until he collected all the juice. Sugar and yeast were then added in just the right proportions, the key to making perfect wine. Then the wine was placed in his cellar to ferment. It was a laborious process, but a labor of love.

While Oscar crushed and strained the grapes, he recalled going through the same processes with his mother, Rakel. He thought of her as he made the wine and how they had talked and laughed together. Wine making was one of the favorite memories from his younger years. Everything else was just work. He thought of her now, speaking his thoughts aloud to her as if she was with him.

"What if she doesn't like wine?" Oscar said, as much to his mother as to himself. "What if she doesn't approve of wine making at all? What would I do d'en? Maybe I could change her mind. Yah, I suppose.

"I t'ink she likes me too. Does she t'ink about me all the time like I t'ink about her? We could do pretty good together, me an' her. She knows farming all right. "Yah" (inhaled), "we'd work pretty good together."

"Missus Holmvik. Esther. That iss a nice name too. Soft sounding, like her. She iss a good woman, Mamma. Takes such good care of her grandson. She iss so nice to me an' cares about everybody at the church, too. So kind. I wish you could have known her.

"D'iss iss really going to be some good wine this year. We never had so many grapes as d'iss. Juicy. Best ever, maybe I t'ink.

"She's nice to look at too, so pretty. Makes me feel... I don't know, special I guess, when she looks at me. Sometimes I... I t'ink it would be nice sometimes... just to hold... her... hand... Yah (inhaled).

"Oh mama, *hva er det å har elsket for en kvinne*?" (What is it to love a woman?) Oscar's thoughts continued on in silence now, as he worked the grapes with the pestle.

"Hilex bottles? What on earth does he want with Hilex bottles?" Esther asked Henry as she took the last loaf of bread from the oven. The coming weekend brought another communion Sunday and the "Host" was ready.

Henry had smelled the bread well before he came in the door and was hungry for the first warm slice as had become their custom. He had mentioned Oscar's request for Hilex jugs as he took a seat at the table.

"Just to carry water in Gramma, that's what he said," Henry replied.

"Well, I guess I've got a few down in the cellar that I don't need anymore."

She set a plate with a thick slice of fresh bread in front of Henry. "You can take a few of them to Oscar tomorrow if you want. How was he today?" Esther asked as she sat down with Henry. "I haven't seen him in a while."

"Good, I guess," Henry said with his mouth full.

"What was he doing?"

"He said he was cleaning and that I wouldn't like to help. He was right."

Esther smiled, catching the underlying message the boy did not get.

"Everybody has chores to do, Henry," she said. "Maybe it's time to pay him a visit again. We can bring him a loaf of bread along with the Hilex jugs tomorrow."

"Gramma, do you like Mr. Halvorson?" Henry asked in his forthright youthful way.

"Why, of course I do, Henry. Mr. Halvorson is a good man," Esther replied trying to be as direct as her grandson.

"Do you love him Gramma?" the boy asked again.

"Why, Henry, that's not a question you should... Why do you ask?"

"I don't know. I was just... thinkin,'" Henry's voice trailed off. "Can I have another piece of bread?"

"Yah sure. Let me cut it for you," Esther said, and got up from the table. Did she love Oscar? Yes, of course, if these feelings she had were those of love. It was different than with Carl, but being with Oscar made her feel good, and it was good to have that feeling again. If love could also mean having someone to hold, especially when things seemed uncertain, someone strong and gentle to share difficult times, then she could love Oscar. It would be nice to not feel lonely anymore. Now it was apparent to Esther that her grandson had come to love the old farmer, too.

"I suppose school will be starting again soon, Henry. Are you anxious?"

"Naw, I don't wanna go back to school. I just wanna be a farmer someday," Henry said.

"You'll need to have an education if you're going to be a farmer, it's getting more and more important," Esther pointed out.

"You said Mr. Halvorson didn't go to school and he's a farmer. Why can't I just be like him?" Henry said with typical boyhood logic.

"It was much different when Mr. Halvorson started farming," she replied, "and I think if he could have, he'd much rather have gone to school. You can't be a good farmer today without getting an education."

"Well, I guess I'm ready to go back to school, but I won't like it much."

"Won't you be glad to see the other children there? You haven't seen some of them since last spring. And how about Miss Engebretson? You like her don't you?"

"Yeah, I guess," Henry admitted. "But Mr. Halvorson is gonna harvest his corn in a couple weeks an' I sure don't wanna miss that. He needs my help."

"Mr. Halvorson forgot about your going back to school," Esther said. "Besides, I think he's gotten along without your help in the past. If you want to help him, it will have to be after school."

"Aw, Gramma," Henry protested, but he knew it was to no avail.

"Let's visit Oscar—uh, Mr. Halvorson tomorrow and bring him a loaf of bread along with the Hilex bottles. Then we can invite him to come to church for communion this Sunday," Esther said changing the subject. "Maybe he'll come this time."

It was mid-morning when Esther and Henry arrived at Oscar's farm, just as he was heading out to plow the wheat stubble under for the year. He was half expecting to see Henry, but not Esther Holmvik. He got down from the tractor to talk to them.

"We brought you the Hilex bottles, Mr. Halvorson!" Henry shouted over the noise of the tractor as Oscar approached.

"Oh, eh, yah, t'ank you," Oscar said, grateful but feeling a little awkward about Esther bringing the bottles, too. "T'ank you both very much. Nice of you to come, Missus Holmvik. I wasn't expecting you today."

"Nice to see you too Oscar," Esther said. "We didn't intend to keep you from your work, but Henry said you needed these Hilex bottles. Whatever for, if you don't mind my asking?"

"Well, eh... that's, that iss, eh..."

"Oh, Gramma, I told you he wants them to carry water in," Henry interrupted.

"Yah, yah, the boy iss right. I'm eh, going to keep water in them. In the winter time. So I don't need to go to the pump so much."

"Oh, good idea," Esther said, her curiosity satisfied. "Thinking ahead I'd say, but a good idea. By the way, Oscar, we brought you a loaf of bread."

Oscar was always pleased to get a loaf of her wonderful bread, and he accepted it gratefully.

"It's communion Sunday this weekend," Esther added, "won't you come join us in church again? It's been a while, and we, I just thought it would be nice to see you there again."

Oscar looked at the ground and shuffled his feet, perhaps feeling a little uncomfortable about having deceived Esther and her grandson about the jugs. The wine was already "working" in a crock, safely hidden in Oscar's cellar.

"Ahh... sure t'ing," he said, "I guess I could do that. Communion, eh. Yah, well, it has been a while."

"Oh good," Esther said, "we'll see you there then."

Esther returned home but Henry wanted to watch Oscar plow for a while. After putting the loaf of bread in his kitchen, Oscar climbed up on *Gubbe* and headed off to plow, with Henry riding along, no longer resigned to the rock pile.

Sunday morning Oscar got up early. He'd bathed the night before, and now shaved and combed his hair before coffee. He put on his good bib overalls and dark suit coat, always feeling a little uncomfortable whenever he got that dressed up. He drove to church and arrived early, but Esther and Henry were already there.

Esther, of course, had to open up and get the communion things ready for Reverend Ellerby. First she polished the silver chalice and silver tray that held the bread. Then she cut the loaf of her bread into little cubes, placed them on the tray and covered them. Reverend Ellerby always brought the wine in a special silver pitcher, which he poured into the cup himself. After everything was prepared for communion, Esther liked to practice a while at the organ.

Oscar arrived to the strains of music floating out the open front door of Eidsvold Church and on up to heaven. He enjoyed music, but all he knew was a few old folk tunes from the old country that he'd learned as a boy. He was only slightly acquainted with church music but was an attentive listener. Watching and hearing someone actually make music on any instrument always fascinated Oscar, and Esther's playing was no exception. He loved the sound of it.

During the service, Oscar did not sit in the back, but took a place with Henry in the front row. He was uncomfortable there, right in plain view of everyone, but he determined this time to not let what others might think bother him. When she was not playing the organ, Esther stepped down to join Oscar and her grandson in the pew, a move not missed by a single pair of eyes in the congregation. It confirmed a lot of the speculation already going on at ladies aide meetings and over coffee around Aasness Township. Opinions varied, of course, but people thrived on their perceptions and a late-life romance was pretty interesting, if somewhat controversial.

A few bitter old maids thought it indiscreet the way that widow woman seemed to carry on with that bachelor, and in church yet, while those more charitable were making guesses as to if and when the two would ever tie the knot. Most farmers had become indifferent, unless their wives influenced their opinions. Those who knew them thought they were "a team that would pull well in the harness." Even the men noticed that Oscar seemed different and was paying more attention to Esther than common business interests required. They thought she was a pretty nice catch too, and Oscar could be an uncommonly lucky bachelor.

Reverend Ellerby's sermon was of the "boilerplate" variety, and the congregation anxiously awaited the salvation Holy Communion would bring long before the good Reverend had summarized his message.

Throughout the service, Oscar shifted uncomfortably. When it came time to go forward and receive the bread and wine, he was hesitant. Oscar rarely attended church and had not taken communion since his mother was living. After such a long time, it evoked memories of her and old family feelings. Now as he took the bread and wine, these old issues seemed to take on a new perspective and Oscar felt a very subtle, if gracious, sense of release. It was a sense of freedom that brought a slight apprehension of the unknown, but it felt good. And he felt he now knew what he should do about Esther.

Reverend Ellerby seemed genuine when he said he was happy to see Oscar in church as they shook hands while going out the door. Then the Reverend leaned forward and said that he needed to talk to Oscar sometime soon. Esther overheard, and realizing the community interest in their relationship, was curious why the Reverend wanted to see Oscar, and asked him about it after church.

"I don't know Missus Holmvik," Oscar said, "I'm sure it iss nothing much."

"Well, before today I wasn't sure Reverend Ellerby even knew who you were, and now he wants to meet with you. I wonder why..."

Oscar remained demure over the incident, but Esther had the feeling he knew something. She hoped it didn't concern silly gossip about her relationship with Oscar, but perhaps she needed to have a word with the pastor herself. For the time being, she determined to be patient.

After church, Oscar gave Esther and Henry a lift the short distance home and along the way they stopped to admire the flax. The beautiful blue field had long since transformed now, dried up and looking more like a crop waiting to be harvested. The little blue flowers had turned to a dark tan field of seed bolls rustling in the breeze, turning more ripe with each passing day. Oscar took some time to check the condition of the crop, with Henry at his elbow asking his perpetual questions. He plucked some of the pods and ground them open in his palm, carefully examining the dark brown, almond-shaped little seeds. He repeated this in several different areas of the field and everything looked fine. It would be over a month before he'd harvest the flax, but it still looked like an excellent crop. Oscar was pleased with himself about the whole flax project and the promise it held. Before the flax could be harvested however, he would need to bring in his corn.

About half of Oscar's corn would be cut and chopped into fodder for his cattle, and later he'd pick the ears of the other half to keep in his corncrib. A lot of work for one man. Just maybe, Oscar thought, Esther's grandson could be of some real help when it was time to pick the corn, but, of course, the boy was starting school.

Esther called to them as they stood in the flax, inviting Oscar to join them for coffee and a little something to eat. He accepted.

20

The corn harvest went well. Esther even talked to Miss Engebretson so Henry could get out of school a couple days to help Oscar. Best of all for Henry, Oscar taught him to drive *Gubbe*. He was soon 10 years old after all.

Henry was afraid of driving the tractor at first, but Oscar patiently went over each step as often as necessary, letting the boy practice driving in a stubble field to get the feel. He learned the press of the pedals and how the iron beast responded to the way various levers were set. Of course, he only drove *Gubbe* in the field, in low gear, and with no fancy maneuvers.

Henry moved the Massey-Harris ahead a few yards at a time, pulling the wagon along the rows of corn while Oscar picked and tossed the ears into the wagon box. Oscar was very fast at picking corn by hand, but it saved him a lot of time and effort to have Henry move the tractor so he could keep picking. They worked well together and made fast progress.

For his part, Henry was pleased to no longer be sitting on rock piles watching the real world pass him by. It was grand sitting high on the tractor seat and doing what real farmers do. He might have bragged about it at school, but it seemed most boys his age were learning to drive a tractor and help in the field so they talked authoritatively about which brand was the best tractor.

Oscar and Henry grew closer while working together during the corn harvest. Oscar learned patience and tolerance and Henry learned about responsibility and how to drive a tractor. It was over all too soon, and Henry was back in the classroom before he knew it. Oscar, though, had one more crop to harvest.

It was the third week of October and the flax was ready. Time to bring in the cash crop and pay E.A. Stordal his due. Everything had gone perfectly for Oscar this year. His farm had escaped serious damage from the summer hail, he had just bottled the best vintage of wine he'd ever produced, flax prices were strong and it was time to harvest what looked like a bumper crop. Then there was Esther. Not being romantic, Oscar didn't use the word "love," but he had come to accept the new emotion, whatever it was. He'd become comfortable with the feeling though still lacked the means to express it. Once he had the flax sold and the check in old Stordal's hand, everything would be stable again and he would work up the courage to tell Esther what was on his heart. Oscar believed she felt the same way he did, and that gave him some confidence and a level of optimism he'd never felt before.

The eastern sky was flush with the promise of the new day by the time Oscar finished his milking. He headed directly to the machine shed to hitch *Gubbe* to the reaper and head over to his field of flax. He'd already made arrangements for Hoffmeier to thresh his flax later that week, and given him the screens. Now the crisp, clear autumn air in his face made Oscar all the more eager to get at the day's work. He pulled open the creaky door on the machine shed, braced it with the fence post and went inside.

The reaper was in position. All he had to do was back *Gubbe* up to it and connect the hitch. Going directly to the tractor, he set the choke and throttle, then turned on the switch. He went around to the front end of the machine, inserted the crank handle and gave it a few vigorous turns.

Maybe he'd set the choke too rich or maybe it was the cold morning. Maybe it was just *Gubbe* being stubborn again, but the powerful engine on the temperamental iron beast chose this day to kick back.

The backfire sounded like a gunshot inside the shed, unexpectedly loud in the morning peace. It was accompanied by a violent blow to his right forearm that spun him away from the crank.

Too stunned to move, Oscar stood confused as the noise resonated in his ears. Then came a deep, tingling ache that traveled from his forearm up through his elbow and into his shoulder, awakening him to a new level of consciousness. As the pain registered, he cradled his shattered forearm and stared bewildered at the starter crank now lying on floor, then backed away from the rebellious beast. The broken bones grated inside the sleeve of his mackinaw as he sat down on a cream can and beads of sweat broke out on his forehead even as he felt chilled.

Hektor came and whined sympathetically, putting a paw on Oscar's knee.

"I didn't say no bad words Hektor," Oscar said in voice so calm he didn't seem to recognize it. "I didn't say a t'ing."

"It happened to fast," he said to Hektor in honest amazement. "I didn't have time to even t'ink about it. Uffda, it does smart some now." Hektor was obviously concerned, knowing something was seriously wrong with his friend and frustrated by not being able to help. The dog could only whine in sympathy.

Oscar sat a while as the familiar reality re-entered his mind and he began to take account of his situation. His arm was going to need medical attention. He'd have to drive to town and see Doc Crowley. It was not going to be easy to drive the truck. Shifting would be the biggest problem. The machine shed seemed confining and he needed to breathe. Still carefully cradling his arm, Oscar got up and walked out into the still morning air and sat down on the tongue of the hay wagon.

The realization came to him that getting to the doctor was just the beginning of his problems. If simply driving his truck with a broken arm was going to be difficult, how could he possibly work his farm? How would he milk, feed or care for his cattle every day? Then there was the matter of harvesting his flax. There was no way he could cut, harvest, and deliver his cash crop with a broken arm, and Stordal wasn't likely to be very sympathetic.

The more Oscar thought about it, the more dear the consequences of this little mishap became. Until now, everything had been going so well. Throughout his life he'd done everything himself, including surviving the Depression years. He'd even figured out the last step needed to save his farm from E.A. Stordal by getting Esther Holmvik to let him work her land. He got credit for the seed from George Kruger and done all the work, survived the hail, got the separator screens, all while keeping the rest of his operation going. Everything he had done on his own, everything he had worked so hard for and achieved on his own, not just for this season but for his whole life. Now everything was about to slip through the fingers at the end of his broken right arm.

"Whatcha doin', Mr. Halvorson?" Henry didn't usually stop by on his way to school. The timely interruption drew Oscar out of his thoughts.

"Oh, ah, hallo d'er Henry. On your way to school d'en?" Oscar said slowly, in a distracted tone.

"Yeah, an' we got an arithmetic test. Boy I wish I could help ya t'day."

"A test, eh. Yah well, that sounds pretty important."

"Well, Miss Engebretson thinks so, but I don't know why I've gotta know all those number problems for anyway. I just wanna be a farmer, like you," Henry reasoned.

"Farmers have problems too, Henry," Oscar pointed out. His voice was absolutely calm. "I t'ink I got one right now."

"What's that?"

"I just busted my arm Henry, an..."

"You did what?"

"My arm... I went an' busted my arm," Oscar repeated quietly.

"Wow! Really? Mr. Halvorson! You broke your arm? Let me see!"

"No, Henry. I just know..."

"Does it hurt? Is it bleeding?" The boy and his questions again.

"Yah, it hurts some," Oscar said patiently.

"How did you do it?"

"Listen to me, Henry, listen carefully," he said slowly, ignoring the questions, "I t'ink I maybe do need you to help me today."

"Sure, sure, Mr. Halvorson. What can I do?" Maybe it was the odd tone in the old farmer's voice, but Henry realized this was serious.

"I need you to run an' ask your gramma... if she could come here. Can you do that?"

Henry turned immediately to leave.

"Wait Henry," Oscar called him back. "Don't tell her I busted my arm, okay?" he instructed, not wanting to upset her, "You just tell her... tell her I need her."

Henry turned again and left at a dead run. Oscar could only wait, trying to ignore the deep, nagging ache in his arm. He tried to flex his hand, carefully opening and closing it, but it was no good. He cursed the pain, evoking a sympathetic whine from Hektor. Wrapping himself in a relentless swirl of second guesses, Oscar gradually became mired in depression.

How could he pay off Stordal? Even if he could hire someone to harvest his flax for him, he didn't have the money to pay them as well. He was out of ideas to save his farm, and now time was running out. Oscar tried to visualize the likely possibility of a future other than farming. There was nowhere else to turn, nothing else he knew how to do. The hard times and difficult struggles he'd faced before had never been easy, but that was just the way things were in his life. He'd always managed. Just as every success had been his alone, he now would have to accept his failure alone as well. This time he would lose it all, and he did not want to go through it alone. This was too big and he had no right to wish someone would share in his failure. He felt he was coming apart and there was nothing he could do, there was no one to hold the pieces of him together. Sitting on the wagon tongue in the brisk morning sunshine, Oscar felt he understood Bergstrom a good deal better now.

"Gramma! Gramma!" Esther heard her grandson calling long before he reached the farmyard. What now, she thought. He should be in school by now. What's he doing back home again? She met him at the back door, drying her hands on her outer apron.

"What brings you home again so soon?" she asked, but Henry wasn't listening. He was trying to talk but was completely out of breath for anything to come out.

"Settle down child. Come in the house and tell me what's the matter." Esther took Henry inside and gave him a dipper of water. The boy didn't want it, but she made him try to drink to slow him down.

"Gramma..." he wheezed, "Mr. Halvorson... his arm... hurt his... his arm," he managed to get out between breaths.

"Take another drink Henry and slow down. Tell me about Mr. Halvorson again," she said.

"He's hurt, Gramma."

"What? How?"

"I'm tryin' to tell ya... He hurt his arm, ...said it was busted."

"He, he broke his arm? Are you sure?" Esther's voice was intensely focused now.

"He said so," Henry said taking another drink. "He didn't show me, he just said it was broke an' that...he needed you to come. You better come right away!"

"Of course. Let me get a few things and we'll be on our way." Esther went off to get some rags she could use for bandages.

"Did you see any blood Henry?"

"No, he didn't show me his arm, he was just holding it real careful."

"Did he tell you anything else?"

"He just said to say 'he needed you, Gramma, and I came runnin' to get you as fast as I could."

"You must have run fast to get here so quickly, too, Henry," Esther said. "You did a real good job of that. I'm just glad you didn't fall and get hurt so I'd have two of you to help."

Henry set out running again, but Esther called him back.

"Wait, wait Henry. I can't run like you. Your gramma isn't young anymore. Just hold up and we'll get there soon as we can," she pleaded. "No sense in us getting there so out of breath we can't do anything, anyway."

But Henry was relentless, forcing Esther to move as fast as she could despite her protests. Along the way she kept asking her grandson questions about Oscar's condition, how it happened, was he doing anything for his arm, where he was when it happened, and how he looked when Henry saw him. She hoped to slow down the boy, as much as learn about Oscar's condition.

Like all farm women, Esther knew all about the risk of accidents and injuries from working around machinery or animals like horses or bulls. Missing fingers, amputated hands or arms, broken bones, crushed ribs, all were simply hazards of the occupation. Injuries were a serious problem when they happened to any farmer. She understood as well that a major injury happening to a reclusive, fiercely independent bachelor farmer could have even more serious consequences. In these critical times, if Oscar couldn't work his farm now, he was likely to lose it. She remembered Theodore Bergstrom and realized more than Oscar's livelihood could be at stake.

The Halvorson farmyard seemed unusually quiet when Esther and Henry arrived. Henry led his grandmother directly to the hay wagon tongue where he had left Oscar, but he wasn't there. They went inside his machine shed and called for him, but he wasn't inside.

"Henry, go check the barn," Esther said, "I'll see if he's in the house."

She noted the door to the house was open and she went inside.

"Hello! Hello, Oscar! Are you home?" There was no reply. She looked in the kitchen and called his name again. He was not in the house.

"He's not in the barn, Gramma," Henry called.

They walked around the out buildings calling his name, but there was no answer. After checking the machine shed once more, they went back to his house and waited a while by the door. Esther began to worry.

"Where could he have gone, Gramma?"

"I don't know, Henry. Not far I think, since he's hurt, but I don't know where. We'll wait a while and see if he comes back, then look some more." They went inside the house and sat in the kitchen.

They didn't wait long before they heard Hektor barking outside. Esther went to the door and there sat Oscar on the steps. His back was to her and she could tell something wasn't right.

"Oscar, for goodness sake where have you been?" she said coming out the door and down the steps. "You've had me worried sick. Henry says you've been hurt." She knelt beside Oscar. His face was pale and damp with perspiration in spite of the cool autumn air. Holding his arm close to his body, he seemed older and more vulnerable than his normal, robust self.

"Esther..." he said. "Esther, I need you... to help me." He spoke slowly, his voice detached from the situation. He'd never called her by her first name before.

"Oh Oscar, what's happened here?" she said kneeling beside him and reaching for his arm. "Let me have a look."

"I'll be all right. *Gubbe* just... decided to kick back today. Happened so quick I didn't have time to t'ink about getting out of the way."

Oscar let her gently remove his mackinaw, and he clenched his teeth as she carefully pulled up the shirtsleeve from his injured arm. There was swelling and an unnatural turn above the wrist, which told her all she needed to know.

"I just... don't know what I did wrong," he continued as she looked for signs of blood. "Guess I always knew it could happen sometime but I sure didn't expect it. Not now..."

"Oscar, we need to get you to the doctor," Esther said quietly. The tone of her voice seemed to bring him back to reality.

"Yah, I know that," he said, sounding more like himself again. "I t'ink you got to drive me."

"I don't know how to drive, we'll have to..."

"You can drive. I will shift the gears. You'll see."

"But Oscar, I don't think I can..." she protested.

"Esther," he interrupted, "I need you to help me now." He looked into her eyes. "You can do this."

She had Henry bring some wood slats from the kindling box in the kitchen. With her grandson's help and the rags she brought, Esther splinted Oscar's arm as well as she could, then used a dishtowel for a sling to support it.

"Oscar, where were you? We looked all around the farm for you but you were gone. You had us worried. Where did you go?"

"Oh, I was down to the pond," Oscar said, sounding vague and distant again. "I was just, uh... let's go get the truck."

Esther frowned a questioning look and shook her head but let it pass, as they needed to be on their way.

When Esther was satisfied they had done all they could to hold the arm together, she told Henry to go on to school. He protested of course, wanting to go along and see that Oscar was taken care of, but Esther insisted. She assured her grandson that he had done well and the doctor would take over from now on, and that his place was in school. Henry headed off reluctantly but got no further than the rock pile beside the stubble of Oscar's wheat field, where Hektor joined him.

Esther got behind the wheel of the truck and Oscar got into the passenger side for the first time in his life. After starting the truck, Oscar put it in gear, held onto his arm and told Esther to let the clutch out. They lurched out of the shed and after several stalls, headed out the driveway and down the road toward town.

Esther faced up to the challenge of driving, though it was hardly a comfortable trip for Oscar. Her apprehension at being behind the wheel was matched only by concern for her passenger's welfare, though her driving didn't suggest it. Had she been more attentive to the task of driving, it might have made for a less excruciating experience for both of them, but Esther was in a hurry to get Oscar to the hospital.

She was unacquainted with judging the appropriate speed for going into curves or over rough spots in the road. The trip was punctuated by a couple brief tours of Aasness Township ditches (fortunately dry this time of year), numerous sharp jolts over unnoticed ruts or potholes, and nonstop side-to-side swaying from over-steering. Oscar remained stoically silent behind clenched teeth, though his pale face beaded with sweat.

It was about a 10-mile drive into Foster Falls and Esther ultimately got them there and to the hospital, albeit neither safely nor soundly. Oscar never criticized her driving once, in fact never spoke a word the entire trip, but was extraordinarily grateful to get there. They arrived not a moment too soon, as the tension that registered on his face was not entirely from the pain of his broken arm. In later years he'd confess to folks that it was Esther Holmvik who brought him closer to the Lord, and referred to this trip to note the specific event.

For her part, Esther later found the experience "exhilarating." She'd always felt "machinery was better left to men," but found driving offered a liberating sense of freedom she had never known before. Driving, she decided, was something she'd like to try more often, once they'd survived this trip.

They checked in at the emergency desk in the hospital and Doc Crowley came to see Oscar. Doc Crowley was a short man with salt and pepper hair, a thin, mustached face, and thick glasses in round, tortoiseshell frames. He greeted them in his conventional white lab coat with his stethoscope hanging from his neck like an exclamation point accentuating his occupation.

The doctor complimented Esther on her good job of splinting the arm. After removing the shirt and cutting away the long underwear sleeve, he took a close look at Oscar's swollen and discolored crooked forearm and clicked his tongue.

"That's a pretty nasty break all right. Both radius and ulna. How did it happen?" he inquired.

"Tractor backfired," Oscar stated flatly.

"I might have guessed. This sort of thing happens more than you'd think, particularly after the weather gets colder.

"I'll set it Mr. Holmvik, but then I'm going to have to put it in a cast and immobilize it for a while."

"Halvorson," Oscar replied. "My name iss Halvorson."

"I'm afraid it's going to be a little inconvenient for you, but I suppose harvest time is over now anyway." Oscar was withdrawn, and just looked away.

"We'll put him under ether while we set the bone," he said to Esther, "and then we'll put the cast on. The ether can make people sick when they come out of it, so I don't think he'll feel much like traveling or doing much else today. It's a severe fracture and he's gone into shock a little, so I'd like to keep Mr. Holmvik a while for observation, if that's okay," Doc Crowley said to Esther.

"It's Halvorson," she said. "This is Mr. Halvorson."

"Sorry Mrs. Halvorson. You can come to take him home tomorrow morning first thing, if that's okay."

"You want to keep him overnight?" Esther seemed surprised. "What's wrong? Is he all right?"

"Nothing is wrong. It's just that he may be in shock and we just want to watch him a while, Mrs. Halvorson."

"Holmvik."

"Yes, of course. He's fine. Just routine observation. He's not likely to feel very well afterward anyway, so we'd just like to keep him comfortable after we set the arm and let him rest."

Esther had to drive home alone. Along the way, she managed to make a few stops at neighboring farms near Eidsvold Church and received some much appreciated driving instruction, as well as help with a number of other matters.

The next morning, Esther arrived at the hospital to pick up a despondent Oscar. She seemed more upbeat and pleasant than usual, which only annoyed Oscar. She was talkative and he was reticent, wanting to retreat to his farm to mull over the bleak prospects of his farm and future.

As they drove with much better control and comfort, Esther spoke of everything from Henry's school progress to the weather, which was crisp and pleasant for a late October day. Oscar did his best to ignore her and remained mostly unresponsive. Couldn't she see what seemed so obvious to him? He was crippled. His arm hung useless in a plaster cast with a big white sling. He couldn't care for his cattle, let alone harvest his flax. He couldn't farm and would probably lose it now to Stordal anyway. Didn't she realize that? All these years he had made it work. His own efforts, his own planning, his own sweat and blood. He'd done it all alone and now he was alone in his misery.

They were approaching the intersection in the road to turn toward his farm but Esther turned the wrong way, towards her farm.

"What are you doing? I need to get home to my place."

"We'll get there Oscar," Esther said in her still cheery voice "I just want you to see something first."

They were headed toward Eidsvold Church and Esther's farm where his flax stood waiting to be harvested. Oscar noted the activity well before they stopped on the road beside the field of flax.

The field had already been cut and bundled, and Hoffmeier's threshing machine was all set up, with him in command of the ongoing operation. Farmers from the area, men Oscar recognized from church, were busy around the field hauling bundles to the separator. Other men pitched them into the hopper of the great churning machine. Great clouds of dust and chaff spewed from the end of the thresher and flax poured from the chute into a waiting grain wagon.

Oscar stared at the operation in disbelief.

"What's going on...? I don't... I can't afford to pay..." he stammered, shaking his head.

"Hush," Esther said sternly. "Of course you can't pay for this Oscar. It's called grace, and it comes from the Lord by way of the heart."

Hoffmeier broke away from the operation and approached Oscar.

"We're saving the straw too Oscar," Hoffmeier said. "Thorvald said there's a good market for it for linen this year and he knows where you can sell it. A little extra profit shouldn't hurt, I guess."

Oscar nodded, unable speak.

"Your cows were milked and fed this morning, Oscar, and they will be taken care of this afternoon, too," Esther said. "The Torgerson boy is going to be helping with the milking this week, and after that I think I can lend you a hand. We'll see that you get through this, Oscar. We'll get through this together."

He nodded again and managed to choke out an inhaled "yah" as he watched the field of activity with tears streaming down his cheeks. Oscar realized these men were more than busy with farms of their own to tend. Without their help he'd have lost his. He had been concerned that Esther wouldn't be interested in him without his farm. It dawned on Oscar that now she and the others were working, not so much to save Oscar's farm, as to save him. The unfamiliar taste of humility was both rich and bittersweet.

"*Mange takk* Esther," he finally said quietly, "*mange tusen takk*," (Many thousand thanks), and with his good hand he reached for hers.

21

Oscar did away with the sling after wearing it the first week because it was a nuisance and he couldn't tolerate being "all wrapped up". He learned to work with the restriction of the cast but it continued to be an annoyance.

A few weeks later, the cast made shifting gears somewhat awkward as he drove into Foster Falls. Oscar didn't mind because today was special. It wasn't just the fresh, crisp air and autumn glow of the sun. His cattle were all milked and fed, his granary was full, and with the help of friends and neighbors his flax was harvested and delivered. All over the country things were improving and it looked like President Roosevelt was gradually bringing the nation out of the long Depression. Driving into town today was different than he'd expected. Today had been a date Oscar dreaded for a long time and had even come to accept with a dark resignation. Instead, his spirit was as bright as the morning sun at his back.

All the color had dropped from the trees and the crisp clear October air played with the bright leaves, blustering them across yards and down the gutters of streets in Foster Falls. It was the last day of the month and the earth had brought forth its bounty to compensate for the past year's labors. Payment in full.

His truck rolled down the main street of town and he pulled into one of the diagonal parking spaces. Oscar shut off the engine and sighed. Made it this far, he thought, the moment has come. He got out and walked down the block to the entrance of the bank.

"I come to see Mr. Stordal," he said.

"May I tell him who's calling?" the receptionist asked.

"Yah, it iss me, Halvorson," Oscar said, removing his hat. He couldn't understand why they never seemed to remember him.

"Just a moment Mr. Halvorson, I'll tell him you're here," she said and went back to his office.

Oscar shifted his weight from one leg to the other and looked at the pictures on the wall as he waited, uncomfortable in the business atmosphere of the bank. Fortunately he didn't have to wait long.

"Mr. Stordal will see you now," the receptionist said as she returned, and she led him back to the dark-stained door to E.A.'s office.

"Mornin', Stordal," Oscar said flatly, his expression not betraying a single thought or emotion. He'd intentionally dropped the formal "Mr." before the name. Stordal looked up over his wire rims from the file of papers on his desk.

Stordal put down his cigar and smiled his golden smile. "Why, good morning, Halvorson, what a pleasant surprise," he replied with polished professionalism. "What brings you in today?"

"Yah well, I t'ink you know what that iss," Oscar said, clutching his hat with both hands and feeling out of place.

"I trust you have brought me good news then?" Stordal raised an anticipating eyebrow and smiled again.

Oscar dug into the breast pocket of his old mackinaw, pulled out a folded business envelope and handed it directly to Stordal. He had mentally rehearsed all kinds of things to say to Stordal at this moment, some appropriate, some not. Now that the time had come, he could find nothing to say at all. The moment, and his satisfaction with it, spoke for itself and it was enough.

E.A. took the envelope and removed its contents while indicating that Oscar should take a seat. Oscar remained standing. The papers were a copy of the loan contract, terms and all, bearing both of their signatures and dated several years ago. The terms stated that the collateral for the loan was Oscar Halvorson's farm and that full payment was due on this very day, the last day of October. Stordal looked the papers over briefly, knowing full well what they said, then looked up at Oscar, still smiling expectantly. Oscar's good hand dug into the front pocket of his bib overalls again and found nothing. Just for an instant his expression of calm demeanor faltered as he quickly patted himself down looking for something. He quickly located another folded envelope in a shirt pocket inside his overalls and produced it. From the envelope Oscar pulled out a Farmers Co-op Grain Elevator check made out directly to the bank for the exact amount of the loan, including interest, and handed it over to Stordal. This time, the smile was on Oscar's face.

E.A. accepted the check and examined it, then examined the loan papers, comparing the amount and numbers, which was unnecessary since he knew full well what every word, every condition and what the exact amount was. He looked up at Oscar, then pulled a file containing his copy of the documents from a tray on his desk. After opening the file, E.A. took a rubber stamp from his drawer and stamped both copies of the loan contract "paid". He signed both copies of the loan agreement and gave Oscar his copy, placed the check with his copy in a file folder and put it in his out basket. That was it.

Stordal rose from his chair and offered Oscar his hand. For a moment, Oscar looked at it and hesitated, remembering the last time they'd shaken hands. His right limb being in a cast, Oscar reached out his left hand to the banker. It was only then that Stordal noticed the cast extending from the right sleeve of Oscar's mackinaw, and the awkward moment forced him to present his other hand. As their hands clasped, Oscar allowed himself the momentary satisfaction of giving the banker's soft, weak hand a little squeeze, knowing he could easily crush it. His grip was more than what would suggest earnest sincerity, and was meant to convey a change had taken place in their relationship. The banker's eyes grew large and Oscar let go abruptly.

Stordal took his hand back and rubbed it, then smiling at Oscar said, "Guess it's a good thing I didn't shake your right hand. How'd you break it?"

"Arm wrasslin' wit' my tractor," Oscar replied, "just part of farmin'."

Stordal smiled again. "You know, I've been keeping an eye on you Halvorson, your crops and all. You're a good farmer, Halvorson, I knew you were going to make it all along."

"Guess you knew mor'n me d'en," Oscar replied flatly.

"Oh, come now, don't be so modest. That was a smart move, growing flax," Stordal continued. "It was a bit of a gamble but it paid off. You did it. It was the flax crop that pulled you through all right. I knew it would though," he said.

"Yah, well, it wasn't the flax that pulled me out, Stordal," Oscar said, "it wasn't that at all. It was... eh... something else. I don't t'ink you'd..."

Stordal furrowed his brow curiously but Oscar knew he couldn't explain grace to the man, could never make him understand.

"Well, whatever you did, you did it right, Halvorson," Stordal said with assurance. "Tell me, though, what made you decide to grow flax? Hardly anybody grows flax around here."

"Yah, well, some have tried it," Oscar replied. Stordal didn't push it further.

"Just remember, if there's ever anything we can do for you here at the bank, if you ever need a loan again, I'd be happy to help you out."

Oscar nodded. "D'at iss good to know, Stordal," he said quietly. He dreaded the thought but realized that with farming, you put your trust in the Lord but sometimes have to make deals with the devil.

"No, I got to be going though," Oscar said turning for the door.

"Have a good day, Halvorson, a pleasure doing business with you," Stordal said to his back.

Before he got to the door, Oscar stopped and turned around.

"Oh, I almost forgot somet'ing," he said returning to Stordal's desk. Once again he dug around in his pockets and eventually pulled out another folded piece of paper, all smudged and frayed from being in his overalls for a long time. He unfolded the paper over the ledgers spread on Stordal's desk and something delicate and golden plunked out.

"I t'ink you should have d'is Stordal," Oscar said.

Stordal looked down at the locket on his desk and his face went suddenly pale as he immediately recognized the necklace. His smile was gone and his professional demeanor suddenly dropped like a veil and he sank back down to his chair.

"Where did you get this, Halvorson?" he asked in a hushed tone.

"That don't matter anymore, does it," Oscar stated. "I just t'ink more than anyone else, you should have it."

E.A. picked up the delicate locket letting the chain dangle through his fingers. He seemed almost afraid to open it, but he did. Oscar watched the man's countenance soften and his chin began to quiver slightly. His eyes blinked rapidly as he stared at the slightly charred pictures of the pretty young woman and handsome young man looking back at him from the locket. A single seed of flax fell out onto his desk.

As he watched Stordal's reaction, he had that feeling again that he was intruding on a private place where he didn't belong, and he turned toward the door to leave. Before he could go, Stordal spoke again.

"I loved her first, Halvorson, you know that don't you?" he said softly.

"Yah," Oscar inhaled, "I figured d'at. So d'at iss why I t'ought you should have the locket," and he walked out the door.

22

The loud, urgent banging at the kitchen door startled Oscar so much he almost dropped the kettle. He'd finished his chores early as a mid-November storm was brewing and was stoking up the kitchen stove to boil up some potatoes for supper. "What brings someone here in d'is weather?" he thought.

"Have you got Henry here?" Esther blurted out as soon as he opened the door. Anxiety showed in the strain and pitch of her voice, and she was out of breath from the fast pace of her walk. Oscar took her arm and pulled her in before taking a quick look outside at the weather before closing the door. It was snowing harder now and the wind had picked up, already starting little drifts in sheltered places. It was the start of a full-blown, early winter storm.

"No, Esther, I ain't seen Henry at all today," Oscar answered, quickly sensing her concern with this weather. "Didn't he have school today?"

"Yah," Esther said, pacing about Oscar's kitchen, "but I thought he might have stopped at your place on the way home. He never goes to anyone else's place without asking, and his friend, the Mueller boy, has been sick," she explained. "He should have been home over two hours ago, even if he dawdled along the way somewhere. It doesn't take him that long. I've been waiting and hoping he'd come home but he hasn't. I've been watching the weather and I think this storm is going to be a big one. When it started to snow I..."

Esther was getting more agitated as she spoke and Oscar could hear the strain in her voice. Glancing out the window at the gathering snow and fading daylight, Oscar couldn't blame her for being concerned.

"Oh Oscar," she said, "Henry knows his way here but he doesn't understand about blizzards out here. He doesn't realize how easy it is to get turned around in a white out."

"Yah," Oscar agreed, "but I t'ink he'd have made it here from the school before the weather got so bad. At least if he could have."

Esther looked up at Oscar as he stood over her, and her pretty eyes grew larger.

"What do you mean? Do you think something might have happened to him? What are you saying?" she asked with a panicky edge in her voice.

"I don't know, Esther. Calm down. I don't mean somet'ing did happen; maybe he just stayed after school or stopped to play. You know how the boy iss. And even if he got turned around, he probably iss gone over to one of the neighbors. I don't t'ink we should get too worried for him just yet."

His attempt to reassure her wasn't working.

"I just came from my place, Oscar, and it wasn't easy going. Every minute the weather is getting worse and now it's getting dark soon too. I've been praying the whole way as I walked. Oh, if anything happened to Henry I just don't know what I'd do. Isn't there anything we can do?" It was a desperate plea.

"Well, I'll go look for the boy along the way he goes to school," Oscar said, "That much I can do. If I don't find him, I'll stop an' check at the neighbors." Oscar didn't like going out with a winter storm coming on. It was common knowledge that people died getting lost in winter storms. A blizzard was a deadly force of nature to be reckoned with. But he couldn't bear the thought of the boy out in it alone, and he could see how it affected Esther. He went to get his heavy wool mackinaw, mitts, cap, and scarf.

"I'll come too," Esther said. "We can cover more area that way."

"No, Esther," he replied, putting a reassuring hand on her shoulder, "I t'ink you should stay here. There should be someone here if he shows up. What if he comes home to your place?"

"I already thought of that. I left a note on the door saying I'd be here with you and he should stay home and wait there," Esther said.

"That's good," Oscar affirmed, pulling on his huge 5 buckle overshoes. He tucked in his overall legs and buckled the boots to the top. It wasn't an easy task with his right arm still in a cast. At least he had rid himself of that "damn sling" weeks ago.

"I'll see what I can fix to eat so you've got a hot meal when you get back Oscar," she said. "I'll go crazy if I just sit here waiting."

Oscar said he had been starting to prepare something for supper and a good hot meal when he returned would be nice, along with some fresh coffee. He quickly told her where she could find the necessary things. It would probably take him a couple hours to search his land and he told her to be patient until he returned.

With that, Oscar worked his mackinaw on over his cast and wrapped a scarf around his neck against the weather. He took a few matches and lit a kerosene lantern that hung by the door. Hektor knew something was up and stood alert and waiting beside the door. Before they left, Esther took Oscar's hand and touched his face.

"God bless you Oscar," she said, her voice thick with emotion. "Be careful out there." Oscar nodded, then man and dog headed out into the gathering stormy dusk together. Esther closed the door behind them, went to the kitchen table and sank into a chair before bowing her head in a silent prayer.

Oscar pulled his collar up high as the wind blustered through the treetops around his farmyard. He headed past the barn and through a fence, then off over his pastureland toward the northeast, in the direction of the schoolhouse.

The snow was not deep yet but was gathering quickly and starting to form drifts, and the biting wind tugged at him like a pack of worrying hounds. Periodically, he bellowed Henry's name, but the wind carried the sound away. Oscar knew the wind was his real concern. Wind was a physical presence that touches without being touched. The wind could steal warmth and breath while blocking the senses of sight and sound.

Heading over a hill and into a wood, Oscar found some shelter from the wind in the trees, but the noise in the branches muffled his calls. He thought Henry might have taken shelter in trees somewhere, but this was close enough to the farmhouse that he should have found his way there while it was still light. Hektor scurried around sniffing at thickets of brush and moving on, always looking for some scent or sign. They continued on and soon were out of the patch of woods. Following a fence line, they watched for smaller footprints in the snow, or signs that someone might have been there recently. When they reached the corner post, they followed along another fence line heading straight north, still in the general direction of the school. That was the last known point of reference where Henry should have been that day.

After following the fence awhile, Oscar cut across the open field in an easterly direction. Hektor ranged out around him, nose to the ground, always searching. Knowing the lay of the land, Oscar headed towards another thick woods that he knew was to the south of the school.

Visibility was closing in and, between the blowing snow and it being nearly dark, he could see only about twenty to thirty yards in any direction. The wind blew his lantern out in the open field, but he continued by intuition until he reached the shelter of the trees. Oscar was thankful his feet had walked these fields for so many years that it seemed he could almost tell where he was by the feel of the earth beneath him. The going was tricky and difficult and anyone else would undoubtedly have been hopelessly lost. The lantern light was of little help to him now, but he reasoned it might make him more visible to Henry, and with the trees helping to block the wind he knelt to relight it.

Working their way through the woods and along another fence line, Oscar and Hektor eventually made it to the country schoolhouse. The building was closed and dark and the tire tracks of Miss Engebretson's departing car were nearly drifted over. After circling the schoolhouse looking for any sign of Henry, Oscar stood in the lee side of the building trying to think of where the boy might have gone when he left school. As he thought, he heard Hektor whining and barking over the wind near the south edge of the schoolyard. Maybe the old dog understood they were looking for Henry and had actually found some sign. Oscar headed over toward Hektor and, sure enough, there were small, child-size footprints, already half-filled with drifting snow. Time for following the tracks was running out, and he knew they'd have to move quickly.

"*Ja, Flink hund*, Hektor, (good, clever dog)," Oscar said patting and praising his friend. "*Nå søke ham*, (now seek him)," and they set off following the tracks directly south along a shelterbelt. Oscar periodically called Henry's name into the night.

He tried to reason which way the boy would have gone as they trudged along. It seemed that Henry had headed toward the pond southeast of his farmhouse where the grapes grew. It would be a short cut to Oscar's house for the boy, though out of the way to his grandmother's place. Henry must have had just enough daylight to see where he was going when he passed this way. They were soon past the thin row of trees and walking became easier with the wind behind Oscar's right shoulder, urging him along.

Hektor led Oscar along the fence line straight south to a corner post, then crossed through the fence and started up a hill over a plowed field.

The lantern blew out again when they reached the top but Hektor was on the boy's trail now, nose to the ground. The old dog continued in a roughly straight line until he came to an area of tall weeds and grass that Oscar knew skirted the woods on the north side of the pond. The footprints led into the trees, and once again in their shelter, he relit the lantern before moving on. It was a relief to have a little protection from the relentless wind but the snow was deeper and made walking slower and more difficult.

They climbed over a hill in the woods and Oscar reckoned by the terrain and even a familiar tree now and then that they were just over a mile east and south of his home. The pond and his vineyard were at the bottom of the hill and to the right. Hektor started descending through the trees, following tracks that were now just faint depressions in the snow.

Oscar called out at the top of his lungs again and listened carefully for a reply, but only heard the wind roaring through the treetops.

Eventually he heard a faint sound in the wind. It could have been a child's voice but he wasn't sure. They continued along, the footprints now following an old cow path Oscar recognized, and he called again. Waiting for the reply, he listened longer, straining to hear over the wind.

They approached the pond from behind the thick cover of the grape vines and followed the tracks through an opening. Hektor stopped at the shoreline and began barking and whining, causing a chill to run through Oscar's veins. This early in the winter the ice was not safe and the old dog sensed it. Oscar understood why he did not want to follow the tracks further. Blinking snowflakes from his eyes, he lifted the lantern trying to see through the gray-white blur.

The dim light, diffused by swirling snow, barely revealed the footprints leading out onto the pond. Oscar carefully ventured out a few steps and the ice hissed a warning. There was a dark spot on the white surface forty or fifty feet out. Between gusts, he could just make out a shape at the edge of the hole.

"Henry!" he called, but there was no reply. "Henry, hold on, I'm coming!"

He set down the lantern and tore off his heavy wool mackinaw, scarf and cap. Gingerly, Oscar started out onto the ice, but about twenty feet out he plunged through to his waist. The frigid murky water took his breath away, but he ignored the biting chill. He struggled to get on top of the ice to slide on his belly but it wouldn't support him, breaking through as soon as he put his weight on it. In desperation, Oscar mustered all his strength and focused on the figure out ahead of him. In frustration he pounded on the ice before him with both arms like a raging bull, and pain shot from the cast up through his broken right arm. Using only his left arm he continued smashing his way through the ice. He made progress but it was getting deeper. He was close now, but still out of reach of the boy. A small ice bridge a few feet across barred his way, and he was now chest deep in the numbing icy water. Pushing off the bottom with his feet, Oscar gave a lunge onto the ice shelf, which broke under his weight and he went under. He bobbed sputtering to the surface and struggled to regain his footing, looking around in a panic.

Suddenly a churning shape moved past him in the dark icy water, covering the last few feet to the figure clinging to the rim of the hole in the ice. Hektor clamped his jaws on the boy's coat collar, turned and towed the passive figure toward Oscar. By this time Oscar had regained his footing and, as the struggling dog approached, he seized the boy and moved toward shallow water. Clutching the boy close to him, he wallowed back through the path of broken ice.

On shore, he removed Henry's soaked, heavy coat and wrapped him in his own dry mackinaw. In the lantern light, he could see Henry's eyes were wide open in a fearful stare but not seeing. His skin was stiff, pale and waxy. Oscar's own mind was far beyond the pain in his right arm, and though he was shivering violently there was no time to think about being cold. He left the lantern and Henry's soaked coat, and gathering the boy close in his arms, he headed up the hill through the white out of the storm. Oscar squinted through freezing eyelashes into the blinding snow, concentrating to keep his eyes on Hektor as the faithful old dog led the way home.

"What could be taking so long?" Esther said to herself. She was struggling to control her anxiety, frequently going to the door and peering out into the swirling snowy night. After filling the wood boxes and making sure Oscar's furnace was well stoked, she placed kerosene lamps in all the windows in case Oscar needed help seeing the house in the darkness.

As Oscar had requested, she'd cooked potatoes and found a few other vegetables and made *lapskaus*, a stew for supper, and also made good batch of broth from the juices. Now all she needed was someone to feed it to.

The wood box for the kitchen stove was almost empty and she put on her coat to go out to a woodpile on the porch for an armload. She deposited the load in the kitchen wood box and was just going back for another armload of wood when she was startled to see a monstrous white bulk coming towards her out of the darkness.

"Who is that? Oscar? Is that you?"

Oscar was unrecognizable as he struggled up the steps. He was caked with ice and snow and staggering with a large, odd bundle. When she could see his figure more clearly, Esther dropped the load of wood and screamed.

23

"Oscar? Oh dear God...! Dear God...!" Esther cried, "You're frozen! What happened? Henry! Henry! Are you alive? Can you hear me?" Esther's eyes were wide and her voice rose to an unnatural pitch. She somehow realized she was on the edge of panic then suddenly, from deep within, found the hidden strength to act. She helped Oscar up the steps and through the door, where he collapsed on the floor with Henry in his arms.

Oscar was caked with ice. His hair was clumped into icicles and covered with snow and his blue eyes peered out desperately from under frosted brows. The color was gone from his face and his lips had a bluish cast. He probably would not have made it another fifty yards with the boy.

Esther pried the frozen bundle from Oscar's stiff arms and opened the heavy mackinaw.

"Oh Henry, we've got to get these wet clothes off of you." Immediately she began peeling wet and frozen clothing from his small, unconscious body. It wasn't easy, as the boy was beyond cooperating and the clothes were stiff with ice. Esther struggled valiantly to keep her panic under control.

While she focused her attention on Henry, Oscar struggled to get up but his muscles were too cold and stiff to give him the coordination to do it. His hands were numb and frozen in a position that made it impossible for him to do anything, and his speech was only incoherent sounds.

Esther stripped blankets from Oscar's bed and wrapped Henry in them, then laid him across kitchen chairs in front of the open oven door. She built up the fire and set a washtub on top of the stove and poured in water to heat. She found more blankets and placed them on the open oven door to warm.

By now Oscar was lying in a puddle of swampy-smelling melt water still struggling in vain to get out of his wet clothing. As heat from the open oven door reached him he began to shiver convulsively, and Esther thought that was a good sign. She turned her attention to him. This was no time for modesty she realized, and began pulling off Oscar's soaked clothing. As she pulled at his right shirtsleeve he winced in pain and she noticed the cast on his arm was broken.

"Sorry about your arm, Oscar, but I need to get these wet clothes off you."

When he was undressed, she wrapped a heated blanket around his shuddering naked body.

"Listen to me, Oscar. You've got to get warm. You've got to help me. I can't do this alone! Please help me!" she pleaded. "I need you, Oscar!"

After setting another kitchen chair next to the oven she practically dragged him across the floor and, with his minimal help, managed to wrestle him onto it. She lifted the washtub of warm water from the stove and put Oscar's feet into it, gradually adding more warm water from the stove reservoir and the teakettle.

Returning her attentions to Henry, she opened the blankets and checked his skin color and temperature. Still no significant change.

"Oh Lord, he looks dead. Don't let him be dead, Lord. He's so cold," Esther desperately prayed aloud. "Help me, Lord. Help me know what to do. Don't let him die. Don't let them die. I need them, Lord."

She scurried around the kitchen, alternating warm blankets and re-wrapping them again, then placing the other blankets in the oven to heat. Esther held the boy's deathly cold face in her hands and searched his eyes for a sign of life. There was no visual recognition, but neither was there the glazed look of death in them.

"Oh, come on, Henry," Esther pleaded, "You've got to come back to us. You're going to be okay. Can you hear me Henry? You're going to be okay."

Esther kept alternating Henry's blankets with those heating in the oven, and did the same for Oscar, who still sat shivering. When he seemed to be improving, she went to his bedroom and found a dry set of long woolen underwear and helped him into them. She was a continuous whirlwind of activity, stoking the fire, heating water, exchanging warm blankets, and tending to both the boy and the old farmer. In the midst of it all, she managed to pour some of the warm vegetable broth she'd made into Oscar, but Henry remained unconscious.

"I think you're doing better, Oscar," Esther said, and he nodded.

"*Yah, mange takk* (many thanks)," he managed to say through chattering teeth. "I was in a bad way d'ere. I t'ink you saved my life, Esther. I couldn't have done a t'ing for myself, sure iss a good t'ing you was here. How iss 'da boy doing?"

Esther was pleased to hear the tough old farmer communicating again, and felt confident that at least his immediate danger was past. Oscar was self-conscious about being in his underwear. She noticed he made efforts to keep himself covered with the blanket as he sipped the broth. It was a good indication that he would recover just fine, but Esther was concerned about the way he carefully cradled his broken right arm. Still, Henry's condition remained her greatest worry.

By the time the warm blankets were rotated again, the fire in the stove needed to be stoked up. The kitchen was getting quite warm, and Esther removed her sweater, folding and placing it under Henry's head.

Oscar suggested maybe a warm bath might revive the boy, and Esther added hot water to the tub. Though he still ached with chills and desperately wanted to sleep, Oscar managed to help her immerse the boy while she carefully supported his head. They kept Henry in the tub of warm water for at least an hour but he remained pale and unresponsive.

"You know," Oscar finally said, "I heard stories about the old country, that if someone was found frozen, people would lay close to d'em in bed... to warm d'em. Sometimes it would bring d'em back to life. It didn't always work, but..."

Esther was desperate to try anything. They lifted Henry from the tub, dried him and then carried him to Oscar's bed where they wrapped him in a heated blanket. Then Oscar and Esther lay down in bed, snuggled close under the covers on either side of the boy.

Esther lay awake praying aloud for God to spare her grandson's life and giving thanks that Oscar was going to be all right. Oscar listened along until exhausted; he slipped into a deep sleep. Esther, worried about her grandson, slept only fitfully. Outside the November storm raged on as the northwest wind howled around the farmhouse, sculpting snow into deep, graceful drifts. Neither the farmer nor the widow noticed, but sometime in the middle of the night Henry moved between them, and smiled.

It was early morning but still dark when Esther first became aware of the wind still clawing for a grip on the corners of the house. She had slept some, but only for brief moments. Now she was aware of Henry's warm body beside her. She touched his cheek and felt its flush glow in the darkness. Emotions welled up inside her and she resumed praying where she had left off, now giving thanks that her grandson would be all right.

Another awareness in the dark was of a steady, soft snoring sound from the other side of the bed. Esther realized she was in bed with a man who was not her husband, and not only that, she had undressed him. She smiled a little smile of embarrassment. What feed for the gossip mill that would make. She didn't care. She was warm and secure in bed with the two men in her life that meant the most to her at this time. She was not lonely.

Esther lingered awhile, absorbing the warmth and comfort, the happiness that everything had worked out so well. But she was not a woman to remain idle for long, and silently she slipped from the bed and went to the kitchen. What a mess. The place smelled of wet wool and pond water. After stoking up the fire, she found the coffee and got water heating, then found a mop and began cleaning things up and making herself familiar with Oscar's kitchen.

Oscar emerged from the bedroom fully dressed while she was cleaning up and began pulling on his wet overshoes, carefully favoring his right arm.

"Got to take care o' the cows," he said quietly.

"Yah," Esther inhaled. She knew that feeding and milking had to be done regardless of weather, even when the barn couldn't be seen through the snow.

"If you could bring some fresh milk back, I'll see if I can fix something for us to eat," Esther responded in similarly quiet tones.

He affirmed with a nod.

"Oscar," she said, "be careful." It was stated simply, with only vague sentiment, but it made him pause. She'd said it yesterday before he went into the storm then saved him from freezing to death last night. No one had ever been around to care about him since his own mother died. Oscar didn't respond. He wasn't even sure if or how he should, but it settled in his heart.

It was no idle concern on Esther's part. Everyone in that country had heard of men getting lost and freezing to death on the way to their barns in the whiteout of a blizzard. Some farmers strung ropes from the house to their barn to help them find the way. The shapes of familiar trees in Oscar's yard guided him to his barn, and his feet just seemed to know where to go.

Along the way he realized something was missing from the familiar trip. Hektor. He'd forgotten about his dog in his stupor after he struggled to carry the boy home through the storm last night. But Hektor often took shelter in the barn when he wasn't in the house with Oscar. Maybe that's where he was now.

Snow had drifted half way up the barn door and Oscar had to kick and scrape it away before he could let himself in. Once inside the barn it wasn't too bad. Out of the wind, the body heat from cattle kept it somewhat warmer than outside. After lighting a number of lanterns he set about milking his little dairy herd, setting aside a pail of milk to take to the house.

It was a slow task, working mostly with his left arm since using the right one for anything caused deep, aching pain. Even so, he put his broken arm to some use and noted it still worked, but it was too painful to be much help. After milking, Oscar climbed to the loft and pitched hay down to distribute to the cows, keeping watch for Hektor the whole time and calling his name periodically.

He kept it up until it was obvious Hektor just wasn't in the barn, and Oscar became concerned. He tried to reason that animals had an instinct for finding shelter from the elements, but this was different. The dog was old and arthritic, and after getting soaked in the pond last night, he'd be in no shape to survive exposed to this weather. Looking for him in this storm would be futile, even if he knew where to start. Oscar had a bad feeling about his old friend.

After making sure all the cows had water and fresh straw, he blew out the lanterns, took the pail of milk and headed back to the house through the blowing snow. Along the way he called to Hektor, but the dog's name was carried away on the wind.

"I found your flour and I've got a batch of bread dough rising, Oscar," Esther said by way of greeting. She had fresh hot coffee ready when he came in, stomping and shaking the snow from himself. "I wasn't sure you'd have yeast but I found some. Do you bake much?"

"Uh, no, I don't bake."

"You don't bake?" she said. "Why do you have yeast if you don't bake?"

"Oh uh, well, I... I might bake, sometime," Oscar said. She didn't need to know the yeast was for his wine. She didn't need to know that at all. Or did she?

The kitchen was made nice and tidy, and Oscar sat down at the table with a steaming cup of coffee in front of him.

"Here, I'll take that and make us some mush for breakfast," Esther said, taking the pail of milk from him. Oscar hated milk mush.

"Oh, let's have pancakes and sausage," he replied. "Don't you t'ink that would be better? I helped a neighbor butcher a pig last fall and he gave me some sausage."

It sounded wonderful to Esther, especially the sausage part. She and Henry didn't often get to eat meat. Oscar lifted a small window that had an egg case nailed on the outside providing a natural ice box and showed her where he kept the sausage. Soon the kitchen was filled with the heavenly smell of cooking sausage and pancakes. The aroma brought Henry out of the bedroom and his grandmother greeted him with hugs, kisses and damp eyes.

Oscar watched quietly as Esther showered her grandchild with affection. He felt similar emotion as he recalled the events of the pond and previous night. Her tenderness sent his thoughts back over the years to his own childhood and the last time he'd experienced such tenderness himself. Thoughts of his own mother emerged from his past as he remembered her soft, loving touch. She had been the closest thing to an angel he'd ever known, and now another loving angel was caring for another child in what had been his mother's kitchen. Not having had much of a childhood, the good memories Oscar did have were of his mother, her songs, the laughter they'd shared walking the fields together, and of course picking the grapes. The grapes. The wine! Esther needed to know. How would he tell her?

After a delicious breakfast they spent the day together, holed up from the storm as the snow grew deeper. Henry explained that he had stayed after school to get some help from Miss Engebretson with his arithmetic. He took a short cut across the pond on the way home in the storm. He remembered falling through the ice and not being able to climb out, but couldn't remember anything after that.

Esther told Henry how Mr. Halvorson and Hektor had gone to search for him and, finally rescued him from the pond after falling through themselves. She told him how Mr. Halvorson had carried him through the snowstorm, and how they finally made it to the house, covered in ice and snow. Then she told Henry how she had tried to warm him with blankets and a warm bath, and finally how they put him in bed between them to warm him. That was what finally brought him back to life, she said. That and God's grace, Esther said.

"I could a' died there in the pond, huh," Henry quietly remarked.

"Yah, you both could have," Esther told him. "It was a miracle you didn't"

It was a lot for the boy to take in, and he sat silently listening to the story of his rescue and their efforts to revive him. Esther was punching down the bread dough as she told Henry, and Oscar sat sipping coffee at the table. As she finished, Henry went to Oscar and threw his arms around the old farmer in a childish bear hug. Oscar, gently at first, patted the boy's back, then wrapped his arms around the child and held him close, feeling a strange, hard knot in his throat. Esther rubbed at her tears ineffectively with the back of her wrist. She used her apron to blot at them and ended up with four all over her face.

Oscar's broken cast was a problem and she knew the man was in a good deal of pain. There wasn't much she could do about it, but she found some old dishtowels and tightly wrapped the broken cast. Then she made a sling and told Oscar sternly that he'd just have to wear the "damn thing" for awhile. The doctor would have to look at it when the weather permitted travel again.

Esther helped Henry practice some arithmetic problems and they laughed and told stories to each other as the house filled with the scent of baking bread. Henry was quiet most of the day, but Esther put him to work churning butter for a while. Afterward he occupied himself looking at old farming magazines and drawing pictures of tractors and threshing machines working the fields. His young body was still recovering and he spent much of the day sleeping. Esther knew he needed to rest after his ordeal and encouraged his naps. But Oscar seemed withdrawn, often going to the frosty window to peer into the blowing snow; looking for something he couldn't see. Esther sensed he was troubled.

"It's Hektor," he said when she asked what was wrong. "He wassn't in 'da barn and I ain't seen him since last night."

"Do you think he'll be all right?" Esther said, knowing how much the dog meant to Oscar.

"I don't know. He iss getting pretty old," he answered, looking at the whiteout framed by the kitchen window.

"Esther, it was that dog that saved your Henry's life last night," Oscar said. "Both our lives. I fell t'rough the ice and couldn't reach him, but Hektor swam out an' dragged the boy close enough for me to grab him. After that, I walked behind him all the way home in the snow. He knew the way when I couldn't see. I should go out an' look for him, but in d'is weather, I just don't know..."

Esther understood his relationship with the dog and reached to embrace him. "Maybe he took shelter somewhere. He's probably hiding somewhere snug, just waiting out the storm. I hope your friend will be okay." Oscar realized to himself it was the first time they had embraced.

"Yah, me too," Oscar said, but he was skeptical of the chances. They stood together holding each other a long time, immersed in the feel of each other.

"Oscar," Esther said softly, "what are you thinking?"

He paused and they looked into each other.

"Esther, I... ," his statement faded into a kiss, cautious at first and somewhat awkward, yet tender and loving. Esther responded by taking Oscar's face in her hands to hold a longer kiss, one that suggested there was something more behind it. Their first kiss, more eloquent than words, expressed the mutual need in their hearts. They held each other close for a long while, simply enjoying the feel of the other.

"The bread is done," Esther said after a while. She felt flushed as she pushed away from Oscar and went to the oven. She removed the bread and set it aside to cool while reheating the coffee. When it was ready, she called Henry and Oscar to come have some. Oscar went to the cupboard and took out two juice glasses, then from a low corner cupboard pulled out a Hilex bottle with a rich, dark liquid inside.

"What's that?" Esther said when she saw him with the jug.

"Wine, Esther. I made it myself. Would you like some?"

"Oh, I don't know, I... well, I suppose. Why not?" Oscar poured her some, then poured a glass for himself.

"Yuck," Henry said, though he wasn't offered any.

Esther took a sip and a puzzled look came over her face. She took another sip and cocked her head, letting the sweet warmth fill her mouth before sliding down to warm her heart. There was something oddly familiar about the taste, but, how... She sat in quiet thought a moment, staring at the rich garnet color of the wine, glowing warm in the late afternoon light. Esther felt she had experienced this taste somewhere before. Oscar held his glass and watched her closely. One more little sip. The taste was extraordinary.

"You know... this tastes familiar to me... the wine," Esther eventually said. "It tastes like, well..." she sipped again.

"Yah," Oscar inhaled with a nod, then took a sip from his glass too, and looked at Esther again. Their eyes met, and she understood.

"How long have you been making the communion wine for church Oscar?"

"A long time. Since several pastors back," Oscar replied a bit cautiously, like he'd been caught doing something he shouldn't. "It was my mother who started doing it, and I... well, I guess I just kept doing it for her. It's a secret, where it comes from, that I make it. So maybe it's like it's a miracle or somet'ing."

"Yah," Esther said as the new revelation sank in, "it maybe is at that. I never would have guessed that you, well..."

"My mother taught me how to make wine when I was a boy," Oscar explained. "We started a little vineyard together down by the pond. She told me even Jesus made wine," he said a little defensively. "Do you like it Esther?"

She nodded. "Yah, I always have. It's really good."

He poured her a little more.

"*Skål*," he said, clinking her glass.

"Amen," she replied, and offered him a slice of fresh bread.

The storm outside was not letting up, and as evening drew near the intensity of the blizzard outside brought darkness earlier than usual. Lamps were lit before they ate their dinner of potatoes, salt cod, and fresh bread.

Sleeping arrangements would be different tonight. Still somewhat weak and tired, Henry had stretched himself out on the old sofa after dinner and was soon sound asleep. Oscar found a heavy old quilt that smelled a bit of mothballs and covered the boy for the night.

"I've been in these same clothes for the past couple days," Esther said. "There's hot water in the reservoir on the stove and I could heat more. Do you mind if I wash this outfit? I could wash some of your things too." Oscar was a little surprised but had no objections and rigged rope clothesline in the kitchen where things could dry by the stove overnight.

"Ahmm, Oscar, do you have anything I could wear while I'm washing these things?" That was a puzzle for him, but he checked his closet and offered a pair of overalls that were far too big for Esther's slender frame, a large flannel plaid shirt and a heavy pair of wool socks. It would have to do.

They hung a blanket over another rope strung across the kitchen so she had some privacy while she changed, and Oscar remained in the parlor room where Henry slept. He passed the time fiddling around with the battery-powered cathedral radio, trying to get some news or music, any sort of diversion, but the reception was poor and nothing stayed tuned in.

Esther soon had the clothes washed and hanging to dry. She used the wash water in the laundry tub to bathe in, and clean water to wash and rinse her long hair. When she asked if he had a hairbrush, Oscar searched a few drawers and brought her one that had belonged to his mother. He watched in fascination from the parlor as she sat at the kitchen table, wrapped in a towel, brushing the tangles from her hair. In the glow of the lamp, Esther looked radiantly feminine, beautiful in the way of women who know themselves and are comfortable with who they are.

Then it was Oscar's turn. He had to stoke up the fire in the stove again as the kitchen was cooling off in the drafty old farmhouse. There wasn't much water left and it was barely warm, but it was enough. He put on a clean union suit and overalls for modesty sake, then banked the fire in the furnace for the night.

"You can sleep in my old bedroom, Esther," he said, and gave her an extra quilt from his bed. Oscar had long ago taken over his parents' bedroom, which was bigger and had a view of the farmyard. For some reason, Esther had become quiet and a bit withdrawn, but Oscar figured she was just tired.

Outside the wind continued to moan around the corners of the house and the old building creaked and cracked with the cold, letting drafts in here and there that crept across the floors and down the walls.

There was nothing to do but go to bed and wait out the storm, so they retired to their separate rooms.

Oscar lay on his back staring at the ceiling, unable to sleep. He thought about Hektor and where his friend might be. He thought about his cattle but felt they were secure enough. He thought about his mother and he thought about Esther. Then he thought about Bergstrom. "Yah," he inhaled, "it iss getting late," he said quietly to himself.

A soft light appeared at his doorway, followed by the figure of Esther in his old flannel shirt. She stood framed in the opening a moment, then spoke.

"I'm cold, Oscar," she said softly, cautiously.

Oscar sat up and drew back the covers to get up, but she quickly came to his bed and sat down on the edge so he couldn't. She set her lamp on the nightstand. In its glow, he could see the flannel shirt was unbuttoned and she was naked beneath it. Oscar had never seen a naked breast before, and Esther's breasts were all creamy golden in the lamplight. She looked into his eyes, took his hand and placed it on her breast. It was softer than anything Oscar's hand had ever known, and he gasped a little in awe.

"I don't want to be cold anymore," Esther said.

Oscar lifted the bedcovers and moved over to make room for her and she crawled into bed with him. They pulled the flannel sheets and heavy quilts over themselves and she snuggled close to him. Oscar didn't know what to do, so he kissed her. Esther responded with another kiss, a long passionate one. He caressed her breast marveling again at its softness, and soon they were all entangled with each other, feeling and becoming acquainted with each other's bodies. Nature took its course and they made love naturally, beautifully, as a man and woman do.

Afterward they just lay together, completely content and still wrapped in each other. Oscar wasn't sure of what just happened or what he should do or say. Finally he turned to her and said the words that had been on his heart for so long. "Esther... *jeg elske du.*" It was a huge relief to let it out.

"I love you too, Oscar," she replied. "I think I have for a long time."

"Yah," Oscar inhaled, "I t'ink I have loved you a long time too, but..."

Esther put a finger to his lips and said, "Shhh... it's okay."

With Ester's head on his arm and shoulder, they fell into a sleep of long-sought peace and contentment, a sleep where nothing else mattered now that they had each other. Outside the frustrated wind groaned and eventually blew itself away in the night.

Esther awoke to Oscar's hand softly stroking her breast again. She smiled and turned toward him. It was very early in the morning and still dark outside. It was so cozy in bed neither wanted to get up, so they made love again just as passionately as the previous time, and it was good.

Oscar was reassured that their night of intimacy had actually happened, but he could still hardly believe it. Esther got up and quickly hurried downstairs where her clothes were hanging, and got dressed before making a fire in the stove. As Oscar dressed, his head was swimming with so many thoughts that he almost put his boots on the wrong feet. When he joined Esther in the kitchen, they looked at each other's glowing faces and embraced again. Despite the storm, the world now seemed a different place, familiar yet new to both of them.

24

Henry's chest rattled like a box of rocks with each breath after sleeping a restless night. He coughed with nearly every breath after getting up and Esther was sure the boy had come down with pneumonia. Oscar suggested he might have taken in some water from the pond. Listless and tired, Henry was much different than the day before. They kept him warm by the stove, applied liniment to his chest and made him inhale medicated steam under a towel. A trip to see Doc Crowley seemed inevitable for both of them, but it would have to wait until the county plow came and cleared the road.

Gradually the snow and wind abated throughout the morning, replaced by clear blue skies and blinding sunshine on the pure white landscape. The temperature sagged below zero, cold for November even in Minnesota. With the roads impassable, returning to their home would mean walking over the drifted fields for Esther and Henry. Henry's winter coat was still by the pond where Oscar had left it after hauling the boy to his house that terrible night, and in his present health he was in no shape to venture outside anyway. But Oscar was happy to extend his hospitality until the weather and roads improved, and Esther decided they could wait a day or two longer. Besides, it meant they could share the tender warmth of each other in bed.

She mentioned concern for her home and Oscar insisted she stay and watch over her grandson while he walked over to check it out. When he got there, he found the furnace had gone out but it had not yet frozen inside Esther's home. Oscar rebuilt the fire and banked the furnace, fed her chickens and checked to be sure everything was all right. At her request, he brought Esther's basket of mending on his return, so she could keep her hands busy. "A woman's hands should never be idle," she said.

Along the way both to and from her house, Oscar kept thinking about Hektor. He worried about his old friend, and his eyes scanned the distance periodically. Now and then he looked over his shoulder, half expecting to see the old mongrel's dark silhouette emerge from some shelter, patiently working his arthritic limbs through the deep snow as he approached.

When Oscar returned, he told Esther he was going to walk back to the pond and look for Henry's coat and any sign of Hektor. On reaching the pond, he noted the hole in the ice where Henry had fallen through was frozen over, showing only a dark patch of ice set in the snow-covered pond. It sent a chill through him and, he shuddered involuntarily, as if recalling some bad dream. Oscar kicked away the deep snow around a clump of stunted willows where he vaguely recalled bringing Henry ashore. Underneath, he found the boy's coat, frozen stiff, and his lantern. It really had happened, it wasn't some grim figment of his imagination. He called for Hektor and searched the area for signs of him, but finding none, headed back home.

Along the way, Oscar tried his best to follow what he felt was their route that awful night, still searching for any sign of his dog. Their tracks were obliterated of course, so he wasn't certain but felt sure they would have followed their regular path to the pond. A path that, on that night, would have been virtually invisible in the darkness and blowing snow.

Walking the route that morning, Oscar could just barely recall the aching cold that had gradually numbed his mind and body. He could barely recall that and the vague shape of Hektor leading the way home through the billowing haze of snow that night. Oscar was sure he'd followed his dog home, but maybe his mind was playing tricks and maybe his feet simply knew the way. Maybe, but not likely. And where was Hektor now?

Oscar spent part of the afternoon on *Gubbe* making a path through the snow on his driveway so he could get his truck out to the road after the plow came by. By the end of the day the driveway was open, but the plow would not come until afternoon the next day. Oscar's arm ached, though he tried hard to favor it as much as he could. It was clear he needed Doc Crowley to check it and put a new cast on as well. Since Henry's cough and breathing hadn't improved, they would go see the doc together when the roads were open.

The visit took longer than Oscar had anticipated because Doc Crowley was amazed at Oscar and Henry's story of survival and how Esther had nursed them back to life. He was so amazed he called his nurse into the room and made them repeat it to her. Then he listened to

Henry's chest and prescribed some medications with careful instructions to Esther about caring for the boy. After tending to Henry, he turned his attention to Oscar's arm.

Crowley was pretty sure Oscar had re-broken the bone, but the ends of the bones were in their proper place. After intensely studying the arm and palpating the tender break sight for a while, he put a new cast on Oscar and told him to not use the arm for at least a week. Oscar muttered something in Norse that the doctor mistook for an acknowledgment; Doc Crowley wasn't from the area. Esther and Henry waited patiently while Oscar's cast dried before they crowded back into his truck for the drive home.

Snow snakes undulated across the road as Oscar drove over the rolling white Aasness countryside under the cold, clear winter sky. Oscar was quiet the whole time, his mind wandering off down a somber, now familiar path. Esther and Henry chattered about Foster Falls and things to see and do there next time they went.

Oscar knew the road home took them past Bergstrom's place, which looked even more forlorn out amidst the desolate, untracked snow drifts as they approached it. Having been unoccupied for months now, the farm appeared all the more unkempt and rundown. At the end of the driveway, the door to Bergstrom's empty mailbox hung wide open, like the silent, sagging jaw of a skull. The sight brought back memories of Bergstrom and Oscar's mind was drawn back to thoughts of the man, his flax, and his wife. He'd spent a lot of time pondering Bergstrom and his flax and the fire. Since Bergstrom's suicide, Oscar had felt that the man wanted him to figure out what had happened, to know the truth with all its ugliness, as though it might help Bergstrom and his Nora rest in peace. Now Oscar thought perhaps he understood.

It was late afternoon when they reached the "T" intersection that turned left toward his place or right toward the Holmvik farm, and he turned right instead of heading home. It had been several days since Esther had been home and she was anxious to get back. She and Henry gave out a cheer as Oscar pulled the truck to a stop at the unplowed Holmvik driveway.

Inside her house, Oscar restoked the furnace and banked it up so the fire would burn long and slowly. Soon warmth began to fill the house and seeped through the iron floor grates throughout the house to the upstairs. Though tired, Henry was glad to be back in his own home and occupied himself with a toy tractor beside the warm grate in his room.

Soon the whole house was warm again and Esther made coffee and told Oscar to make himself comfortable at the kitchen table.

"It's late, Oscar, why don't you stay for dinner?" she said. Oscar agreed, mostly because he now didn't want to return to his own empty house, all the more empty without Hektor.

The clean new sling hung empty and unused around Oscar's neck as he rested the new cast on the table. His furrowed forehead suggested to Esther that the arm still caused him some discomfort.

"Say, shouldn't you be keeping that arm in the sling?" she reminded him.

Oscar pulled it over his head and set it on the table. Esther just shrugged. She'd come to know the man, and knew something was on his mind.

"It's good to be in my own home again," she said changing the subject. "Oh, not that I don't appreciate your hospitality Oscar, but you know it's always good to get back to your own place.

Esther roasted a chicken for their dinner, boiled some potatoes, and opened some vegetables she had canned the past summer. For dessert they had strawberry rhubarb sauce she'd canned over a cake she hastily baked. Oscar ate like a king.

After dinner, and after Henry had gone to bed for the night, Esther and Oscar sat together in the little living room of her farmhouse and she took up her knitting. He could have left, or Esther could have said she was tired and needed to go to bed, but she knew by his mood that something was on his mind. An old clock on the wall ticked away in the quiet room, bringing him closer to expressing what was on his mind. Finally, he spoke.

"You know, Esther, I been t'inkin' a lot about Stordal an' Bergstrom since he died last summer."

"Yah?" Esther said without looking up from her knitting. A pause followed.

"When I went to Bergstrom's place to get d'em flax screens I found somet'ing that didn't seem to belong, somet'ing Bergstrom had kept wit' him in his shop for a long time."

Esther looked up at him from her knitting.

"It was a necklace wit' a locket on it. You know, wit' the pictures inside," Oscar said. "Pictures of Nora an' Bergstrom. The pictures were burnt a little from the fire, but not too bad. An' the locket was engraved too. Anyway, I gave the locket to Stordal. He said 'I loved her first', an' I told him I knew that. See, I t'ink Nora chose to marry Bergstrom, an' that made Stordal jealous. What do ya make o' that?"

"Hmmm, that's interesting Oscar," Esther said thoughtfully. "So then, do you suppose Stordal could have started that fire that not only burned up his flax but Nora too?"

"Yah, well I t'ink so," Oscar inhaled, "but I don't believe he meant for Nora to die. D'at was by accident."

They sat in silent contemplation for a while.

"Anyway, I gave the locket to Stordal. I figured it would mean somet'ing to him," Oscar finally stated. "I know d'er iss no evidence, but do you t'ink I should say somet'ing to the sheriff?"

"Oscar, it's over," Ester replied quietly as she put down her knitting. "It all happened long ago and it's not our burden to bear. I think we shouldn't tell anyone about it, just keep it to ourselves. If Stordal did do it, he will have to just live with it."

"Yah," Oscar inhaled.

25

(Epilogue)

In the spring as the snow melted and Oscar began to get restless again about the coming season, he began walking his land again. Eventually he made his way down to inspect how the grape vines had survived the winter. While there he walked along the shore of the pond, recalling the drama that had happened there the previous fall. Now the pond ice was melting and had receded out about twenty feet from shore. As he walked along, he found a soggy mass of dark, wet fur that was Hektor's remains submcrgcd a short way out from shore. Oscar took an old tree limb and dragged the old dog's body to shore. Then he sat himself on a stone and, all alone in the privacy of his remote little vineyard where no one would see, no one would know, Oscar wept his heart out.

He sat for a long time grieving for his friend, but eventually he pulled himself up and trudged back to his shop to get a shovel. He returned and set to work digging grave for Hektor among the grape vines. It wasn't easy as the ground was still frozen just a few inches down, but Oscar took his time. Later, Oscar selected a large stone from along the pond shore, and with a hammer and cold chisel, carved in the stone: "*Takk for Alt min kjære venn*" (thanks for everything my dear friend), and placed it on the grave.

As he worked he tried to put together what had happened that stormy night, but things did not fit well. After the old dog pulled Henry from the grip of the icy pond so Oscar could grab the boy, he had led them home through the blinding snow. Afterward there had been no trace of Hektor around the house or barn or anything to suggest the dog had been with Oscar when he carried Henry home all caked in ice that night. Esther was certain Hektor had not been with them or she would surely have brought the dog in the house, too. Hektor would have had no reason to return to the pond in the storm. Besides, soaking wet and covered with ice, the old dog would not likely have had the stamina to do it.

The truth, it seemed, was Hektor had saved the boy, but the tired old dog had not survived the cold swim himself. Oscar had been so concerned for Henry he had not noticed his dear friend had never made it to shore. Hektor must have died in the freezing pond that night. Still, Oscar was certain he remembered following his dog home through the snowstorm that night, or at least a vision of his dog.

A pragmatic man for the most part, Oscar never told others how he had followed a dog's ghost home through the blowing snow and darkness. People around Aasness Township were realistic and skeptical by nature and would never accept his story. But in his own heart Oscar knew, and nothing would change that. It was his dear old dog's last act of friendship. He did tell Esther, and she believed him and comforted him, standing by him in his grief, realizing that even though Hektor was just a dog, he had been the only family Oscar had. That would soon change.

Esther and Oscar's wedding was in May before things got busy again for the farmers. It was a joyous occasion, well attended and celebrated by friends and neighbors from all around Aasness Township. It was not a typical wedding, as marriage of older couples was unusual. But that was precisely what seemed to make it special among so many of the farm wives in the area, who put out their finest efforts. Of course, there were a few old biddies who disapproved of the couple as they felt such relationships were improper and unbecoming at their age. And as the story of Henry's close call got around, there was some gossip about Esther spending a few days at the home of a bachelor when she and Henry were stranded at Oscar's place by the storm. But as word got around of Oscar rescuing Henry from drowning in the pond, and of how they both nearly froze to death and Henry's miraculous recovery far overshadowed any negative rumors.

Arthur came home on furlough from the Army to walk his mother down the aisle of Eidsvold Church and Henry was Oscar's best man. Henry was so proud to see his father in uniform he could hardly contain himself. It nearly broke the boy's heart later when his father had to return to duty, but having "Grampa" Halvorson there made it easier.

Reverend Ellerby happily joined the couple in holy matrimony. He asked the blessing on the bread and wine, and then in a radical twist with a conspiratorial wink, he had Oscar and Esther serve Holy Communion to the congregation. Afterward, Gus Thorvald carelessly quipped within his wife's hearing that he'd like to get back in line for seconds. That remark fetched a threatening look from his wife and her assertion that if anybody needed a double-dose of salvation, he did. As Oscar had wished, the congregation would never learn where the wine came from until after he had passed on. No one ever really inquired, since it was a "miracle" after all.

After the wedding, people crowded the basement of Eidsvold Church for the reception to escape the chilly spring weather outside and to socialize with each other, and of course the bride and groom. The women buzzed around Esther and she glowed radiantly with the attention.

Oscar took refuge outside with the men most of the time, receiving many well wishes and pats on the back enduring their wry, good-natured ribbing, and giving it back in like manner. A couple rascals even "decorated" Oscar's old truck for the occasion and tied on a tail of tin cans to trail behind it.

The return of spring brought with it the greening of the earth and a fresh new start as the cycle of life with the land began again. Once more farmers began preparing the soil, sowing with hope and nurturing with faith that another harvest would come forth in its season.

That Memorial Day Oscar and Esther made their annual trip to the cemetery to decorate the graves of their families and remember those who had gone before them. They visited the graves of Theodore Bergstrom and his wife and scattered a handful of flax seeds over them. Later that summer, for a brief period, the sky-blue flowers of flax bloomed brightly on the Bergstrom graves. No one really noticed them waving there in the breeze as everyone was busy making preparations for harvest time.

That following December brought the attack on Pearl Harbor and the United States entered World War II. Arthur's regiment was called into the fight and he wrote as often as he could from somewhere in North Africa. Esther noticed his letters developed a melancholy tone. Still, he always mentioned how happy he was that he had sent his son to live with her on the farm, and that she and Oscar were raising Henry together. In early 1944, she received a telegram saying her son had been killed at a place called Anzio, somewhere in Italy, a place neither she nor Oscar had ever heard of or knew where it was. In good times or in bad, in sickness or in health, it was good to not face life—or death, alone.

And so Henry continued to live with Oscar and Esther and he learned to love and care for the land. He grew in stature and skill, eventually taking over the Holmvik land and later, Oscar's farm too. Henry became a successful and prosperous farmer and when the time was right, he learned how to make a fine and righteous wine.

Author

Jack Kraywinkle is a retired copy writer and graphic designer who finished his working career in the medical imaging field. These days his creative outlet is mostly wood carving and wood sculpture, but he still likes to write. Jack is a bit reclusive and enjoys being alone in nature and the outdoors whenever he can. His parents nurtured a love and respect for his Scandinavian heritage and culture, and he has always kept a place in his heart for the Ottertail County area where his grandparents settled upon coming to this country.

Jack and his wife Kay moved to the Brainerd, MN, area after he retired. They enjoy spending time with their children and grandchildren.